CURSE OF A DRAGON HEART

CURSE OF A DRAGON HEART

DRAGON DESCENDANTS OF DRAKKOIA
BOOK 0

BONNIE JACOBY

COSMICDRAGON PRESS

For anyone who has ever struggled to accept a part of themselves.

I believe in you.

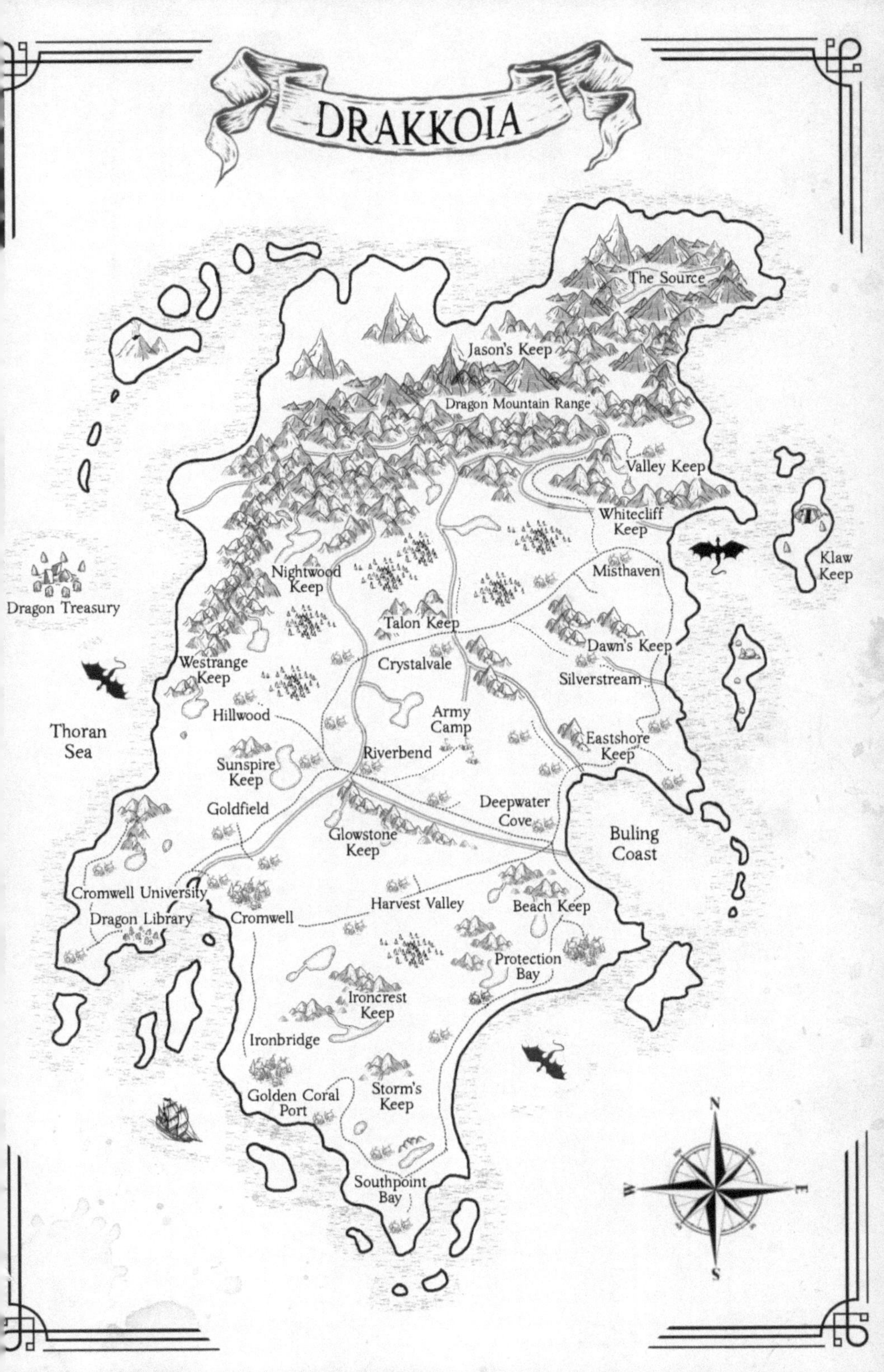

DRAKKOIA
The Source
Jason's Keep
Dragon Mountain Range
Valley Keep
Whitecliff Keep
Klaw Keep
Misthaven
Nightwood Keep
Dragon Treasury
Talon Keep
Dawn's Keep
Westrange Keep
Crystalvale
Silverstream
Thoran Sea
Hillwood
Army Camp
Eastshore Keep
Sunspire Keep
Riverbend
Goldfield
Deepwater Cove
Buling Coast
Glowstone Keep
Cromwell University
Dragon Library
Cromwell
Harvest Valley
Beach Keep
Protection Bay
Ironcrest Keep
Ironbridge
Golden Coral Port
Storm's Keep
Southpoint Bay
N
S
E
W

SCORCH MARKS

JASON

Magic brought only pain and death.

Jason couldn't believe that three months ago, having a magical ability made him special. It did. But not in a good way.

A shout from one of the younger boys pushed dread into Jason's throat. At the distinctive sound of a fist hitting flesh, he dropped the empty bucket and raced through the field of broken corn stalks. His thirteen-year-old brother tended to be at the center of conflict.

Dust swirled around the circle of silent boys next to the barn. They parted to let Jason through. But he was too late. His brother lay on the ground, his jaw locked and fury in his eyes.

Barnaby yanked Charlie to his feet and dragged him toward the farmer standing at the gate.

The bruises on his brother's gaunt face ignited Jason's magic. Heat rushed to his palms, pulsing with his anger. He clenched his fists, trying to control the rush of power.

Barnaby had gone too far this time. No matter what Charlie had done, there was no excuse for beating him. The heat in his head agreed. It wouldn't take much to set it free and burn Barnaby's fists, so they never hurt anyone again.

But as Charlie stumbled past, he shook his head, his eyes pleading with Jason to let it go. To keep his magic contained and hidden.

Charlie was right. It wasn't worth the risk. But once the heat rose within Jason, it had to be released. He choked on a growl, unable to even speak without losing control.

He ducked behind the barn and brushed his fingers along the aged wood, reciting the spell to control the heat that wound through his body. His magical ability. His curse.

"Burn short and fast. Hot to cold. Release the fire. Breathe and rest."

It wasn't elegant, but it worked. His father had helped create it years ago when Jason's ability manifested. There'd been no need to adjust the spell, or even use it much. But everything had changed three months ago. Maybe it was the death of his parents or turning sixteen. Didn't matter. For the past month, he'd struggled to control the heat coursing through his head.

There was no one left to help. No parents. No aunts or uncles. Only Charlie. And taking care of Charlie was a full-time job.

The smell of burnt wood soothed Jason's anger. His magic settled into a low thrum in his chest, his shoulders dropped, and he sucked in a calming breath. A quick swipe of his palm obliterated the words etched into the wall, leaving a scorch mark next to the others. With a little dirt, it wasn't even noticeable. Unfortunately, hiding his magical ability was becoming a daily battle.

Jason couldn't expose his magic. Not in Riverbend. Not anywhere.

Everyday magic was fine. Illusions for entertainment. Small spells to make life easier, like lighting candles or calling a soft breeze. But people with true magical abilities were rare now. Capable of accessing their abilities to fuel spells, they could become witches. If they excelled at battle magic, they trained as war mages. But the Great Wars consumed power. So instead of going to Cromwell University to learn spell casting, they were conscripted.

The war mages had drained his parents of their magic, killing them in the end. Few survived, becoming mere shells of the people they once were. So maybe it was better this way.

At least no one knew that Jason had a magical ability. His parents had died before arranging the Ability Test, and he and Charlie had been sent to the orphanage with nothing more than the clothes they wore. No mementos of their life before. Nothing to identify them as children of witches.

The reward for reporting someone with core magic was substantial. And during the famine, people were desperate for trader coin.

Joining the farming crew had been a mistake. The promise of food and shelter had lured Jason into believing they'd be better off than at the overcrowded orphanage. But the food was nothing more than scraps from their harvest. Not enough to feed the ten boys ranging from nine to sixteen. As the eldest, Jason had no trouble getting his share, but Charlie had always been too sensitive, helping the younger boys. More like their mother in that way. He'd withered into a walking skeleton from losing his share to Barnaby or giving it away to the younger ones.

Jason's chest tightened at the unfairness of his parents' death and the impossible task of keeping Charlie safe. It wasn't Charlie's fault that he was scrawny and an easy target. But sometimes Jason wished his brother didn't care so much about the injustices of their world and would realize he was no fighter.

Jason sighed. Charlie had no sense of self-preservation. That was Jason's responsibility. In another time, he might admire Charlie's courage, but not now. Not when boys like Barnaby needed to rule. Not when Jason's magic leapt so easily to his hands, ready to burn anything that angered him.

It wasn't his brother's fault that Jason was angry all the time and that his magic longed to be set free. In winter, it would be easier. His magic shifted with the temperature and would cool down.

In full control of his emotions now, Jason strode out from behind the barn. Time to soothe Barnaby and fix whatever injustice Charlie had uncovered.

But as he approached the boys clustered around the farmer, the warning bell sounded.

Visitors.

Men's voices floated on the hot, dry wind. Soldiers from the barren wasteland to the east of the village.

"Line up," the wiry farmer growled in a baritone voice. They'd learned early to obey immediately. Supposedly, he'd had kids of his own and lost them to the Great Wars. But you wouldn't know it. He treated the boys like cattle. Rounding them up, sending them from pasture to pasture, and locking them in the barn at night.

Jason hurried to the front of the line, next to a scowling Barnaby and a tight-lipped Charlie. They stood in order of height and not age. Despite his lack of bulk, Charlie was almost as tall as Jason.

Two soldiers stopped next to the farmer—a man who favored his right leg, and a younger man, maybe twenty. A woman leaned against a horse-drawn cart, probably filled with provisions from the village.

Jason stood taller, pulling his shoulders back. The soldiers looked healthy. They didn't go hungry. Charlie wouldn't last another month on the farm. Jason didn't want to fight. He didn't want to die. But joining the army couldn't be any worse.

"That all you got?" The old soldier sounded weary.

The farmer grunted. "Better than no one. Crops don't harvest themself."

"We need soldiers, not pathetic crops. Boys and girls over eighteen. These are just kids."

Jason's hopes fell. It had been a slim chance, anyway.

The farmer rubbed his jaw, as if thinking over the soldier's assessment.

"Slim pickings in Riverbend. But you already know that. Now, if you loaned me a soldier for a week ... the silos would fill up faster." The farmer pointed back toward the main outbuilding.

Jason stifled his smirk at the soldier's eye roll. If the farmer thought he was being clever, he was mistaken.

The old man turned away. "Just load up what you have."

Jason lurched forward. This was his chance. "Wait, take us with you."

"Shut your mouth, boy." The farmer's elbow slammed into Jason's gut.

Pain doubled Jason over, and he wheezed, unable to speak. Not the strength he'd hoped to impart.

But it had been enough to attract the younger soldier's attention. "We could use a runner back at camp. That one could bulk up a bit with some food and training."

Jason straightened, ready to turn down the offer. He couldn't leave Charlie.

The older soldier snorted and then slapped the younger soldier's back. "Gerry got to you, huh? They're pretty scrawny. Fine. We'll take half."

The farmer sputtered. "What? You can't take my crew."

"Be thankful I'm not taking them all."

His protest died at the stern look from the old soldier.

Jason, Charlie, Barnaby, and two others were sent to gather their belongings and wait at the barn. Jason couldn't help worrying about the other boys. The oldest was only twelve. They couldn't possibly do all the work the farmer needed. But it wasn't his problem. The farmer would find more orphans to replace them. Probably by supper.

Despite the farmer's protests, the wagon was loaded with everything he had. The old soldier had told him, "You could join the front lines if you can't farm anymore." And that shut him up.

At least he had a choice.

As Jason followed the wagon out into the wasteland, he gave Charlie a reassuring grin. "Soon we'll have a proper meal and a place to sleep." He didn't know if life would be easier, but the food had to be better than what they'd been surviving on.

Charlie frowned. "It wasn't like they gave us a choice. But you gotta be careful."

He was scared. Problem was, so was Jason.

The Great Wars couldn't last much longer. Over the past thirty-four years, villages had been destroyed, cities abandoned, and forests reduced to burnt stumps. There was no land worth having, and magic to fuel the battle spells was disappearing.

As long as Jason hid his magic, they would survive, and he'd find somewhere safe for Charlie to laugh again.

RUNNER

JASON

Life was both harder and easier at camp. The boys shared bunks in the supply tent and ate two full meals a day. But Jason rarely saw his brother.

While Jason delivered messages, Charlie tended the horses and cleaned tack on the far side of camp. By nightfall, they fell asleep before they could talk.

At least Charlie looked better after three weeks of filling meals. With all the chores, Jason had feared his brother would weaken. Some soldiers grumbled at their smaller servings, but they grinned whenever a boy was sent on a task, allowing them to sit. Food was a small price to pay to avoid grunt work.

Jason jogged through the men saddling up the horses and packing up the camp. This would be the third move since he'd joined. A horse sidestepped into his shoulder, and Jason gripped the paper tighter. Dropping the requisition in the mud would earn him a whack to the ear.

A squeal split the air, and he whipped his head to the left. A massive dark brown horse pawed the air inches from Charlie's face. Instantly, fear ignited Jason's power. Heat rushed through his body, and the paper in his fist disintegrated.

Jason grunted and unclenched his hand, afraid of startling the killer horse and injuring Charlie.

"Whoa. Easy, Warhog. I got you." Charlie's voice was calm and soothing. Not a hint of fear.

The horse snorted and shook his head, but he kept his hooves on the ground. Charlie rubbed the horse's neck, murmuring something Jason couldn't hear.

The sounds around Jason resumed. Men talking. Horses snorting in the cool morning air. Steam rising from the horses' backs. Charlie led the now tame horse to the waiting stable hand. Together they put on the saddle pad and saddle and tightened the straps. The horse snorted and shifted but let them be.

Jason groaned. The list was gone. He'd have to run back and get another one. His power had lain dormant since they left the farm. He'd been fine. And now. Damn it. He thought he'd mastered it. This couldn't happen again.

Charlie waved. Jason smiled and gave him a thumbs-up. Then he turned and ran back to the quartermaster. He'd say he lost the list in the mud and take the punishment. No way he'd reveal that he'd burned it with magic.

That night, after the camp was resettled, he caught Charlie outside the supply tent.

"Hey. That horse was wild this morning." Jason figured if he eased into the conversation, his brother wouldn't get upset. Lately, every conversation ended in an argument, and he didn't want to fight.

Charlie shrugged. "I could handle him. Seems I have a calming influence on the horses. That's what Arthur says, at least. Gets me out of latrine duty."

"You doing all right? Getting both meals?"

Charlie rolled his eyes. "I can take care of myself."

"Yeah, right." The sarcasm popped out, despite Jason's resolve to not fight.

Charlie punched him in the shoulder, hard. "Stop fussing, Mom."

Jason bit his lip, holding back his retort. Charlie was fine. He should be happy about that. "You managing to avoid Barnaby?"

"I never see him. You?"

Jason shook his head. No, he hadn't seen Barnaby and had assumed they worked different schedules.

"The stars remind me of Mom." Charlie leaned back and gazed at the millions of pinpricks in the black sky.

Jason didn't want to remember how his mother used to tell stories with the stars. She was gone. Her beautiful illusion magic had gotten her killed. The night sky was just another reminder of what he'd lost. He swallowed the lump in his throat. Charlie was the only family left. And even though he knew it might annoy Charlie, Jason reached over and hugged him tightly.

For once, Charlie just squeezed back, then let go.

They didn't need to say anything. A hug said it all. Mom would've been pleased.

Jason followed Charlie into the tent and crawled onto his bunk. He needed sleep. Soon enough, he'd be running across camp with messages. But sleep didn't come.

Instead, the stars danced behind his eyes as his mother's voice recounted the story of the dragon mating flight she'd seen as a little girl. The world had been different then, distant, little more than something to gossip about. Dragons had lived near her village, and she'd trained to be a dragon rider. But life had other plans for her. And the Great Wars grew, stealing dreams and destroying her village.

She'd turned her attention to strengthening her magic, certain her illusions could make a difference. Bring joy instead of ruin. But she'd been wrong. Magic destroyed her.

If Jason didn't control his magic, it would destroy him too. And he wasn't sure Charlie could survive without him. He had to keep them both safe.

They'd moved camp so many times in the past month that Jason couldn't keep track anymore. It wasn't like they followed a road or went in a straight line. One day they went north, camped for a day, and the next they went back to the area they left. Then they'd head west.

Yet the rumors continued about settling in for a huge battle soon. Jason now served the officers food and water in the war tent. Another boy had become their runner. Supposedly, it was a promotion, but he missed sprinting around camp. Stale smoke and rancid body odor filled the tent. He missed fresh air.

And now, Jason ate scraps, never having enough time to grab his own meal. He'd caught sight of Charlie sitting with another boy, leisurely slurping stew.

Occasionally, the cook, Susan, convinced him to eat while she assembled the tray for the officers. He cherished those times. It was the only time his food was hot. It wasn't a hard job, but it involved long hours of standing at attention and lurching forward with wine or water at a moment's request.

Every day, Charlie looked less like a skeleton and more like a growing teen. Once they settled, Jason would get to spend more time with his brother.

"Dig the latrines deep." General Riley pointed to a spot east of their current location on the map.

Jason's ears perked up. That was a good sign. It meant they'd be there longer than a day. The soldier nodded and left the tent.

The general held up his mug, and Jason hurried forward to fill it. The water carafe was almost empty, which meant he might be able to slip into the food tent before the lunch rush.

"Boy. Grab the stores report."

The request was unusual. Not that the general didn't know his name. He doubted he'd ever be called anything other than boy. But the runner had just left, so maybe this was too important to wait for his return.

Jason grabbed the empty plates and metal cups so he could drop them off on the way. He scurried out of the tent. Susan waved him to the bin of dirty dishes where someone else would clean them.

He dumped his load and jogged to the storage wagon, certain the general was already impatiently waiting for the report.

As soon as the wagon was in sight, he slowed to a walk. A long, raspy cough stole his breath, and pain shot through his chest. Sheepishly, he ran his fingers through his hair as he straightened, hoping no one had noticed.

Another series of coughs caught him by surprise. Jason bent over, his face turning red with the effort of trying to breathe through the barrage. Finally, he gasped a rattling breath of air and rubbed his aching throat.

"That's a nasty cough. Get some sweet tea from the cook. She'll fix you up. Maybe don't run so fast back to General Riley." The soldier held out the report.

"Yes, sir." Jason grabbed the paper and whirled around, mortified. He didn't need tea.

He jogged back to the tent, rubbing the growing ache in his chest. He must be fighting a cold. A few days of rest should help. Luckily, the army camp was settling in the sparse forest. From what he gathered, the front line of the magic war was just over the rise. General Riley intended to make this their last battle.

By nightfall, he'd lost his voice and his throat felt as if he'd swallowed a sword. Pain stabbed through his head whenever he turned too quickly. He wasn't even aware he was swaying until one of the soldiers caught him by the shoulder.

"Hey. Are you all right?" The man's voice seemed far away, and his face floated, detached from his body.

Jason turned his head to see if the general had caught the interaction.

But stars fell from the sky, turning into strange creatures that opened their mouths and screamed.

Jason clamped his hands over his ears and closed his eyes. "Stop."

Then his throat ripped apart as he coughed, and everything disappeared.

When he woke, he was on a cot inside a large green tent. Coughs and moans filled his ears.

Charlie leaned over him, a black mask over his nose and mouth. His eyes reminded Jason of their father. There was something sad and worn in them.

"Don't speak. It's my turn to take care of you. Drink this. It will help."

Jason opened his mouth and licked at the sweet tea. Even that motion hurt, as if his tongue was yanking out his throat. How long had it been since he was last in the officers' tent? He must've said something, since he was sure Charlie couldn't read his mind.

"That was yesterday. You've been asleep." Charlie's concerned expression was odd, as if he was seeing death.

Fatigue dragged Jason's eyes closed. He wanted to tell Charlie not to worry. It was his job to take care of his brother. Not the other way around. Once he rested, he'd get back to work. He didn't want the army to kick them out. Charlie needed him.

Ragged breathing filled Jason's ears as visions of rock creatures chased him through a sea of tents.

SORCERER
CHARLIE

Jason might die today, and there was nothing Charlie could do to stop it. Instead, he trembled in the corner of the officers' tent, wishing they'd never joined the army.

The past two weeks had been hell. He'd never seen dragons up close, and now they flew over day and night. If he weren't so terrified of losing his brother, he'd be amazed at their power and skill. But he just wanted to return to the farm, despite the hard work and lack of food, to the time before Jason got sick.

"We're losing the war." The leader of the war mages, Sorcerer Bloodstar, sounded exhausted.

General Riley slammed his fist onto the table. "It's those dragons. The enemy has more than we do."

Screams filled the air as another dragon flew overhead and arrows rained down on the soldiers holding the border just half a mile up the road. Charlie didn't know why they bothered fighting at all. By nightfall, the soldiers would return and fill the infirmary with blood and moans. He'd help patch them up, and they'd go out in the morning to fight again. Fewer came back each night.

The sorcerer looked up. Charlie hadn't had this position long, but he knew the drill. He lurched forward. The jug shook as he filled the cup at the man's elbow, and water spattered the map. But the battle group was too intent on their strategies to notice.

Charlie backed away and tried to stand still as they continued talking.

"Boy." No one in the tent called him by his name. "Who's the sickest from the plague? Someone who won't last another day." The sorcerer's question was unusual. What did he care about sick soldiers?

"Why does that matter?" General Riley could barely contain his impatience, his hand poised over the map.

Charlie held his breath in the long silence that followed. More powerful than war mages, the sorcerer could flatten the entire camp with his magic. He'd arrived the day before and had taken over. The general was still adjusting to his change in status.

"Do you want to win this war or not?" Bloodstar's voice oozed disdain.

General Riley gulped and nodded at Charlie to answer.

"Jason, sir. He's been sick for two weeks." His brother might not be the worst, but he was close enough, and he'd survived when others had died. It made sense that healing the soldiers would help win the war. The general claimed it was a numbers game. If the sorcerer could cure his brother, it was worth the tiny lie. Even if Jason wasn't technically a soldier.

"Take me to him." The tall sorcerer glared down at the general. "The captive is mine. Ensure no one disturbs me while I work." The warning in his voice was obvious. There would be no second chances.

Before Charlie could wonder who they'd captured, Bloodstar pushed him out the door, and Charlie led him through the maze of tents.

Harsh coughs and agonized moans filled the air. A strange illness had swept through the camp, infecting many before they'd even realized what was happening. Jason had been one of the first to succumb, along with a dozen others. It was a plague unlike any other in history. Faster and more deadly. Charlie couldn't believe it had only been two weeks. It felt like forever. Two died on the first day. It happened so fast.

Jason was barely holding on. The Healers had already given up on him, working on the people who still had a chance of surviving. Once the illness lasted more than five days, there was nothing they could do.

Charlie stopped at the largest tent. These victims were too sick to moan. He grabbed a black mask from the bin beside the door and covered his nose and mouth. Bloodstar put one on too.

There were no beds inside. There was no need. Rows of blankets on the ground held dying soldiers, those beyond help. When they died, the blanket became a stretcher. At night, Charlie would grab one end of a blanket and help toss the bodies into the pit. The fires blazed through the night, cremating the dead, while the blankets were boiled and laid out for the next plague victim.

Jason's chest barely moved. Each agonizing rasp pinched Charlie's heart. He'd seen this stage often enough to know that his brother wouldn't make it to nightfall. A chill swept through his soul.

He didn't know what he would do if his brother died. His entire family would be gone.

In this war, death was the only escape from grief.

But while Jason still breathed, Charlie had to believe in a better future. One where he and his brother went on adventures together and had full lives. The sorcerer had a plan and Jason would survive.

Bloodstar lifted Jason into his arms and then strode out of the stench of death. They climbed the hill behind the camp and stopped at a large tent that faded in and out of sight.

Pain stabbed behind Charlie's eyes, and he groaned as he lost his balance. A lot of magic was being expended to conceal the details of this tent. He might not have his ability yet, but he'd always been sensitive to magic.

There was no room for fear. Whatever was hidden inside didn't matter. It couldn't be worse than the plague stealing Jason's life.

As soon as the tent flap closed behind them, the chaotic sounds of camp disappeared, replaced by the deep breaths of a dragon shackled to the center post.

Candlelight danced on the walls, reflecting off the dragon's glimmering red scales. The dragon's eyes swirled in a head that was bigger than Charlie's chest.

He fell into her gaze. The tent spun as anger, fear, and sadness beat at his mind. He stumbled back, gripping his head to stop the onslaught.

The sorcerer chuckled. "Try not to look into her eyes. They say a person could get lost in the things reflected there." The melancholy in his voice disturbed Charlie. It was as if the sorcerer mourned the dragon.

He settled Jason on a narrow cot and then gripped Charlie's shoulder. "It must be done. We cannot win as long as dragons help our enemies."

Over the next hour, Charlie fetched supplies from a large chest in one corner of the tent. He cleaned Jason and dressed him in a ceremonial green robe. Finally, Charlie sat beside the cot and held his brother's limp hand.

Each labored breath barely moved Jason's chest.

"Hang in there. You'll feel better soon." Charlie hoped he was telling the truth, because it looked like his brother had given up already.

Bloodstar circled the dragon, chanting ancient words and swinging a ball on a chain. Blue smoke poured from the ball and obscured the dragon. The smoke engulfed Jason and lifted him from the cot, his hand slipping from Charlie's grasp.

The smoke dove for Charlie, but the sorcerer chastised it with a loud clap. The smoke subsided, leaving the dragon and Jason suspended in a blue mist.

The air was thick with magic, filling Charlie's chest with dread. A deep, unnatural pulse overpowered his own heartbeat, causing so much pain he had to blink through tears to watch.

With a guttural roar, the sorcerer plunged a curved dagger into the dragon's chest. A hole burned through the scales, exposing her beating heart. No blood fell. The blue smoke gently pulled her white heart out until it floated between the dragon and Jason.

Charlie trembled. He'd made a terrible mistake. This wasn't going to heal anyone. But he sat frozen, unable to move. The magic in the tent was so thick the spiciness burned the back of his throat.

The dragon's heart glowed with every beat. Charlie expected her to die, but while she didn't move, her eyes still swirled, and her breath rasped. She was alive without a heart.

The huge heart hovered above Jason. Charlie wanted to close his eyes, but he couldn't. He'd offered his brother for this sacrifice. It didn't matter that he hadn't known. If these were Jason's final moments, Charlie had to be there for his brother.

But there was no knife. No stabbing. No blood.

The smoke seeped into Jason's chest and peeled the flesh away to expose his beating heart.

Jason gasped and opened his eyes, and the smoke yanked his red heart out.

The sorcerer roared again, and the dragon's heart slammed into the hole in Jason's chest.

It should've been too big, but magic made it fit. The tent twisted, then snapped back into place. Charlie swallowed the bile that rose as his head spun.

But it was done. A white heart beat inside Jason's chest, pumping red blood through his body.

Lines of black and yellow shot through Jason's former heart as it floated to the dragon. The heart doubled in size, and a slow, painful thump, the heart's pulse, filled the tent. The smoke slid the red heart into the hole in the dragon's chest. But the tent didn't twist, and the heart didn't grow to fit. Instead, yellow strands connected the small heart to the cut vessels and pumped magic through the dragon.

With a single clap, the sorcerer sealed both hearts into their new homes.

A green glow surrounded Jason. He sucked in a huge breath, the rattle gone from his throat. Hope filled Charlie's chest. Maybe his brother wasn't going to die.

A yellow glow surrounded the dragon, and she coughed the long wet raspy cough of the dying. And Charlie felt the wrongness deep in his soul, as if the world had changed. As if this one act had destroyed something important.

The smoke lowered Jason onto the cot, his breathing deep and clear, and he settled into a healing sleep.

The sorcerer had done it. He'd cured Jason. But why? He couldn't hope to heal all the infected soldiers with one dragon. Her heart was inside Jason now, and her new heart looked like it could barely keep her alive. Unless he was going to transfer Jason's new heart into the next sick soldier. Charlie's head spun, certain that Jason couldn't survive another spell.

Without a word, Bloodstar disappeared, along with all traces of smoke. Sounds were muffled, and exhaustion pulled at Charlie, as if his energy had been drained. The dragon's wheezing filled the room, but Jason slept peacefully, a pinkness to his cheeks that hadn't been there before. Charlie wrapped his arms around his brother as sleep dragged him into oblivion. After so much magic, Jason had to live.

DRAGON PROMISE

KARYN

Karyn was dying. Phlegm filled her lungs, making each breath a struggle. The boy's tiny heart fluttered in her chest. It couldn't keep up with pumping blood through her body, infusing her organs with life. Magic couldn't make up for what she'd lost.

Strength seeped from her muscles, leaving her weak and unable to move. Even opening her eyes took effort.

When they'd captured her, she hadn't worried. Nothing could hold a dragon for long, and she'd survived the cave-in when she'd been but a youngling. Other younglings had not. So her confidence had been high.

They'd only landed because Brian needed help to extract the arrow from his back. If he'd been shot anywhere else, he could've removed it. So she'd flown to the embankment, and he'd slid off with a groan. He'd been tired, sore, and angry.

She'd kept her thoughts to herself, since he didn't like her hovering. But when she'd yanked the arrow out, he screamed. The barbs on the arrow had ripped something inside. She'd sensed it. His blood poured from the wound.

Before she could grab him and fly to the village for help, a wave of dizziness had altered her vision. She hadn't been hit. Only later did she realize the sorcerer had muddled her mind with magic. By then, an entire day had passed in a blur.

She couldn't sense Brian at all. He was too far away, or dead. It had hurt too much to try to communicate with the others to find out. So she'd rested, certain the magic would ease, and she would escape.

But then the sorcerer appeared with two boys. Charlie caught her gaze, and she'd felt his desperation to save his older brother, Jason. She'd tried to delve into his mind, but the sorcerer's spell stifled her thoughts. Or maybe the boy's thoughts. Either way, she wasn't able to communicate.

Then a blue mist surrounded her, numbing her thoughts and slowing her heartbeat.

Bloodstar stabbed her in the chest, the knife easily slipping through her tough hide. As he removed her heart, shock held her in its grasp. Her heart was gone and yet she lived. Only a huge amount of magic could explain such an incredible feat.

Her rage was enough to free her mind of the sorcerer's hold. But before she could call her coven for help, the sick boy's heart was inserted into her chest.

Karyn fell into a deep sleep.

When she woke, the tent was quiet, though she didn't know how much time had passed. The sorcerer was gone, and the two boys slept. Even though her mind was still foggy, she called out to her coven, hoping someone was near enough to help.

"We thought we'd lost you. Where have you been?" Ackenar sounded far away, but the image in her mind showed he hid near the battlefield.

She told him what happened, not sure any of it made sense, but he would see the images in her mind and understand. *"I'm getting weaker. But Great Torin, I'll try my best to survive and return home."*

"I'll free you." His anger soothed her confusion. No human should hold a dragon captive.

But Bloodstar had, and she didn't know how. They couldn't risk him capturing another from her coven.

"No! You must warn the others. This spell has stolen enough."

His disbelief only made her feel alone. If she hadn't experienced it, she wouldn't have believed a human could wield such magic.

"Please, Ackenar. Stay away. At least until I discover the source of Bloodstar's power or destroy him." Saying it made her stronger, more like herself.

But the moment was fleeting as another long cough disconnected her from mind-speech. She could feel her body deteriorating more rapidly than it should. Dragons should never have taught humans how to wield magic.

She didn't know how to stop the spell attacking her body. For the first time, she wished she had powers like the younger generation. Maybe magic could counter magic. But she didn't. She only had her determination and her years of survival.

Killing her wasn't the sorcerer's goal. He'd put her heart into the boy for a reason.

Over the next few days, Charlie cared for her, giving her water and mopping up the discharge from her nostrils. His thoughts were easy to access, even when he slept. The ritual had horrified him, but it was worth it to save his brother. He didn't know anything useful about the sorcerer's intent or his magic.

The sorcerer stayed away, so she couldn't delve into his mind. And the other boy ate and slept, barely awake enough to do much more.

Why exchange hearts? Bloodstar wanted to stop the war. That had been clear, even through the magic-induced haze.

As Jason improved, Karyn's body faltered. Another day passed, maybe more. She tried to speak with Ackenar but couldn't reach him. At least she still felt her coven's bond. They were there, holding her in their hearts. Too far to communicate, but that sense of belonging kept her calm. She wanted to leave. To return home. But she was too weak. She'd been wrong to send Ackenar away. There was no more to fear from Bloodstar. He hadn't returned to the tent.

She missed her coven. They must feel her demise. She slept, knowing they would come for her, so she didn't have to die alone. But they might not make it in time.

Visions swirled, obscuring reality and time. Colors and dragons. Fires and death. Sorcerers and magic. None of it made sense. Her connection to her coven was a thread of green that slowly turned yellow, thickening and pulsing.

Something was wrong with it. But it took too much effort to focus.

The visions swept her back to life as a hatchling. Back to that cave-in, when she'd been only three, trapped, unable to move. Unable to breathe. The coven had come for her.

But they were taking too long. Breathing was hard.

"I'm sorry." Jason's mind-speech was gentle, as if his recent bout with the plague had made him sensitive to noises.

She clung to his mind, an oasis of solid ground in the visions that cast her adrift. There was something about him that grounded her in reality.

"Not your fault. You're as much a victim as I am." His pain felt like her pain, so she tried to ease it.

"But I'm cured, and you're sick with the plague." Guilt flowed from him to her.

So that's what happened. Dragons didn't get sick. She tried to shake her head, but the ground held on too tight. *"Not sick."*

"You are. Please don't die."

His mind was sharp and clear. Certain. Almost draconic.

She longed to tell him she wouldn't die, but something stuck in her throat, cutting off her breath. Coughs racked her body as thick yellow-green phlegm spewed from her mouth, and she lost her connection to reality.

Sometime later, Jason rubbed her forehead. A deep ache eased. How had he known she hurt there?

"We're connected." His thoughts felt like her thoughts, just like coven thoughts. His sadness was hers, and somehow he loved her. It was as clear as dragon emotions. Human emotions were usually scattered, their thoughts a chaotic swirl that took training to focus. Jason didn't need training. His focus was already there.

"I think it's your heart. It connects us." Jason rubbed his chest.

It was as if he lived inside one of her minds.

Every muscle ached. Karyn blinked and realized she couldn't see from her own eyes. She saw herself prone on the ground, through Jason's eyes. Maybe their hearts did connect them. The coven link was gone, or she couldn't find it. She missed her family. Grief engulfed her, and she clung to Jason's mind. He understood her pain.

As Charlie cared for them, she recounted her life to Jason, feeling the connection grow.

She slept again. Visions filled her head. Jason's dreams. Dragons didn't dream. Their seers had waking visions, but dragons slept deeply, needing the time to heal and replenish their bodies. With six minds, sleep made the connections they needed to survive.

But Jason dreamed, and she experienced his hopes, his fear of magic, his love for his brother, and the resentment that he buried deeply. For once all these strange human emotions made sense.

When Jason woke, his energy made her head ache. He glowed, healthier than before. Changed. She could sense it, even without sight.

He wasn't the boy he'd been before.

A dragon heart controlled the blood flowing through his veins, changing him.

Maybe Bloodstar's wanted to create dragon-powered humans. But why?

Karyn needed to figure it out, to destroy his plan, but her lungs filled with that horrible phlegm, and she could no longer breathe. She had only minutes. Her fight had ended.

Jason's mind was all that connected her to reality.

"Tell my coven what happened to us. Find the spell that captured me. They need to know." Ackenar would've told them. Warned them about the spell. But she needed the coven to know exactly how she died, to see it in Jason's memories, and to see the change in him. They would figure out what it meant and stop Bloodstar. This story had to be stored in the dragon archive. As a warning. As a legacy.

Humans had too much power. They didn't know what their wars were doing to magic. But she knew, in these final moments, that the world's magic had been transformed into something to be feared. Dragons had to understand it, if they hoped to survive.

"Promise me you'll find them."

She felt his tiny body lean against her neck.

"I promise."

There was so much more behind his vow. He would tell the coven what had happened to her, to him. And once he discovered Bloodstar's plan, he would protect dragons over humans. She felt it in her soul. He feared magic as much as she did.

The other covens had been right to stay out of the humans' war. She didn't regret helping Brian, but she wished they'd moved his family to safety until the wars ended.

Jason would keep his promise. The coven would be safe.

Karyn closed her eyes as the plague finally took the last of her breath. She could rest now.

POWER OF SCENT
GREGOR

The putrid scent of rot woke Gregor. He sneezed, trying to clear his nostrils, but it only made it worse. He gagged as he scrambled out of the sleeping alcove, certain something had died next to him while he slept. The keep walls spun.

Gregor clutched his head. Something was terribly wrong. The other younglings slept, unaffected by the overwhelming stench. Blinking steadied the swirling, and he searched the worn indent. But there was nothing. No decaying critter. No reason for the smell.

Automatically, he reached through his mental connection to the coven to center himself. If there was anything to fear, someone would know about it.

Pain stabbed through his skull, and he doubled over as tears filled his eyes. He could feel the other dragons, but he couldn't communicate. He scanned the keep, but every dragon slept in the moonlit night.

Fear pushed his heart into a staccato pulsing through his mind.

Run. Flee. Escape.

He couldn't think around it. He had to get away from the rot, from the coven, from his home.

Energy coiled in his legs, and he leapt for the sky, pumping his wings to gain height over the dragons sleeping in the keep. As soon as he cleared the forest, he flew east.

The scent chased him. Every time he tried to turn back or called out to the coven, decay and death drove him to fly faster. But when he headed north, the sense of dread eased a little. So he flew toward hope, where the stench lessened.

The sun raced across the sky, into night and then back out again, but still he flew.

Eventually, each breath scraped his throat raw and cramped his lungs. His wings ached, forcing him to ease into a glide through the cloudless sky.

The land below was unfamiliar. Younglings weren't allowed to explore too far from the keep due to the shifting human wars.

He was so tired. The scent was weaker now, not so overpowering. But there was no way he could continue flying. He didn't know how much time had passed. It could've been hours or days. He did remember seeing the moon at one point.

The wind shifted, and Gregor tilted his wing to catch the thermal, but a cramp shot through the membranes. His wing folded in protectively, and he fell.

Frantic, he tried to correct, but with only one wing he spun head to tail toward the ground.

He bounced off the top of a tree and landed with a splash in a lake. Water engulfed him and slowed his descent.

His mind was clear. The fear still pulsed through his veins, but he could think. The cold water eased the ache in his limbs. Gregor swam for the surface, letting his wings settle along his back as he whipped his tail.

He was alive. Not that he'd thought he'd die. Gregor was glad no one could hear his thoughts.

When he broke through the surface, his stomach growled. He dove back underwater and filled his mouth with fish and lake grass. He ate more than twice his usual fare, and still couldn't ease the ache in his belly. But even a youngling knows not to overeat.

The edge of the lake was covered in snow. His talons sunk into the crusty covering, leaving prints as he shook off the water. Snow dropped from a pine tree, loud in the silence.

Gregor concentrated on reaching the coven. He focused on the coven bond, stretching out his awareness, but couldn't sense anyone. Not a dragon or a scout, or even a human nearby. The connection was there, deep in his heart, but he couldn't reach anyone with mind-speech. Obviously, he was too far away. He'd never been out of range of their thoughts before.

It felt strange, but also quiet. The only time he'd had his mind to himself was when he hatched. He couldn't remember much from that chaotic experience, other than days of starving and a driving need to find something. He'd found his coven, and they'd been in his mind ever since, a constant hum.

The silence in his head wasn't unpleasant, but it felt wrong, like something was missing. No matter. He could still feel them, even if he couldn't hear them.

The horrible scent was gone, and his thoughts were clear. Even the gnawing hunger had eased. Now, he felt only embarrassed that he'd fled from an odor. The other younglings would make fun of him. Being the youngest at sixteen meant he was always doing something wrong.

As if his body realized he was now safe, a warm lassitude swept through him. He would rest, let his muscles heal, and in the morning he'd fly back home.

Gregor slept.

He didn't know how long. He woke to sunlight and snow, and the chirps of curious birds. He smiled. They'd probably never seen a dragon. He was small compared to a grown dragon, but he was still bigger than the deer they were used to, and a brilliant green. He probably looked like moving grass, or a ferocious shrub.

Gregor stretched and winced at the ache in his wings. They hadn't healed yet. His stomach growled, reminding him he was still hungry, though not as ravenous as before. He sniffed and caught the scent of rabbits, a fox and her pups, and a badger, burrowed under the snow.

Rabbits would do.

He quickly caught his prey and ate, easing the ache in his belly. Now that his head was clear and he'd slept, he could start the journey back to the keep. At least his chest didn't hurt, and the cool lake water had soothed his sore throat.

The foul stench that had started his headlong flight was gone. Just thinking about it made his heart race. So, he made an effort to focus on the sky, the land, the air. Everything around him. It was time to go home. A hint of rot disagreed with his plan, but he ignored it. If he didn't focus on it, it would go away.

Hoping he'd eventually see a familiar landmark, he flew south. Worst case, he'd fly east to find the sea and follow the coastline. His coven lived in the cliffs inland from the sea, but he'd traveled there many times to explore the warm water and feast on salty fish.

The setting sun marked the passage of two days of flying, hunting, and the inevitable sleep that slowed his progress. Gregor hadn't left behind the snow. It was sparser, the trees no longer covered, but the forest floor below still held a couple of inches. He was in for another cold night on the ground, maybe two. He'd been too exhausted to notice before. But now he craved his warm sleeping alcove.

His wings quivered with the effort of flying. No way he'd admit he felt weakness. It wasn't the dragon way. But maybe a little rest would help. Hunger drove him back to the ground to hunt.

With his belly full, Gregor slept. But when he woke, more than a night had passed. The ground was clear, with no hints of the snow he'd fallen asleep in. He must've slept through at least one day of sunshine to melt the snow. He was losing time.

Hoping that he'd flown close enough to reach his coven, he stretched out his mind. Instantly, the stench of decay filled his snout. He sneezed and it dissipated.

It didn't make sense. Why would communicating with the coven cause him to smell something that didn't exist? He sniffed deeply. There were many kinds of rot, though he'd never smelled anything quite like this. Seaweed and decaying fish had a distinctive odor. The corpse of a half-eaten deer had another scent. This was different, stronger, yet also spicy. For some reason, it reminded him of humans.

He'd only met the riders who flew on the older dragons, but sometimes they smelled of sweat and fear when they landed. There was a bit of that in this scent.

Again, it dissipated as if shy of his attention, but he knew how to invoke it now.

Calling to the coven was too much, so he decided to narrow his focus. He sent his mind-speech to Rancor, an older dragon who'd taught him everything he knew.

The scent was strong, but not as overwhelming. He analyzed it, identifying something within that made his heart race again. Underlying the sickly spicy decay was the distinctive odor of dragons.

But dragons fly away to die. Even if they're badly injured, he'd heard, their coven would carry them somewhere special. He'd felt the loss of one of their coven once. A 200-year-old dragon had left them in the night. Gregor didn't know where he'd gone, but he'd felt the dragon's death. A whisper of emotion. A goodbye with no regrets. And then nothing. An absence in the coven link. It was gone in moments, as if the coven bond closed itself to the pain.

What if one of the coven was sick? Humans got sick all the time. The riders spoke of a plague causing a horrible sickness in their war camps. Their fear had a hint of this type of odor.

He shook his head at his foolish thought. Dragons didn't get sick. They died from old age, injuries, or the lack of will to live. Rare infections were treated immediately, and recovery was swift, nothing like human illnesses. Or at least that's what Gregor thought. But maybe the coven didn't tell the younglings everything. Maybe there were things that could make a dragon sick.

If that was the case, and he'd smelled it, he should've warned the coven so they could help the dragon. Instead he'd flown far away. Shame filled Gregor's chest, and his throat ached.

He was a coward. Weak. At the first hint of his power, he'd run away. The coven had told him he might develop a powerful ability. Many younglings did, but he hadn't expected his power to enhance his sense of smell. His ability was different, and instead of using it to warn the coven, he'd fled.

He hoped he wasn't too late.

With renewed purpose, Gregor jumped into the sky and flew south. He would find his way home and save the sick dragon.

POWER OF FIRE

JASON

Jason sucked in a deep breath. And another. Gone was the rasp that had torn his throat raw and filled his lungs with phlegm. Gone was the cough that rattled his brain. His awareness of himself came slowly. His body, no longer racked with pain, could move. His arms were heavy, but he could lift them.

For too long he'd been trapped in horrific visions. Only Karyn had been a lighthouse in a world of distorted shapes and sounds. At one point he'd been certain his mother was there. But then her face had melted into a monster, and he'd fled, unable to find reality. Charlie's voice had come and gone, begging him to live.

And through it all, Karyn had been with him in the chaos, her thoughts crisp, soothing the heat that threatened to consume him. Without her, he was certain his magic would've won.

As he cooled, she glowed hotter. Sixty years of life, from hatchling to the powerful dragon she'd become, seared through his mind. He didn't have time to process it all before she'd released him with her request. Her mind left his, and he woke.

"I promise to tell them what happened."

She was too far into the plague visions to hear, but he hoped she sensed his vow. Her family would want to know of her death. The dragon keep wasn't far, for a dragon, but even if he left right now, it could take a week to travel there on foot.

"Charlie." His brother was always nearby. Even during the most chaotic visions, Jason had felt him.

Scrawny arms wrapped around him. "I'm here. You sound better." Charlie's voice cracked.

Jason sat up. Strength pulsed in his arms and legs. The bright brown walls of the tent, the scent of crushed grass, the damp air on his skin, and even the stench of Charlie's sweat bombarded Jason. He blinked, trying to reset the world to normal.

But this wasn't a vision from the plague. This was something else.

Karyn's body lay across the huge tent, a chain around her neck. Her red scales still shimmered, as if defying the plague. She was larger in person than he'd imagined. But one thing was clear.

She was dead.

He felt it deep in his soul. He didn't know if she'd left his mind before or at that moment of death. But he could tell she was gone.

Grief enfolded him, a heaviness in his chest that had nothing to do with illness.

Charlie's words were lost in a roar of agony that filled Jason's head. The soulful cry of hundreds of dragons.

"What's wrong? Do you need water?" Charlie's face swam into view. His concern buffered Jason from the primal connection.

Jason stood, tossing the blanket onto the cot. He didn't know if the dragons had felt her death or if the pain had been something else, but he didn't have time to mourn. Bloodstar was bound to return soon to check on Karyn.

"We must hurry." He yanked on a pair of britches and a clean shirt, tucking it into the waistband.

Charlie grabbed his arm. "Wait. You almost died. Get back to bed."

Jason yanked free and ran to Karyn. He leaned his head against her forehead. "I'll tell them, Karyn."

Even though she was still warm, there was no response. He didn't want to let her go.

"You've been talking to her?" Charlie's demand didn't make sense.

Of course he'd been talking to her. Jason rubbed his chest. "She's part of me."

Somehow, that didn't describe the intense connection he felt. Her heart pumped his blood, and her mind had allowed him to feel her coven. Later, he would figure out what it all meant. But for now, she would live on inside of him. "We have to leave before the sorcerer returns."

"Why?" Charlie's confusion broke through Jason's focus. His brother didn't understand. Couldn't understand. For Charlie, Jason had been deathly ill for … He didn't know how long he'd been sick. Time had no meaning in the plague world.

"I'm healed. See?" Jason jumped and sucked in a huge breath to demonstrate his new vigor and clear lungs.

His brother didn't look convinced.

"The spell cured me."

"You might feel fine now, but what about in an hour? You need to rest. To eat. It will take time to recover. Going anywhere is ridiculous." Charlie crossed his arms, his mouth in that stubborn line that used to enrage their father.

"I'll explain later. Please. We need to leave now. Can't you just trust me?"

Charlie's face crumpled. "You almost died."

"But I didn't." Jason felt a shift in his brother. A desperation to believe everything would be fine.

With a curt nod, Charlie pushed Jason aside and dug through a large chest. He pulled out a leather travel pack and stuffed it with supplies. "Where are we going?"

"To Karyn's coven. I promised to tell them what happened to her."

"You've been sick for three weeks! You can't hike up a mountain. She's dead, and killing yourself won't bring her back." Charlie jabbed his finger into Jason's chest.

Jason didn't know how, but he could feel Charlie's exhaustion, his joy, and his fear. Charlie had fought to save him and now he was terrified that Jason was going to collapse again. To leave him.

The sorcerer's spell must be responsible. He hoped it faded soon, but he didn't have time to figure it out now.

Jason added extra blankets to the bedrolls and pulled the straps tight.

"I know. But I can warn her family about the spell Bloodstar used to capture her. I can tell them her final thoughts." He couldn't explain the sense of urgency or his connection to her coven. Thoughts buzzed just outside of reach, but he could sense their presence at the back of his mind.

Charlie threw up his hands and yelled, "Obviously, it doesn't matter that I'm trying to help you. Stay here. I'll get a horse." He ran out of the tent, taking his anger with him.

Jason turned back to Karyn's body. *Find the dragons. Warn the dragons. Live.* Her words pulsed in his chest. A promise he had to keep. A way to repay her for keeping him sane in the chaos.

Sadness and pain rolled through him in waves. More intense than all the grief he'd endured. His heart was her heart, and it wanted her to live. Jason stroked her chest, where his battered heart lay silent. The world had lost something with her death.

Anger ignited his magic, filling his head with heat. Bloodstar's spell had destroyed her while it healed him. Guilt at surviving fueled his power into an inferno swirling through his body.

The shimmer in Karyn's red scales dulled. Her body sunk into itself, her ribs showing through her dehydrated skin. Bloodstar had done this to her. He was a monster.

Jason's magic pulsed in his fingertips, aching for release. He wanted to revive her. To undo the spell. But he couldn't. That wasn't his power.

What would Bloodstar do with her now?

Images of her body being hacked up for more spells tortured Jason until he cried out.

Heat pulsed through his body, wave after wave, his mind nothing but fire. Magic surged through his palm, burning her chest. Scorch marks spread to encase her underbelly. The pungent odor of burnt flesh caught at the back of his throat.

Jason yanked his hand away and gagged. What was he doing?

Frantically, he pulled the heat back into himself. But his magic was in control. It burned through his revulsion. Through his fear. And suddenly it felt right, as if she'd given him permission. He couldn't leave her like this. Couldn't allow Bloodstar to harm her anymore.

Closing his eyes, Jason cradled her head and released his magic, to set her free.

Heat consumed him, hotter than any sun. There were no flames. No thoughts. No control. Only pure magic.

Moments later, he felt himself become solid. Human. Heat no longer pulsed through his body. Instead, he sat in a pile of red sparkling ash, drained of all emotion.

He should be terrified. Instead, he felt hollow. Empty.

Bloodstar's spell had changed him.

Jason's magic was gone, poured into Karyn to cremate her. He wasn't sure he wanted it back. Not if this was the result.

Karyn's heart beat in his chest. He didn't know what it meant, but he was certain he wasn't completely human anymore. Not a dragon. Something else.

He scooped the ash into a leather sack and pulled the ties tight. Bloodstar wouldn't use any part of her in his spells. Not even her ashes.

Sadness, anger, and fear swept through him, stronger after being absent. His hands shook. Maybe he was a monster now.

Only his promise kept him from lying down and giving up.

Jason sucked in a bracing breath. He'd dealt with grief before.

One day at a time.

But first he had to find the spell that Bloodstar had used to capture Karyn, so no other dragon endured her fate. That, he could do.

Digging through the chests, he found blank papers, bottles filled with bits of animals, plants, and other things he couldn't identify. Finally, he grabbed a small leather journal that looked promising.

The sound of rustling grass and heavy footsteps outside told him he'd run out of time.

He stuffed the journal into the pack and strode confidently out of the tent, hoping anyone who saw him wouldn't realize he was the same sickly boy who'd slept there.

The soldiers walked past him without even pausing. "Don't know why we have to stand guard on a hill."

"Don't complain. We get to sit here and enjoy the sunset."

Jason looked back. The tent was gone. A few trees sat on the rise. If he hadn't just left the tent, he wouldn't know it was there. Bloodstar was using a lot of magic to keep his experiment hidden. Even a sorcerer didn't have that much power. Another mystery for another day.

It was easy to avoid the few soldiers Jason encountered as he jogged through the empty camp. Charlie had told him that hundreds of soldiers had fallen ill. But the eerie silence, punctuated by an occasional murmur, did more to convince him of the magnitude of the plague.

As he neared the stables, the horses whinnied, hoping for food or attention. Jason slipped between them searching for Charlie. Everything about this war was wrong. Magic had destroyed a dragon soul. Battle had ruined the land and emptied villages. Now the plague was killing anyone left. Death was everywhere. It was time to stop fighting.

But the best Jason could do was flee with his brother and keep his promise to a dragon.

Jason found Charlie on the far side of the stable, rubbing Warhog's flank. The same horse that had almost trampled him on their first day in camp.

"Whoa. Steady." Charlie's voice was soothing and even more surprising, the horse responded.

"Wouldn't it be better to take one of the older horses?" Jason gestured toward the tame horse in the next stall.

"No. Warhog and I have an understanding. We've become friends. Isn't that right?"

Friends with a horse? Jason opened his mouth, ready to scoff at Charlie's silliness, but Warhog leaned into Charlie and whinnied.

"Won't someone notice him missing?"

Charlie patted the horse's neck as he slipped on the bridle and attached the reins. "Nope. His rider died, and no one else can ride him, but he likes me."

Charlie's attachment confused Jason. They'd never been around animals much growing up, but the horse was obedient now. Not the beast he'd been that first day.

He watched Charlie lift the saddle and tie on the bedrolls and pack. During the whole process, Charlie murmured to the horse. Nothing complicated, but Jason swore the horse understood.

They mounted, Charlie in front of Jason, and slipped behind the paddock into the darkness.

Tension gripped Jason's shoulders as they rode into the moonless night. He kept expecting a shout. Or a blast of magic when Bloodstar discovered they were gone. But nothing happened.

The clamor of camp life faded. Wind whispered through the tall grass, punctuated only by the clop of the horse's steps.

"We should stay off the path." He shifted his weight, and Warhog sidestepped.

"No one will follow us." Charlie sounded so sure.

"How do you know?"

Charlie's sigh was long, exhausted. "Almost everyone is in the plague tents. Those who aren't sick are too busy to care about deserters. The fighting stopped three days ago. Besides, we aren't the first to leave."

A lot had happened while he'd been ill. Jason hugged Charlie's back. "Thank you."

Charlie shrugged. "You're my brother."

They didn't need to say anymore. Jason understood. They were family. He'd do anything to keep his brother alive too.

Charlie's stomach rumbled, loudly.

Jason chuckled when his own belly responded. "We should eat before our hunger gives us away."

"I only have a little bread. There wasn't enough time to raid the cookhouse. You were supposed to stay in the tent."

So now it was Jason's fault they didn't have anything to eat? But Jason didn't want to argue anymore. Karyn's death and his near death had taught him that fighting didn't make life easier. "I had to leave. Two guards showed up."

He stuffed the bread in his mouth and chewed. Later he would tell Charlie about what he'd done. Once he understood how he'd transformed Karyn into ash in seconds without burning anything else. Jason wasn't ready for Charlie's questions or his reaction.

They stopped as the first rays of dawn painted the clouds red. Even though they'd ridden through the night, they hadn't dared let the horse trot or canter. The marsh was unstable for horse hooves and the last thing they needed was a lame horse.

Jason slid off first and groaned. His thighs burned and his legs wobbled. Charlie didn't fare much better.

"There's plenty of grass here for Warhog. I'll hobble him, and we can find something to eat." Charlie took charge. Something he'd never done before.

His brother had changed while Jason had been sick.

It was early enough, they could risk a campfire. They needed a warm meal to keep traveling through the cold fall day. And he could tamp down the fire before anyone back at camp noticed the smoke. He wasn't as confident as Charlie that no one would follow them. At the very least, Bloodstar would want him back. But the sorcerer might not know the effect of his spell. He'd only returned once to check on Jason's health. Charlie said he'd been too busy fighting the war.

Jason's magic had returned before dawn, coiling through his body. He held his hands over the tinder and concentrated on letting the tiniest bit of his power out. The campfire roared to life, flames shooting to the sky over his head.

"Crap." Jason clenched his fists and slowed his breathing, imagining his magic like a faucet, the water dripping instead of flowing.

The flames died down to the small fire he'd intended. He sighed, relieved. He could control it. Just had to set his intention before he used magic.

Charlie bounded up with two fat frogs, a handful of fever weed, and some mushrooms. "I thought we were hiding."

Heat infused Jason's face. "I, uh ... Having some troubles with my power since Bloodstar did his thing."

His brother's look would've made their mother proud. Jason could almost hear her words: That's no excuse. Get it together.

But Charlie didn't say them. He just shrugged. "That's tough."

Jason busied himself with cooking up the feast while Charlie sat and watched.

"You can tell me, you know. I know you're mad."

Jason stopped stirring the mushroom broth. "I'm not."

"Right. You lit a fire that could signal not only the war camp, but the villages far beyond them, for giggles."

The pot boiled, and Jason dumped the frogs into the broth. He settled next to Charlie.

"That's not what's happening. You saw what the sorcerer did."

Charlie nodded, his expression wary.

"It changed me. Having Karyn's heart. Talking to her. Being exposed to Bloodstar's magic. Of course it did. My power has been growing. Since Mom and Dad died, I guess. It was getting harder to control, especially when I was angry. But now, my magic is there all the time. Inside my body. At my fingertips. In my head."

Jason flipped his palms up. They looked so normal but held so much danger. "I'm trying to control it. To stop it. I don't know how, and there's no one to ask. I know why you gave me to Bloodstar. You were right. I would've died. But now, I have this problem."

Charlie grabbed his hands. "I'll help. This is amazing. You're more powerful than a sorcerer!"

Jason stood up. "No. It's too dangerous. I can't control it. What if I hurt you? I have to get rid of this magic."

He stomped away, knowing he'd overreacted. His brother had always worshipped him, but he should be afraid. A simple fire spell turned into an inferno. Karyn had turned to ash in seconds.

Jason was a monster.

DRAGON SENSES

JASON

After three days of travel, Jason's excess energy from the dragon's heart had faded. The meal in the marsh seemed like a distant memory as they wandered through the wasteland left behind from the war. Scorched trees and dirt. That was it. No animals, no plant life, and no shade.

Warhog stumbled on the lead, and Charlie murmured something consoling. They walked beside the horse now, trying to conserve his strength, having run out of feed the day before.

Jason's feet ached, and his urgency to get to Karyn's coven at Dawn's Keep had disappeared, replaced with pain and hunger.

Charlie plodded beside the horse, his head down, guiding Warhog through the holes and rocks in their path.

They needed to stop. To rest. But Jason kept moving, saying nothing. He knew how Charlie felt. He could sense every ache, his hunger and fatigue, as if they were his own. He could even sense the horse's emotions. They battered him, adding to his misery.

He hadn't had much time to talk to Karyn before her mind was lost to nightmare visions, but she'd told him a little about dragon abilities. Between the sorcerer's spell, Jason's own magical affinity, and Karyn's heart, he was pretty certain he was experiencing what dragons sensed. The wind moaned as it passed through the distant patch of trees. Burnt wood and the scent of animal carcasses wafted through his nose. And shades of greens he'd never seen before covered the distant mountain.

But it was more than changes to his vision, hearing, and sense of smell. He was stronger, despite his lack of energy. The night before, he'd thrown a rock to ease his frustration, and it had shattered against a boulder. He felt every beat of his heart pushing blood through his body. He was aware of everything.

Heat whooshed from his head to his arms, leaping to his fingers, responding to his distress.

Jason clenched his hand and breathed out slowly, forcing the heat into a box he'd created in his mind. Karyn had told him that dragons had six minds and could compartmentalize their thoughts and emotions. He didn't, but whenever his magic grew too hot, he pushed it into the box and could keep moving.

So far, it had worked. He was in control of his power. But as hunger weakened his concentration, and the unrelenting sun beat upon his head, the heat came more often.

Karyn's family would have to wait. He needed rest. The pile of ash in his satchel reminded him of what could happen if he lost control. He didn't want to become more of a danger to her coven than Bloodstar.

"There's a river over there. We should make it in a couple of hours. Maybe we'll catch some fish." Jason turned onto a path into the small forest that marked the end of the wasteland. It was in the wrong direction. Didn't matter. He wouldn't make it any farther without a break. Without the chance to release the heat growing within him.

Charlie mumbled something incoherent. Jason wasn't even sure his brother was aware of his surroundings. His exhaustion rolled through Jason, making him stumble.

Jason hated this side effect. He didn't want to feel anything other than his own fatigue.

Once they reached the shade of the trees, the crisp scent of life soothed the ache in his head. Pine trees, ferns, water. They all had an energy that vibrated in his mind.

Jason tied Warhog to a tree, leaving enough lead so the horse could nibble at the grass. Charlie swayed, as if his body wanted to keep moving but his feet had stopped. Jason pulled his unresisting brother to a log and pushed him down.

"What are we doing?" Charlie rubbed his eyes.

"Making camp. You're exhausted. We're both starving. And we need sleep." Jason cleared an area for their bedrolls and quickly set up a tarp. They didn't need the tarp, but it made the space feel more permanent. A home, at least for a brief moment. He needed it and suspected Charlie needed it more.

Charlie perked up. "Does that mean we're here? We made it to the dragon keep?"

Jason didn't have the heart to tell him they still had at least two more days of walking. Or that he no longer knew the exact location. He'd been connected lightly to the dragons ever since the spell. But as they'd traveled, that sense had weakened. Now, there was nothing. The loss felt important, but he didn't have the energy to figure out why.

As soon as they got close enough, he was sure he'd be able to use mind-speech to contact a dragon.

"Not yet. Don't worry about that now. Rest."

Charlie nodded and then slumped over in sleep.

Jason chuckled. He rubbed his hair, feeling the grease and pulling twigs from it. He'd fish first, then wash in the river, before making a fire.

His mother always said everything made more sense when you had a rested mind and a full belly.

Jason carefully released a trickle of his magic to start the fire. After catching a fish, he'd dunked in the cool river water and then had fallen asleep next to his brother. He'd awoken refreshed.

The heat in Jason's fingertips throbbed and his palms turned red. He concentrated on stopping the heat, but his magic struggled to be free.

Heat rushed through his blood, pooling in his skin, aching for release. Even his feet burned. The scent of scorched grass brought him back to the outside world.

Flames licked his boots. He stomped, killing the embers. The fire in the small pit flickered greedily. He sucked in a breath of ash and warmth and concentrated on driving the magic into his mental box. It was getting harder each time. His entire body was heat.

He had to release more magic. It was growing beyond what he could hold.

Jason ran from the camp, back to the burnt wasteland he'd so recently escaped. He grasped a charred tree trunk. Instantly, it turned to ash. He grabbed another one. And then rocks. Every one disintegrated under his touch.

But it was working. The heat was easing. He could think.

His ability shouldn't be this strong or this uncontrollable. It had to be Karyn's heart. Magic needed a source. And he didn't feel as if his power would ever run out. It just kept building. He torched a dozen more trees before he could shove his power into the box.

He slowly walked back to camp.

Charlie stood at the tree line, shock in every line of his body. Fear emanated from him in jerky waves.

"What are you doing?"

Jason didn't want to know that his brother was afraid. He didn't want this power or these new abilities. "I'm overheated from the sun, or maybe from the fever when I was sick. All I know is I feel better when I release the magic." There was no way he'd tell his brother it was more, and that he didn't know if he could stop it.

"That was a lot of power. How's your essence? Are you sure you're all right?"

Jason walked past his brother and stared into the flames. "I released magic daily when we were at the barn. It's no big deal. I have it under control. Let's eat."

Charlie frowned, and his disbelief beat at Jason's mind. "It didn't look like it."

Sensing his brother's emotions wasn't helping with his control. He built another mental box and shoved his brother's feelings inside. Since he didn't have multiple minds like a dragon this was the best he could manage. The pressure inside his head eased and the only emotions he could sense were his own.

"Are you hungry?" Jason placed the fish next to the flames in the fire pit, but Charlie wasn't willing to let it go.

"Why won't you talk to me, anymore. I can help."

Talking wouldn't solve anything.

"There's nothing to say. Just leave it." Jason patted Charlie's head and turned away. He would figure it out and keep Charlie safe.

But the acrid scent of the fire and the cooking fish mocked him with their intensity. He didn't want to lose control of his own power or sense the world in so much detail. It was exhausting. He just wanted to be normal again.

POWER OF EMPATHY
CHARLIE

Charlie was alone again. Jason had muttered something about setting snares and left. Ever since Jason had recovered from that horrible plague, he'd changed. Not once had he thanked Charlie for saving him or for taking care of him when he'd been sick, and now he was burning everything in sight and pretending nothing was wrong.

The expression on his brother's face had been frightening, his eyes closed and lips parted, as if destruction brought him pleasure. But then he'd returned to normal, ignoring Charlie's questions and shutting him out.

Charlie kicked a rock, and it thunked against the log they'd pulled next to the campfire. He didn't have a powerful ability, but that still didn't make it right for Jason to refuse his help. He picked up another rock and threw it against a tree trunk, the sound somehow expressing his frustration and easing it.

Not that long ago, they'd been more than brothers. They'd been best friends. At least once a week, after their chores, they would visit the blacksmith and hear stories of great rescues, amazing buildings, and people from far-off lands. They played games in the park behind the school and practiced illusion magic. Jason used to show him the spells he'd learned from tapping into his temperature ability and had reassured Charlie that his ability would eventually manifest too.

But after the war mages took their parents away, Jason had changed. He stopped being a friend and tried to replace their parents. He became solemn, never laughing, and only speaking of chores. There'd been no more trips to the blacksmith or the park. He refused to talk about magic, pretending his own ability had disappeared and barely using practical spells.

So when Charlie felt the first glimmer of his own ability, he'd kept it to himself. Jason would only deny it or make him stifle his power. But he'd needed his brother, especially on their first day at the army camp, when his power changed. Warhog's fear had swept through him, and he'd lurched to reassure the horse. Later, the stable hand told him that Warhog was dangerous, unpredictable, and violent. Charlie had known that wasn't true, but he couldn't say how, at least not without exposing his magic.

His magical ability had snuck up on him. He'd always been sensitive to emotions, feeling angry when others fought or sad when someone cried. His mother claimed he was more empathetic than most people. But as soon as he'd arrived at the farm, he wondered if it was more.

The other boys were easy to handle, most of them lonely and scared like him. But whenever he was around Barnaby, Charlie found himself reacting, unable to separate his own emotions. The more Barnaby lashed out, the angrier Charlie felt, and he found himself pushing back, trying to stop the feelings.

Jason stuck to himself. He'd always been a loner, but Charlie hated being alone. The boys talked about their families, the lives they had before, their hopes for the future, and he didn't feel so lost. He missed those days on the farm and the friends he'd left behind. But farm life had been challenging too.

Growing up in Cromwell, Charlie had rarely interacted with animals. There'd only been the occasional horse or a cat darting after a mouse. They kept to themselves. It took a while to realize that his empathy had transformed into a magical ability with animals.

Chickens had given him his first clue to the irrational waves of hunger and the desire to run into a corner and hide. They acted out their emotions, so it was obvious where they came from. Hunger abated when they ate, anger dissipated when they pecked at the offender, and their fear disappeared when they left their hiding spots.

Later, he discovered that touching an animal enabled him to discern the source of their emotions. Cows and sheep didn't let much ruffle them, enjoying the sun and munching grass. Their fright always had a cause. Horses and dogs were the most interesting, with emotions as varied as people. They got bored, felt joy, and craved interaction.

Some days, Charlie would lose himself in the simple experiences of the animals. It grounded him in the present, instead of the past, and made him feel connected. But he couldn't turn off his ability, not like Jason with his temperature power. Although, it was obvious that Jason wasn't in as much control as he'd been before.

Charlie plucked a piece of grass and tore it to pieces. Some of the plague survivors had a persistent cough or tremble. The Healers hoped the effect would go away over time, but they didn't really know. Being sick may have changed Jason, broken his ability to control his magic. Or maybe it was Bloodstar's spell. He'd taken Jason's heart.

What if a person's heart was the key to their magic?

He shook his head. There was no way to know what had caused this change. At least he didn't have to worry about his own ability. Touching animals to understand their emotions couldn't hurt anyone, and he only needed to walk away to break the connection completely.

Still, he envied his brother. Jason had powerful magic. He could train to be a witch or even a war mage. He could tap into his ability to protect himself from anything.

Charlie couldn't convert sensing animals into anything more powerful than the practical spells he could already perform, and he certainly couldn't stop a war mage from draining him. Like his parents, he was nothing more than a source of magic. He had even more reason to hide his ability than Jason did. The war mages would be fools to drain his brother when he could be trained to aid the war effort.

Charlie's resentment dissipated. Probably his own discontent had been boosted by his brother's anger. Empathy was tricky to separate from his own feelings.

He had nothing to do and was tired of thinking. He'd done enough of it in Bloodstar's tent.

Now there was a sorcerer who controlled enormous amounts of magic. Despite the horrific spell that saved Jason's life, Charlie hadn't felt anything other than purpose and melancholy from the man. Bloodstar had been in control of his power and his emotions the entire time.

Charlie dug through the backpack for Bloodstar's journal, hoping to find something that could help Jason before he lost control again. Next time, he might start a forest fire and lead the war mages right to them. Charlie wasn't about to lose his brother after everything they'd gone through.

He flipped through pages of intricate dragon drawings, documenting every stage from a tiny creature inside an egg to a full-grown dragon. There were many spells, some scrawled sideways or rewritten above crossed-out passages. Most didn't make sense, a jumble of odd-looking words, but some were simple in their phrasing. Elegant.

The knife that Bloodstar had used to remove Jason's heart was there, but Charlie couldn't decipher the words under it, some containing symbols instead of characters.

The journal portrayed years of research. Tools, locations, and hundreds of spells culminated in the final ritual that Bloodstar had performed. Even the smoke had pages of spell work and references to plants Charlie had never heard of.

It was obvious that Bloodstar respected dragons. His drawings showed their strength and intelligence. One page listed all the reasons dragons were better than people. So, it didn't make sense that he would kill one.

There had to be a reason, but Charlie would probably never know it. He sighed and stuffed the journal back into the sack, unsuccessful at finding anything about controlling power. At least nothing he could understand.

He would have to find another way to help Jason, but first, he had to get his brother to talk about the conflicting emotions that poured from him in waves. His brother was a jumble of resentment, guilt, anger, and sadness. Obviously, denying it wasn't working.

Together, they could figure something out. It would be hard. Jason still treated him like a child. He seemed to forget that Charlie had lost his parents too. Jason wasn't the only one who had to grow up fast.

Charlie leaned against Warhog's neck, allowing the horse's contentment with nibbling grass to ease into his consciousness. Food, water, exercise, and rest were all the horse needed. Maybe that was all Jason needed. Ever since they'd left camp, they'd been running. Hunger had filled Charlie's nights. He hadn't felt safe for a long time.

They needed to settle, to find balance, and do more than exist. They needed a home.

As soon as Jason finished with the dragons, they would find a place where they could live far from the war and be in control of their powers and destiny.

Until then, Charlie would open himself to his brother's confusing emotions and help him accept his power. Fighting a magical ability wouldn't lead to more control. In fact, it might destroy Jason, and Charlie couldn't let that happen.

RETURN

GREGOR

It took two more days before Gregor recognized the mountains below him. The day before, he'd encountered the coastline and followed it southward. The horrible stench was gone, but each time he tried to call to the coven, there was nothing. No sense of them at all.

He'd flown through the first night but then had to sleep half a day to recover. The light was fading, and his energy along with it. The fatigue that sapped his strength concerned him. His hope was that once he returned home, enveloped in the energy of the coven, he would recover.

Once again he reached for the comfort of the coven bond. But he could only sense the island dragons off the coast at Klaw Keep. His coven was missing from his mind and his soul. Something terrible must've happened. Though he couldn't imagine what could take out an entire coven of almost three hundred dragons. As he searched the coast for a safe place to rest, he went over every possibility. A cave-in. Tornado. Tsunami. But even those couldn't make an entire coven disappear.

There were only two explanations. The first was that he was simply too exhausted and was doing something wrong. The other was too hard to believe. That he'd been banished, cut from the coven mind. Every youngling knew the story of the dragon who'd been banished for killing a youngling who asked one too many questions. Some say he flew into the icy mountains to die. Others said he flew south and started his own coven of the banished. Gregor didn't know the truth, but dragons couldn't survive without more of their kind.

He was alone.

No hum of mind-speech. No community of love. Nothing.

He wanted to fly to Klaw Keep and beg them to take him in, but he didn't. He'd never spoken to a dragon outside of his coven. And something inside warned him that he should keep his distance. He wasn't going to question his instincts. His coven must've cast him out, so he must be a danger, even if he didn't know what he'd done.

Gregor landed on the beach and curled up in the sand, but he couldn't sleep. Every crash of the waves felt like regret. Every squawk of a seagull a mournful cry. Even the wind howled rejection.

As soon as the sky turned pink, he flew inland.

Home. The answers were there. Someone would tell him what he'd done.

The scent of rot returned, but he flew through it. He wouldn't turn away this time.

Gregor gagged on the stench, his entire body shaking with the desire to flee. But his heart held strong. Fear wouldn't drive him away.

He tried to call to his coven, but there was only silence. Worry ate at his stomach.

By the time Gregor flew over the mountain and dove into the keep, each breath was a struggle.

The sleeping alcoves were empty, but the floor of the keep was not. Dragons lay everywhere, some on top of each other, some sprawled in unnatural poses.

They didn't move.

They didn't respond when he called out to them.

There was no coven bond.

He wanted to land. To make sure. But the fear, the pain, the odor was too much to bear. Gregor fled, tears drowning his view and grief filling his soul.

The stench was real. This wasn't his power warning him. All the dragons were dead.

He'd been connected all along. Was still connected, even though they were gone. That's why he could smell them.

As he flew over the village of Silverstream, a dragon rider waved and tried to contact him. He closed his mind to the woman's call. He already knew what happened.

He'd smelled rot days ago, when they were alive. He could've warned the coven. Saved them all. Instead, he'd fled, his cowardice ensuring they died.

He flew until exhaustion made his wing tremble, and he rested in a valley. He forced himself to eat, because the coven would want him to survive. And then Gregor gave into the grief.

He curled up in a ball, tail to snout, wings tucked in tightly to hold in the pain, and he howled for his family. For his friends. For his mistake.

He couldn't sleep. Night sounds filled his ears, but he wasn't afraid. Nothing could hurt a dragon. Except something had. Something had turned his coven into rotting corpses. He'd been gone a long time. Five days, maybe a week. What could destroy an entire coven in only a week?

He didn't know, but he would find out. Because if it happened to his coven, it could happen to others.

A new odor drove Gregor to his feet. Something sweet. He didn't recognize it, but it lifted his pain a little. Hope. This time he'd listen to his power, instead of running away from it.

After rising gently into the sky, he sniffed deeply. There. A sweetness that didn't fit. There was no sense of doom. He felt drawn to the scent. It had to mean something.

A subtle connection settled in his chest, and hope made him fly faster. Maybe someone had survived. Maybe he wasn't alone.

55

DRAGON GRIEF

JASON

Jason rested for three days, more exhausted than he realized. He and Charlie slept in between fishing, cooking, and checking the snares. Fortunately, the war hadn't ruined this part of the forest, so they found berries and mushrooms to fill their bellies.

Fourteen days after his heart was exchanged, Jason woke early. The air had a stillness to it that made the hairs on his arm stand. The spicy scent of magic filled his nose and numbed his tongue.

A presence sat in the back of his mind. Close.

Jason's heart leapt. Maybe it was a dragon from Karyn's coven. They weren't even halfway to the keep, and he was still so tired. If he could communicate, maybe he wouldn't have to travel any farther.

As he lay next to Charlie under the tarp, Jason stretched his awareness along the mental connection.

Pain stabbed through his head. He couldn't break the connection, but the pain eased, leaving an impression of youth.

Karyn's emotions had been clear, but these were muddled. Fear, anger, and loss.

Jason's throat tightened, and he swallowed to relieve the ache. This was the same grief he'd felt when his parents died.

Jason slammed his mind shut to block his own memories and lost contact. The only thing he knew for sure was that the dragon was flying toward them.

"Wake up, Charlie. Someone's coming." Jason nudged his brother. A grief-stricken dragon might not be the most rational, and he wanted them to be dressed and ready to run.

Soon, Jason could see a green dragon flying toward them. He was much smaller than Karyn and seemed to struggle with flying.

Jason's heart slowed, as if trying to match the dragon's heartbeat. Wary of what would happen when the dragon landed, Jason breathed in deeply, hoping to remind his body that it was his to control.

The horse whinnied.

"I'm going to hold Warhog." Charlie jogged away, leaving Jason alone in the clearing next to the firepit.

As the dragon flew over the trees, Jason cleared his mind and focused on mind-speech.

"Hello, dragon. I have something to tell you." He tried to transmit calmness, hoping this young dragon came from Karyn's coven. He wasn't old enough to be a scout, and covens didn't allow their young to travel far from the keep. They were probably closer to her home than he'd realized.

A blast of panic made Jason turn, ready to flee into the protection of the trees. But he resisted. His mission was important, and he couldn't let fear stop him.

"Who are you?" Uncertainty transmitted from the young mind.

"Jason. It might be easier if you land over here." Jason projected an image of the space by the river, far from the horse and upwind of the camp.

Acceptance was immediate. Jason gasped when the dragon dove for the ground. He'd assumed dragons circled and slowly descended.

He stood completely still, unsure if showing any sign of fear would incite the emotional dragon to do something rash.

The dragon landed with a quick backwing that blew dirt and leaves into Jason's face, and then he collapsed.

"They're dead." The words burst through Jason's head along with a vision of hundreds of dragons lying on the ground. Some had their eyes open, others with their jaws wide, but most appeared to be asleep.

A putrid odor of rot assaulted Jason, and he gagged.

Before he could ask what happened, the dragon roared, *"Did you do it?"*

Jason stepped back, holding out his hands. *"No! I don't know what happened. I was on my way to your keep to tell you about Karyn."*

The dragon whipped his head back and forth, then pushed himself up on his hind legs. He stood twice as tall as Jason but was only a bit bigger than Warhog.

Fear made Jason's heart race and magic leapt to his fingers. Only his mental connection prevented him from losing control.

Gregor. His name rose from Karyn's memory. He was a youngling from her coven.

"Calm down, Gregor. I can help." Memories of his own confusion when he'd been told of his parents' death softened Jason's fear. Gregor was scared and hurt.

Jason's power receded.

A shift in the wind pushed the scent of the dragon's terror to Jason. He wrinkled his nose, trying to keep the contents of his stomach where they belonged. Then suddenly, he swore he could smell apples.

Gregor raised his head, his eyes whirling his distress.

"You're little for a human. But there's something different ..." Gregor sniffed loudly, and the apple scent dissipated.

He seemed calmer. Sadder.

"Tell me about Karyn." Gregor's mind was closed to Jason now, his emotions no longer transmitting.

The abrupt change made Jason sway. He forced himself to focus on staying calm.

"I promised to let her coven know how she died. A sorcerer cast a spell to exchange our hearts." The story unfolded in his memory, showing Karyn's strength in holding on until the plague killed her.

"That's what happened to my…" Gregor sucked in a breath, and his emotions leaked out. Guilt. Fear. Despair.

"To who?" But Jason knew. No matter how impossible, it was there in Gregor's mind. A plague had killed his coven. *"They're all dead?"*

"Yes." Pain radiated from Gregor.

"But you survived."

"I wasn't there."

"When did you leave?" Bloodstar's spell had been incredibly powerful, but it couldn't have infected the coven. Karyn died many miles away. She never left the tent. But what if it was the same plague spell? Magic didn't always behave in a rational manner.

"I'm not sure. A week. Maybe more. It's taken me three days to return."

"They were healthy when you left?" Jason frowned. The timing fit. They'd gotten ill after the spell. But Gregor was hiding something. He didn't say why he'd left, or where he went, and he seemed confused about the passage of time. From Karyn's mind, Jason had gathered that dragons didn't lose time. Maybe it was because this dragon was young.

"Yes." Guilt poured from Gregor, which didn't make sense. He didn't kill his coven. The spell did. Though impossible, it was the only explanation that made sense. Bloodstar's spell had killed Karyn's coven. Everyone except this youngling.

Another whiff of decay hit Jason, bringing bile to his throat.

"Are you sick?" If the spell infected the coven, then Gregor might have the plague. Jason didn't know what a normal dragon smelled like. Karyn had been sick, but she hadn't smelled this way.

Gregor shook his head. *"I'm not. But I could smell it. I could've warned them."* His self-accusation almost brought Jason to his knees.

"No. You didn't do this."

A tortured snort echoed in Jason's skull.

"I woke to a sense of doom and an overwhelming odor of decay. It forced me from my sleeping alcove, and I flew away from my keep. By the time the scent faded, I was far from home and couldn't sense the coven." A wave of loneliness and loss hit Jason.

This youngling needed his family. There must be more to belonging to a coven than community. It felt deeper than the bond between Jason and his parents.

"When I returned ..." Gregor bowed his head.

Jason didn't need him to say it again. *"They were dead."*

"I thought I couldn't feel our connection because I'd flown too far away. I was wrong." His sorrow was a hundred times more intense than Jason's grief.

"Do you think you smelled the spell?" If Gregor had, then maybe there was a way to detect the magical plague, before dragons died.

"Maybe. I've always had a really good sense of smell."

Even though it was impossible, the spell had infected Karyn's coven.

But Gregor had escaped, so others may have survived as well. Assuming that Gregor wasn't sick. He seemed healthy, but his eyes whirled, and the scent of apples and rot kept wafting from him. His emotions were erratic. Karyn had been calm, even when her mind was filled with plague visions.

"Rest, Gregor. We'll figure it out." Jason felt a deep connection to the youngling, something more than shared loss, something bound to his new heart.

Gregor sighed, his mind clearer. He lay next to the river, curling his tail under his chin, and closed his eyes, falling asleep in seconds.

Jason didn't know what Bloodstar's spell had done to him, but Gregor was his responsibility now. Gregor was family, as important as Charlie, and Jason would take care of him.

OVERLOAD

JASON

Gregor slept until dusk the following day. Jason kept checking on him, but the youngling's mind was clear of the chaotic visions that had plagued Karyn. Gregor wasn't sick, just exhausted. The impression of endless snowcapped mountains kept settling in Jason's mind.

Wherever Gregor had flown, it was much farther north than any human had traveled. The ache in his wings and shoulders made Jason rub his own shoulders.

Charlie hadn't returned from his walk, but Jason could sense his brother's state. Charlie wanted to leave. His impatience grated on Jason's nerves. Charlie didn't understand. He couldn't. He didn't have the connection to Gregor that Jason had.

It was the same as he'd felt with Karyn. Something deep in his chest and at the back of his head. The coven was dead.

Despite the horrific spell involving his own heart, Jason didn't believe that Bloodstar had intended to kill an entire coven. He probably didn't even think the spell would kill Karyn. Jason wasn't sure how he knew this—maybe something in Karyn's thoughts?

Dragons were special. Stories of their heroic deeds had been memorialized in statues. Dragons flew for both sides of the war. General Riley had planned many strategic archer attacks employing the dragons on their side. So the sorcerer wouldn't have wanted to kill them.

Something must have gone wrong with Bloodstar's spell.

Or maybe Jason had been too sick. Not many people survived the plague.

It was his fault. He was the one who was supposed to die. His pathetic heart had killed Karyn. Because he hadn't been strong enough.

Now, he'd destroyed hundreds of dragons. The spell had failed because of him.

Jason poked the fire as shame gnawed at him. He had to do something. But it was too late. They were all dead and only Gregor had survived.

Guilt rolled through Jason and grew, but it wasn't his. It was Gregor's. The youngling had the chance to warn the coven, but he hadn't.

Anger wound through the remorse, stamping it out. And heat rose through Jason, infusing his mind with purpose. Bloodstar had killed all those dragons, but Gregor could've saved them.

And Jason should've died.

If he had, the dragons would still be alive.

Charlie shouldn't have saved him.

"Only one small trout today." Charlie plopped down next to the fire.

Jason clenched his fists, his power rushing through him with his conflicted emotions. Charlie was trying his best.

But the dragons, his brother, the world, everyone would've been better off if Charlie had let him die.

"What's wrong? Did something happen? You look like you're going to explode."

Jason couldn't tell Charlie the truth. He stood, his body vibrating with all the things he couldn't say.

"Do it." Charlie stood with his fists on his hips, facing Jason. The fire snapped between them.

"What?"

"Yell. Throw stuff. Hit me. I don't care. Whatever has you wound up so tightly is only going to get worse. Unless you let it out." Charlie's tone was so reasonable and so like their father's that pain stabbed through Jason's heart. He missed his father the most.

It was enough to settle the roiling inside him. For a moment.

Gregor shifted in his sleep, and his grief crashed through Jason.

That dragon was part of the problem. His emotions were all over the place.

Jason had enough trouble controlling his own. He didn't need a teenage dragon's thoughts in his head all the time.

So he ran.

Away from Gregor. Away from Charlie. Away from the fire inside him that longed to be set free.

He ran until his breath came out in gasps and burned in his chest. He ran until his heartbeat filled his head. And then he stopped, looked up at the stars starting to appear in the sky, and screamed.

Magic burst from his fingers, filling the air with green sparks. His heart pounded three times harder, blocking all sound, all thought.

Anger poured from his soul. At Gregor. At Charlie. At Bloodstar.

Fear of himself, his power, and his lack of control.

And grief for the loss of his parents, Karyn, and her coven. All dead.

Because of him. Because of magic.

Only Charlie and Gregor were alive, and he resented them for it. For living and feeling, when so many had died. For the responsibility Jason felt for ensuring they both survived.

Everything poured out with incoherent grunts, gasps, and shouts. Gregor's mind left his. Jason couldn't sense the world around him. Not Charlie, the dragon, or the forest.

And still it came. Until, finally, the last of the chaos left.

Maybe the sorcerer's magic had been stuck inside him, trapped in Karyn's heart. Maybe his own magic had gotten messed up. He didn't know.

He stood in a clearing, surrounded by tree trunks composed of ash. He hadn't even been aware of burning them. But the fire was gone. The ring of untouched trees showed no sign of sparks.

He'd done it again. Destroyed everything.

But the pressure was gone. The pain too. His anger simmered, but he could think through it. Gregor wasn't to blame. The youngling didn't understand his own power, but it had probably saved him. Jason doubted it could've saved the coven. Bloodstar had made a mistake and dragons had died, but that was the end of it. Karyn's bond to her coven must've killed them. An accident.

Jason was alive. His brother wasn't alone. Those were good things. He could live with his regret. He hadn't forced his heart into Karyn's chest. He hadn't killed her. The sorcerer's magic had done that.

Jason returned to camp and collapsed next to Charlie.

"It's OK now. I'm done."

He was suddenly ravenous. No. Gregor was awake. Jason felt his hunger as if it were his own. *"You should eat."*

Gregor simply blinked and turned away, his apathy evident.

"We need to feed him. He's not sick. He's grieving." Jason didn't blame Gregor for surviving anymore. He'd lost enough already. Now he needed to live, and Jason intended to help him.

"You couldn't have done anything to save them. If you'd stayed and ignored the scent that forced you away, then you would've died too." It felt right. He forgave Gregor. But the young dragon wasn't ready to forgive himself.

Charlie handed Jason a piece of cooked fish. "There's barely enough for us. Don't dragons feed themselves?"

It took a moment to adjust. Mind-speech came more naturally now. It was as easy as thinking. But Jason didn't have the multiple minds of a dragon to keep the conversations separate.

"Yes, normally. He's the same age as us, and he's lost his family." Jason put his arm around Charlie. "You remember, right? We have to help him. If he doesn't eat, he won't have the strength to fly. I don't know if he'll die. All I know is he's too young to be by himself."

"So we feed him. Then what?" Charlie's question wasn't new. They couldn't stay there forever.

Jason chewed his lip. What would they do? The coven was gone, so his promise to Karyn didn't matter anymore. He didn't know anything about taking care of a dragon. But they couldn't leave Gregor alone. His connection wouldn't let him, anyway. They had no destination. No home. They couldn't go back to the army, and he didn't want to. Charlie deserved a better life, and safety.

But Jason couldn't control his magic. So finding a village wasn't a good idea yet. He sighed. Taking care of his brother was hard, but he was glad he wasn't alone. And really, if it hadn't been for Charlie, he'd be as dead as Karyn. There was no way he would have survived the plague.

He didn't know what was next, but for now, they could take care of Gregor until he was strong enough to fly to another keep. Dragons needed covens. Gregor would feel better when he wasn't alone.

"We'll find someplace to live. But Gregor needs other dragons. So let's focus on getting him better so he can fly to another dragon keep." Jason wasn't ready to tell Charlie about his problem with his own magic. Not yet.

Charlie nodded, accepting his big brother's plan. He always did. Which made Jason wonder at the initiative it must've taken Charlie to offer him up to the sorcerer for a cure. What would he be like without Jason around to make all the decisions?

He shook his head. It didn't matter. Charlie was his responsibility. He'd figure out a way to get them both a place to live and a chance at a happy life. He owed it to Charlie and to his parents.

But a secret part of him wished he could drop Charlie and Gregor off somewhere safe, so he could figure out what he needed. His power was a liability, and it scared him. The war mages would use him up in a heartbeat. But he wanted to be more than a source of power for battle magic. He wanted to do more than survive. And he was tired of being afraid of his power. He had to master it.

Charlie had given him a second chance at life. There had to be a reason he lived when so many others had died. Something special to make up for everything the world had lost.

YOUNGLING
ZANTHOR

Zanthor flew beside Ronin and relished the crisp fall air. Rain would come soon and replenish the parched ground below. The humans would seek cover and stop destroying forests in their quest to claim a constantly moving border. Winter always brought a respite from war.

A fierce wind pushed him toward Talon Keep. He'd been away from home for too long. He missed the hum of the coven in his mind. At least Ronin had turned out to be good company on their mission to enlist the other covens in supporting their riders.

With the unending war among the humans, riders were becoming scarce. Too many dragons had felt the loss of their human companions. It wasn't anything like losing a coven member. Dragon riders were special friends, fragile, but with hearts of courage.

The pain of losing his rider over two years ago still took him by surprise whenever he thought of her. Ariel had been with him for ten years. Even now, the space where she'd sat on his shoulders felt empty. She'd died fighting off the invaders in her village. He'd felt her fierceness, her hope, and her death.

Coven policy was to stay out of human politics. They were to leave the riders to their war. Some dragons had defied the rule and become outcasts, no longer connected to the coven. When he'd flown over the burnt remains of Ariel's village, the pain of every dragon who'd lost their rider echoed through his soul. They'd all ignored their riders' pleas, and a war mage had incinerated the village. The battlefield hadn't even been close. The village was attacked solely because dragon riders lived there.

Zanthor rarely used his power of conviction, especially not to influence coven policy. But they could've stopped the slaughter. Dragon riders deserved their protection.

He'd started small, working his way up through the hierarchy of advisers. And the ache in his heart had eased with each conversation. Eventually, he gathered enough support to plead his case to the coven leader, Kruzen.

Other covens had aided their riders, either flying over the battlefield to allow their riders to fight or scaring off invaders when they threatened their villages. Humans rarely denied a dragon. Not when one swipe of a talon could shred a human. Swords and arrows couldn't penetrate a dragon's skin, and even mage spells had little effect, merely causing a minor annoyance with their blasts of heat or ice.

Zanthor's coven could do the same. They didn't have to participate in the war. That was up to each dragon. A choice only they could make. But they could provide safety. There was a high plateau in the mountains where the riders and their families could resettle, away from the war and the mages.

Once Kruzen agreed, Zanthor had pushed for more, convincing him that they should help any dragon rider, regardless of coven affiliation. He hated coercing dragons with his power, but this was too important to wait for leaders, stuck in tradition, to shift their thinking over time. They had to save as many dragon riders as they could, now. Before the Great Wars killed them all.

For the past six months, he'd traveled to each coven, only using his power to push those who would've decided to help in time. Anyone over thirty-four didn't have powers. The seers said it was a side effect of the mage wars. But more younglings demonstrated powers each year. His was subtle enough that most dragons weren't aware he was even one of the powered dragons. Zanthor was able to use this to his advantage, as long as he was careful. An abrupt change of mind could be sensed by everyone in the coven. So he spoke and cajoled and then helped with the relocation.

Many riders didn't want to fight any more than dragons did. Everyone was tired of thirty-four years of war and wanted a life without loss.

No one knew what had started it. Not even dragons. And they had long memories.

It wasn't about land. Armies battled over shifting borders, destroying everything in their path, leaving only wasteland behind. It wasn't about government. Too many cities had fallen over the years. Only three nations had survived by closing their borders and refusing to participate. He didn't know what force kept the humans battling on the ground. But three sorcerers fought over who would control magic. Something even dragons without powers knew was impossible. Magic flowed through the world, as uncontrollable as air or water. Humans weren't rational.

A sensation of fear pulled his attention to the south. Not an animal. A dragon. He stretched his awareness, attempting to identify the threat evoking such a strong emotion.

"You felt it too?" Ronin's voice held a somberness that made Zanthor uneasy. The large blue dragon had a knack for connecting to dragons outside of their coven.

"I sensed fear. Did you get more?"

"Chaos. Shame. A youngling in distress." With these words, Ronin dove for another current, seeking the fastest path.

Zanthor followed. The youngling's coven should be near, but he couldn't sense any other dragons. Dawn's Keep wasn't that far away. Something drastic must've left this youngling alone and afraid.

As they drew nearer, the youngling's emotions pulsed through Zanthor's mind. Anguish now overrode fear. Without a coven shield, the dragon's fragmented memories were easily accessed. Images of dead dragons, wisps of a rotting stench, and an exhausting flight. Zanthor had to tighten his own shields to stop his body from reacting. The youngling's emotions were powerful.

"Shield your mind. We're coming." Zanthor pushed a little of his power into the command, hoping the youngling wasn't too frightened to respond.

Ronin was right about the danger. The youngling's emotions could cause any nearby creature to react mindlessly. They wouldn't know the emotion wasn't theirs.

"Wait. There are humans nearby." Ronin's reach had always been farther, something to do with his power, though they hadn't discussed it.

Zanthor slowed his wing beat, gliding through the clouds. *"I'll warn them of the danger, so they stay away."* Usually, contact without permission was discouraged, but these humans would be affected by the youngling's emotions. They wouldn't know why they felt that way. Few humans understood the effect of transmitted dragon emotions, certain all emotions were their own.

He gently eased into the one mind that seemed calmer. *"Stay where you are. There's danger ahead."*

"Oh, thank the Healer. Are you here to help?" The words were clear and surprising. This mind belonged to a young, male human who spoke with the ease of a dragon rider.

"Jason." The response held mirth, and Zanthor realized the boy heard his thoughts.

Zanthor shielded his mind. It was rare for humans to access dragon minds, especially this young, but none could break through a shield. *"I am Zanthor. There's a dragon in distress nearby. Please keep your distance."*

"That's Gregor. We tried to help, but he's getting worse." Jason's concern for the youngling was strong. There was a connection. Empathy.

Zanthor frowned. It was almost like a dragon rider bond. But that couldn't happen. He'd speak with the boy later, but first he needed to calm Gregor.

He and Ronin landed next to two boys.

Jason was smaller than Zanthor expected, having dealt mostly with adult humans. Next to Jason was a thinner boy. He didn't look nearly as confident, standing as far away as he could while holding the reins of a frightened horse.

Zanthor lowered himself to a reclining position to keep the boys calm while communicating with Gregor. He could shield them physically should the youngling act rashly. Ronin stood, protecting his flank from anything that might agitate the youngling more.

"Gregor, shield your mind. You're harming these humans," Zanthor spoke gently, worried the youngling would flee.

Gregor responded with fear, regret, and a soul-wrenching sadness. Yet there didn't appear to be anything wrong with him. Just those disturbing images.

Zanthor pushed his conviction into Gregor's mind. *"Calm yourself. You're safe."*

There was resistance and an overwhelming stench of decay. Zanthor sneezed and shook his head. This dragon had power, but he had no idea what it meant. There was only one thing left to do, though he hated doing it.

"Sleep, youngling. When you wake, you will be calm." The cooling scent of mint filled his mind before Gregor fell into a deep, healing sleep.

Zanthor turned his attention back to Jason, who immediately launched into an unbelievable story about a sorcerer, an exchange of hearts, and a magical plague that killed the coven at Dawn's Keep.

Jason outlined his encounter with Gregor and the subsequent decline in the youngling's health. Gregor hadn't eaten in three days.

Ronin inserted the occasional snort of disbelief into Zanthor's private mind as they listened to the boy's tale.

It was clear that Gregor was unwell. A sickly yellow wove through his green hide, and his tail was molting. But it wasn't an infection or an injury that had brought him to this state. It was guilt and grief.

"Gregor?" Zanthor lowered his shields and gently prodded the youngling awake.

Gregor didn't answer. Not in words. But his desire for death came through loud and clear. He'd lost his entire coven in a short time. Whether from this magical plague, as Jason claimed, or some strange infection, Zanthor believed the coven was gone. Gregor had no coven protection. Even if he'd flown across the continent, he should still be connected. No coven would force a youngling out of the bond.

Zanthor dove deeper into the youngling's unprotected mind. There was a connection, but with the boy, Jason. Dragons didn't bond with humans until they were adults, and never with human children. This felt different from a dragon rider bond. Deeper. Jason felt Gregor's emotions, even when the youngling wasn't transmitting.

If this was the result of a sorcerer's spell, then dragons had a lot to worry about. Zanthor would have to inform the covens right away.

Magic used to be predictable, but the Great Wars changed everything. If dragons could hatch with powers, it was reasonable to assume that eventually sorcerers could amass enough magic to harm dragons.

He didn't know how the sorcerer had immobilized Karyn, or if he believed the sorcerer could use magic to take her heart. But Jason's thoughts were clear. This had happened. Zanthor couldn't even begin to imagine what a dragon heart inside a human would do, or if it could hurt dragons. But somehow the sorcerer had created a plague spell that killed Karyn and her coven. And if one sorcerer could do this, so could the others.

Dragons were in danger.

"I'll fly to Dawn's Keep. You keep the youngling calm and find out more from these boys." Ronin took off. He was right. They needed to confirm Gregor's story before they panicked. The boy and the youngling might be under the influence of an illusion spell. They needed the facts. Not stories. Gregor had fled after seeing the coven dead on the ground. Jason's story had filled in the rest.

But Gregor wasn't bound to a coven, and he needed one. Banished dragons were always old enough to live as outcasts. No coven would expel one so young. Gregor was only sixteen. Adult dragons could survive without the coven bond, but they rarely lived as long or prospered. If Gregor's coven was gone, Zanthor would take him back to Talon Keep. Kruzen would protect the youngling.

But first, he needed to know everything about this spell. And when Ronin returned, they would know the whole truth.

Dragons must be protected from humans and their abuse of magic. Even the traditionalist dragons would have to agree. It was time for dragons to join the fight.

BROTHER'S REQUEST

JASON

The new dragons were so much more intimidating than Gregor. They were bigger than a house. Karyn must've been similar in size, but she'd been asleep most of the time and Jason had focused on her head. The magic in the tent might've disguised her true size too. Most likely he hadn't noticed because he'd been ill.

They must be older, but not as old as Karyn. Jason wasn't sure how he knew. It was like his connection to Karyn had left residual memories and concepts.

The blue dragon, Ronin, leapt into the sky and spread his wings. Dirt blew into Jason's face, forcing him to shut his eyes and cough. By the time he recovered, Ronin was far enough away that he could be mistaken for a large bird.

"Ronin will check the keep for any other survivors." Zanthor's voice vibrated in Jason's skull, so much deeper and full of meaning than Gregor's.

Karyn had been subdued. Whether by magic or from the illness stealing her vitality, Jason didn't know, but now that he'd heard a healthy dragon, the difference was evident.

Zanthor's hide rippled and his color shifted from the hazy blue of the sky to the deep green and brown of the surrounding forest.

Jason gasped. The dragon was using an illusion spell.

Zanthor's chuckle vibrated within Jason's chest. Everything was in his head. The dragon didn't make any verbal sounds. It was disconcerting that such a large creature was so silent.

"It's not magic. The army camp isn't far, and I don't want anyone to know we're here. Especially not that sorcerer of yours."

Jason didn't like the inference in Zanthor's words. He never wanted to see the sorcerer again. Even now he shuddered when he thought of what Bloodstar would do with his magical ability. But he noticed that Zanthor didn't explain his change in appearance. It certainly looked like magic.

Zanthor stood, towering over Jason, and walked to Gregor.

If they spoke, Jason couldn't hear it. Seemed dragons could block him from their communication. Unfortunately, Gregor's emotions were not stifled in any way. His guilt rushed through Jason.

Suddenly, Zanthor was back in Jason's mind, transmitting curiosity.

Jason tried to hide his reactions to the dragon's probing and to Gregor's emotions. But then an overwhelming wave of defeat ignited Jason's power and it pooled in his chest. He could end it all. He could take away Gregor's pain.

The memory of Karyn's ashes replayed as if in real time.

Zanthor's shock brought Jason back to reality. He would never harm Gregor. The youngling was a part of him. It would be like burning off his own arm.

With Zanthor's attention still on him, Jason tried to soothe his power and send it safely back into his mental box.

The scent of mint and a sensation of coolness made him blink. He didn't know where it came from. But then the tension in his shoulders released, his power settled, and he knew everything would be all right. With Gregor. And with him.

The older dragon wasn't concerned about the sorcerer's spell. Karyn's coven was dead. The spell could do no more damage. There was nothing for Jason to worry about. He was free.

Zanthor's mind left, and Jason wilted, relieved to have his thoughts to himself. The dragon was right. Spells needed magic to power them. Killing hundreds of dragons would consume an enormous amount of power, more than should be possible. Not even Bloodstar could sustain it. The damage had been done.

Gregor stood, his mind clear and focused. He was hungry. Which made Jason realize he was starving too. As Gregor followed Zanthor to the stream, Jason felt lighter than he'd felt since he'd fled the army camp.

Everything was fine.

The next morning, Jason felt more refreshed. The sun was already up, and Charlie was cooking breakfast.

Automatically, he mentally reached for Gregor. The dragon was asleep, his mind free of the emotions that had rolled through him the day before. And he was stronger. Jason didn't understand their connection, but Gregor's state made him feel stronger too.

The other dragons were gone.

The scent of trout frying wafted from the fire, and Jason's stomach growled. Everything seemed heightened. The scent of the trees, the smoke from the fire, even Charlie's body odor.

Jason rolled up the blankets so bugs wouldn't settle in the folds.

Charlie sat next to the fire. "You slept like the dead."

It was supposed to be a joke, but Jason could sense Charlie's anxiety.

"Guess I was tired. I feel better now. Stronger." Remorse at worrying his brother made him a little more enthusiastic than was warranted. It would take many more nights of sleep before he felt like himself again.

Charlie pointed at the sleeping dragon. "Are they going to take him back to their keep?"

"I think so." Jason shrugged. It wasn't like the dragons had told him about their plans. But he assumed they'd take care of Gregor. Dragons cared for their young.

Charlie handed Jason his plate. "We should leave. You've told them what happened. You kept your promise."

There was an odd note in Charlie's voice. Not anger. Jason searched his brother's face. Not resentment, but something.

"Yes. But we can't leave yet." He knew he was being gruff, but he couldn't explain his sense of dread at leaving the dragons, or his desire to explore this strange connection.

"What else is there to do?"

Jason sighed. "I don't know. Gregor is still weak. Maybe we can help." It wasn't like they had somewhere to go.

Charlie's frustrated growl surprised him. His brother rarely got angry, but his locked jaw and killer glare made Jason hold up his hands.

"Fine. Where should we go? Back to the army? Find a starving village and beg them to take us in? At least here we have food and water. We're safe here." Jason was trying his best. It wasn't that he didn't want to find a new home for them. Here, he didn't have to do anything. And after his parents' death, watching Charlie wither away at the orphanage and the farm, the busy life in the army camp, and even being sick, Jason needed a minute to figure out their next steps. He was tired of making decisions and trying to do the right thing. And getting it wrong.

"The dragons will take care of him. You're supposed to care about me. I'm your family. Not that dragon." Charlie flung a stick into the fire and sparks flew.

Gregor lifted his head. *The little one is upset.*

"Yes." Jason rubbed the back of his neck. *"I know."* It was easier to talk to Gregor than to his own brother.

"Argh. You're talking to *him* again. Talk to me." With that Charlie strode off into the woods.

Jason ran after him. "Wait. I'm trying. What's really going on?"

"If you'd listen, you'd already know." Charlie abruptly turned and headed for the river.

"I've had a lot on my mind. Tell me now." Jason tried to wrap his arm around his little brother's shoulders, but Charlie shrugged him away.

"You were going to die and leave me." It burst from Charlie as an angry whisper.

How could Jason explain? He hadn't been able to focus on reality while in the grips of the plague. He had no concept of time or any awareness of how ill he'd been. "I didn't want to."

"I saved you." Charlie thumped his chest, before waving toward their camp. "Not for them."

And Jason heard it in between the words. Charlie had saved him for himself. And ever since Jason had healed, he'd been focused on his quest for Karyn, then on helping Gregor. And now, he was waiting for the dragons to tell him what to do next.

"I'm sorry." And he was, but he still couldn't change how he felt about Gregor. He was as much his family as Charlie. More so, because Gregor had lost everyone he loved, and Charlie still had Jason. But his brother wouldn't want to hear that.

"You're not." Though Charlie mumbled the words, Jason knew he was mollified. This strange ability from the spell was inconsistent, giving him insight at rare moments, while overwhelming him with emotions at other times. For this moment, he'd said the right thing.

Jason hugged his brother, hard. "I'm sorry that you had to save me. I'm sorry that I wasn't strong enough to fight the plague on my own. I'm sorry that I almost left you." Because that was the crux of the problem. Charlie would've been alone at only thirteen, with no family, no home, and no way to survive.

Charlie punched Jason in the shoulder. "Well ... don't do it again."

That odd sense of knowing settled in Jason's mind. Charlie was afraid Jason's preoccupation with the dragons would get him killed.

"I won't." Not a promise, since both of them knew there was no way to keep it. But it was a vow to try.

"So, we can leave?"

Remorse at being the source of the spell that destroyed Karyn and her coven ate away at Jason. He couldn't explain that he needed to do something. To make amends. Not without blaming Charlie for enlisting the sorcerer to save him. His guilt was hard enough. He didn't want Charlie to feel shame too.

"Not yet. I'm connected to the dragons. Maybe it's a side effect of Bloodstar's spell. All I know is that I can't leave until I know they'll be all right. So I'm waiting. I just need you to be patient a bit longer."

Even though the spell had done its worst, killing hundreds of dragons, something felt unfinished. Until Gregor was safely claimed by a coven, and Ronin confirmed that there were no sick dragons wandering around to spread the dragon plague, Jason had to trust his instincts.

Charlie bent his head, his hair flopping over his face. In that moment he looked more mature than his years. After a long minute, he straightened and sighed. "I have nowhere else to go."

He didn't blame Jason, but it still felt like a gut punch. Maybe Jason could leave the dragons to deal with everything. After all, he wasn't a sorcerer. What could he do if there was more to the spell? He couldn't stop an infected dragon from spreading the plague.

There must be somewhere where he and Charlie could hide from the war mages until the fighting stopped. Because Bloodstar was right. With no dragons to aid in the fight, the war would end. The plague was killing soldiers. Villages had no more to give to the war effort, and people with true magical abilities were scarce. That left only sorcerers and war mages to continue the battle, unless the plague captured them too.

The Great Wars would finally come to an end.

He would be safe and could build a home for Charlie. But his power still rolled through his mind, barely contained within its mental box. Even now, the heat grew, craving release.

Jason needed to explore his limits. To learn how to control it and eventually extinguish it. Because his magic was death. To Karyn. To the forests. And Jason feared that one day he'd lose control and burn his brother.

Charlie deserved safety, to have a warm bed and more than one meal a day. But until Jason could control his magic, he couldn't give his brother that.

"After Ronin returns, I'll find a home for you." It hurt more than he expected to consider leaving Charlie. But it was better this way.

"Damn it, Jason. I don't want to be dropped off while you continue on your stupid quest to save dragons."

Charlie's anger battered Jason's chest.

"It's not because of the dragons." Jason had to make him understand the danger.

"Really? Because if it wasn't, we'd already be somewhere else."

Jason sucked in a deep breath. This was harder than anything he'd ever done. Charlie looked up to him. Jason was supposed to be the protector. He'd already failed by almost dying. Guilt tightened his fists as he tried to contain his power. Emotions made it harder.

"My power is out of control. You could get hurt."

Charlie snorted.

"No. It's true. The heat keeps building, and I have to release it. I've burned trees and rocks. It's not just a little fire. Sometimes I'm not even aware of my surroundings, and when it's over, ash surrounds me. It's getting worse. I'm not safe to be around."

Charlie tugged at his hair, his frustration evident. "You are my brother. I will never leave you. We can figure this out together."

Jason blinked, surprised at the relief coursing through him. It might be safer to send his brother away, but he was weak. He didn't want to be alone either.

"Once I know the dragons are safe, we'll go somewhere where I can practice my magic. Maybe in the mountains where it's easier to hunt. But if I'm not myself or I lose control, promise me you'll run far away."

Charlie nodded.

Now that they'd made the decision to stay together, Jason grinned. "Hey. Maybe your power will manifest too."

"Not all magic is worth having. You're afraid of yours. Why would I want that?" Charlie stomped away.

Jason rocked on his heels. When the war mages took his parents, he'd felt the same way. And yes, his magic did scare him. After all he'd reduced a dragon to ash.

But a year ago, they had looked forward to getting their abilities. Charlie had even tried a spell to identify his magic. Their mother had laughed and said he would know when he knew. They couldn't force it to happen before its time. She'd been confident they'd both have wonderful abilities.

Of course, lighting fires and freezing water had seemed exciting then. Especially with Charlie looking on enviously.

Jason had been so focused on his own changes, he hadn't noticed that Charlie had changed too. Charlie had saved Jason from the plague. He'd stolen a horse. And he'd stayed with Jason even when he didn't believe in the quest. His little brother had grown up fast.

He had a right to his wariness.

Without Bloodstar's spell and Karyn's sacrifice, Jason wouldn't be alive. And now he struggled to understand and contain his new powers. Of course, Charlie didn't want an ability. Jason hadn't shown him any reason to trust magic.

He wished he could, but his own fear that he was becoming a monster prevented him from embracing magic. It must be extinguished. Before he destroyed more than forests and rocks.

DRAGON LOSS
JASON

Two days later, Jason no longer felt the young dragon's emotions churning through his body. He was still connected, but Gregor's thoughts focused on food and rest, his grief a quiet hum in the background. His emerald hide had patches of dullness, but he looked better than when he'd shown up. And he slept. A lot. Zanthor had taken him out twice to hunt, which had improved Gregor's mood more than anything else.

Jason strode past the cold firepit on his way to the forest. Hunting, cooking, and sleeping had helped all of them recover, but he couldn't shake the unease tightening the back of his neck.

The noon sun beat on his head, fueling his magic. The cool shade of the forest should help. Otherwise, he'd have to dunk his head in the river again to ease the heat threatening to explode from him. The day before, he'd heated two large rocks into dust before he felt safe enough to be around Charlie.

At least he didn't need to worry about the campfire giving away their position. He'd become adept at cooking with his magic. Releasing the heat in a controlled manner was good practice, despite burning the fish more often than not.

His brother had offered to help, but there wasn't anything he could do. Charlie spent most of his day on the horse, investigating the river up to the mountain. There were two abandoned villages to the east and a huge forest to the west.

Zanthor broke the silence with a roar that vibrated through Jason's skull, then shot to the sky, leaving Gregor behind.

"What happened?" Jason sent his thought to both dragons as he ran back to camp. Zanthor was already a speck in the sky, but distance didn't matter with mind-speech.

"I don't know, but Ronin is on his way back." Gregor's fear filled Jason's chest with dread.

"I'm on my way." The desire to console the young dragon drove Jason to his side. Gregor's will to live was still too fragile. Jason sent comforting thoughts as he settled beside the youngling to wait.

Charlie arrived on Warhog at a trot. After dismounting and tying the horse upwind, he paced the clearing in front of their camp. "Something's happened?"

"I think so."

"The big one didn't tell you?"

Jason shook his head. Charlie didn't understand the intricacies of mind-speech, no matter how many times Jason explained he couldn't hear dragon thoughts. Mind-speech was the same as talking out loud. Dragons used a public part of their brain to speak. Their thoughts remained hidden as much as his own thoughts. He only heard what they wanted him to hear.

"No. He left to meet Ronin." He didn't add his own concerns, or that Gregor's fear had sent his magic coiling in his chest.

His brother and his magic would have to settle down and wait.

The dragons would let them know of any danger. But it was hard to stop his own questions from filling his mind.

He didn't have to wait long. Their presence eased into his awareness, drawing his gaze to the sky over the mountain.

Five dragons flew below the clouds.

Jason felt their emotional upheaval through Gregor. Something had upset them enough that they weren't shielding their emotions from the youngling.

Jason stood, knowing his size wouldn't make a difference, but certain that sitting would show disrespect. Anguish rolled through Gregor.

Jason felt more than heard Zanthor's command to Gregor, *"Shield your emotions, youngling."*

Suddenly, Gregor shut him out completely. No emotions. No mind-speech. Jason swayed, lost without the anchor to the youngling.

Charlie slowly stood, his body tense, and clutched Jason's arm.

Jason steadied himself, sucking in a calming breath, and squeezed Charlie's hand.

"Relax. They can sense your fear, and it will make them think we can't handle the news."

Charlie took a deep breath and relaxed his posture.

Zanthor and Ronin landed next to the camp, while the other dragons settled in Jason's burnt clearing farther down river. At least his control exercises had created space for dragons.

Before he could ask what had happened, he was engulfed in five dragon minds.

Anger. Pain. Confusion.

Emotions battered him like a boat tossed in an angry sea.

His stomach rolled, and he grabbed his head to hold it steady. This was worse than being connected to Gregor. All the adult dragons were inside his head.

Jason gritted his teeth and created mental shields to protect himself.

But the dragon minds tore through his shields like they were cobwebs. They dove through his thoughts, exposing all his secrets, tossing them aside, and making him relive the plague. Chaos and visions finally coalesced into a scene Jason only knew from Charlie.

Karyn suspended in the air, surrounded by smoke, alive with a gaping hole in her chest, until his weak, plague-riddled heart floated from his body to hers. The difference between her large glowing white heart and his tiny red one was beyond disturbing. No wonder she hadn't been able to fight the plague.

The heart in Jason's body suddenly felt too big. Blood thundered through his veins and magic pulsed a deep rhythm. His power rose, eager to obliterate the memory and protect him.

But the dragons weren't done. He relived every excruciating moment of Karyn's demise and death, desperately trying block them from seeing what happened later. He didn't know if he'd succeeded when the dragons roared, and everything went black.

Jason opened his eyes moments later, amazed he still stood. Charlie's arms were wrapped around him, and Jason clung to the sensation, unable to see or hear.

Hatred from one of the dragons made Jason shake. Their emotions were too large, too fierce. His own were pitiful in comparison.

"Enough." The power behind Zanthor's command stopped the pressure in Jason's head.

The spicy, earthy scent of dragons filled the air, as awareness of the world returned. Wind blew against his overheated face. Pain throbbed through his skull, and white stars burst in his vision. Only Charlie's embrace felt solid.

Soothing mint swept through Jason, and he exhaled, his body drained and shaking. The pain receded, leaving only Gregor's comforting presence.

The other dragons were gone. His mind was his again.

Zanthor's eyes whirled, and his regret eased the last of Jason's pain. *"Sorry. I've shielded you now."*

"What was that?" Jason rubbed his forehead. The ache was gone but the memory of it felt physically imprinted.

"There were questions about the sorcerer's spell. But that could've been handled more gently. Most dragons are used to dragon riders who've been trained to shield their minds." Anger simmered

beneath Zanthor's explanation, but Jason didn't know if it was against himself or the other dragons. He was afraid it was both.

His mind had been violated, even though he'd never hidden his involvement in the spell. Neither he nor Karyn had any control, but he'd survived. He focused on his own anger, pushing away the self-blame that soured his tongue. *"Who are they? Survivors from Karyn's coven?"*

The other dragons were listening in, their emotions contained. It made Jason nervous, though he suspected that Zanthor had stopped the assault before the other dragons learned of what his magic had done to Karyn.

Zanthor sighed, his emotions under tight control. *"Ronin flew to Dawn's Keep. They're dead. Then he flew to our coven at Talon Keep. But these dragons hailed him before he got there. They'd lost contact two days ago and some force shields the keep from entry. Ronin tried, but even mind-speech couldn't penetrate."*

Something was wrong with Zanthor's coven. The dread that had loomed in Jason's mind all day grew.

"I fear our coven may also be affected by this spell. I don't know if they live or not. I'm no longer part of the coven bond." Zanthor's pain was sharp and brief, before he shielded it.

Hundreds of dragons. First from Karyn's coven, and now Zanthor's. But the keeps were far apart. The sorcerer's spell couldn't possibly be that strong. No spell could reach such distances. There had to be another explanation.

"How?" Jason tried to keep his self-blame from leaking into his question.

"Possibly, one of Karyn's coven tried to get help and carried the infection. Maybe the same way Ackenar transmitted the spell from Karyn. We don't know. Ronin and I have been too far for mind-speech. And these three were on scout duty. They said they lost communication two days ago. My guess is that our leader blocked

mind-speech before the keep was shielded." Zanthor wasn't telling him everything, but Jason knew better than to ask for more details.

"Ronin brought them back here, but ..." Agony dripped from every word. *"Kruzen, our coven leader, died moments ago. I felt it deep in my soul. The coven bond is gone."*

This couldn't be happening. It wasn't possible. A spell could kill. Yes. It took great power. And maybe, using a dragon as a source of energy had amplified Bloodstar's spell to infect another dragon.

The plague in the army camp had spread through coughing and touch. That's why the infected were put in tents and their caregivers wore masks and gloves. But it didn't kill the whole camp. Some people, like Charlie, naturally resisted the disease.

So, it didn't make sense that a spell converting the plague to infect dragons would be so much worse. The dragons might've gotten sick. Some may even have died. But no spell should be able to kill hundreds of dragons and then travel miles away to another keep. Something had to be powering the spell, constantly feeding it magic.

"Excuse me." Zanthor left Jason's mind.

It was such a human expression, it took him a moment to focus outward. Gregor wasn't inside his head anymore. Jason had been shut out.

"It's so weird when you talk with them. Your face goes slack, and you stare straight ahead." Charlie had moved to the other side of the firepit at some point. He waved at the dragons next to Gregor. "So. What's going on, and why are there more dragons?"

Jason's explanation was brief, leaving them with nothing to do but go back to gathering wood and food. The dragons would let him know their plans when they were ready.

But one thing was clear. Bloodstar's spell had mutated. If it could infect hundreds of dragons far from Dawn's Keep, then it was out of control. The spell should've dissipated by now. But the sorcerer had used a dragon heart. Somehow that changed everything. Now it was a curse.

A spell could be countered. Though considering the amount of magic the sorcerer must've used, it would be extremely difficult.

Jason licked his suddenly dry lips.

There was one way to stop a curse.

Destroy the original components of the spell. If they still existed.

The dragon heart beating inside Jason's chest faltered, and his power wrapped around it, forming a burning shield of protection.

Jason, his dragon heart, and his magic did not want to die.

PLAGUE CURSE

JASON

The dragons' loss sat heavy in Jason's heart.

Years of war had destroyed homes, forests, and fields. So many people had died. But this destruction was twisted in a way that had nothing to do with the war.

If the curse grew, dragons could disappear forever. Jason didn't know what that would do to the world. To magic. It was obvious that dragons were linked to magic as much as humans, maybe more.

Charlie paced. "He kept muttering about making them sick. Slowing them down. How could this happen?"

"Dragons don't get sick." Zanthor's voice rumbled quietly, keeping track of Jason's conversation with his brother.

Jason shrugged. "Something went wrong. Karyn's coven is dead and Zanthor's is infected, if not dead too. That's ..."

"Four hundred eighty-six. But they might not be dead. Some may be fighting this curse. I can only confirm that my coven leader is dead."

"Almost five hundred dragons in twenty days. Even the war mages, using their battle magic to create fires, floods, and tornadoes, never targeted that many people. Usually, people died fighting, or from having their powers drained, like our parents. I thought there was some rule about killing. Or maybe there isn't, and we just never heard about it because the victims were dead.

Either way, Bloodstar's curse is a killer." Jason threw up his hands in helpless frustration.

"Did the scouts find anyone outside of the keep?" He swallowed the bile that rose up his throat when he imagined a decaying dragon, but it might explain how Zanthor's coven became infected.

"I know. My point is I don't think he planned it. I was there. Bloodstar didn't use anything other than that green smoke and the spell. Maybe the dagger had an enhancing effect?" Charlie rubbed his hair, making it stick up.

"No. There were no other dragons, dead or alive." Jason could feel Zanthor's mind working out the timeline.

Charlie growled. "If you want to talk to them, just do it. I can't stand seeing you stare through me when I speak." He stomped away.

"Charlie, wait. I need you both."

But it was no use. Charlie believed what he'd seen and heard. He couldn't imagine hundreds of dragons dead, because he couldn't see their memories. He felt guilty enough that Karyn had died to save Jason. The other deaths were too distant, too bizarre to accept. Because that would mean that saving Jason had possibly brought about the extinction of dragons.

Jason had too much remorse to chase after him.

He turned his mind back to Zanthor. *"Could it have something to do with mind-speech?"*

In the army camp, talking, coughing, sneezing, and even touch had spread the plague. That's why masks and hand washing had been effective at keeping the Healers and Charlie safe. But Karyn's coven hadn't come into contact with her. Right after the heart exchange, she had informed Ackenar of her capture and the sorcerer's spells. But then her mind had been consumed by fever, and she'd asked Jason to tell her story because she couldn't reach her coven with mind-speech.

Even now, having experienced mind-speech, Jason found it hard to understand the complexities. But Gregor, Zanthor, Ronin, and the three other dragons had been too far from their covens for mind-speech. That might've saved them.

Zanthor's hum vibrated inside Jason's skull. *"Possible. But no human could know dragon minds enough to target the area specific to mind-speech."*

"Bloodstar wouldn't have to know where to attack. He transferred the plague from me to Karyn by putting my infected heart in her chest. That was enough to infect her. But he wanted to make her coven uncomfortable enough that they wouldn't help in the war. He would've known that dragons don't get sick." Jason rubbed his chest, the ache in his heart spreading. *"He probably expected Karyn to escape or planned on releasing her so she would infect the others. But he would've built in a failsafe. My father said the most effective spells have at least two vectors. So, maybe Bloodstar modified the illness to pass from dragon to dragon whenever they communicated. We have to be close to talk, but dragons can be miles apart."*

This was the mistake Bloodstar had made in his logic. First, he didn't realize the plague was harder to control than a simple illness. It wanted to spread quickly and voraciously, and second, that dragons used mind-speech to communicate, allowing the spell to infiltrate dragon brains. The spell was a double attack. A disease that affected their bodies and their minds.

He felt Zanthor's mental nod, before the dragon's presence left.

For a moment, the complexity of Bloodstar's spell held Jason in awe. Everything he'd learned about magic settled into balance.

The sorcerer had underestimated the power of the plague, but his spell had been eloquent. Mind-speech, like breathing and talking, took no conscious effort on the part of dragons. The spell didn't have to be powerful. It just had to transmit the disease with as little magical effort as possible.

Which meant they might be able to stop it without needing huge amounts of magic.

For the first time, Jason felt hope.

But then he recalled the vivid visions that had overwhelmed him during his fight with the plague. Reality hadn't existed. Infected dragons wouldn't understand what was happening to them. Any who fled would be in a state of extreme confusion. Their own brains would deceive them.

People protected themselves with masks. Dragons needed to shield their minds somehow.

Zanthor cut Jason out of mind-speech easily, but he wasn't sure it was so easy between dragons. The scouts had said their leader blocked mind-speech. But if they couldn't speak, they wouldn't be able to warn the other dragons. And what happened when a leader died?

Jason's head hurt thinking about it. A dragon would have to know they were infected, identify the magic inside their brain, and then build a wall around it to contain it. But it would still be there, waiting to come out, like his own magic. There had to be a way to eliminate the curse, so dragons could speak again.

So far, the dragons at camp weren't infected. But if they communicated with other dragons, they might catch the curse.

"I think you're right. The curse is transmitted via mind-speech. It fits all the facts. And explains how Karyn's coven could perish in such a short period. The coven leader can access our minds through the coven bond. If the leader were infected, they could spread the spell with a single broadcast." Zanthor's tone was somber. *"I believe Kruzen knew this. That's why we lost mind-speech with the coven first."*

A bit of Jason's guilt eased. That must be what happened. But Zanthor had felt his leader die. *"Are you still connected to the others? Or does a coven bond need a leader?"* He really didn't know much about dragons.

Zanthor's hum vibrated through Jason's skull and pain lanced behind his eyes.

"You've given me enough to think about. Now that we understand how the curse spreads, we can warn the others. We will persevere. Rest. Our conversation is harming you." Zanthor's presence left, and a faint mint scent filled Jason's head, soothing the pain.

Jason nodded, drowsily. He ducked under the tarp and curled up on his bedroll. Rest would help. He would figure everything out later. The dragons had everything under control.

DRAGON COVEN
ZANTHOR

Zanthor hadn't meant to influence the boys, but their minds were susceptible to his power. Possibly because of their weakness, one from hunger and the other from the recent battle with the human plague. Either way, when he'd exerted his power to calm the other dragons, the boys fell into a deep sleep.

The debate about what to do next continued, though less heated. Ronin wanted to return to Talon Keep. Peyton and Fallyn wanted to fly to one of the southern covens and request refuge, certain that distance from the epicenter was the key to surviving, or at least would give them more time to fight the curse. Morgan was keeping her opinions to herself, and Gregor was so lost, his turbulent emotions made them all desperate.

Communicating without the connection of the coven bond was frustrating. Zanthor had to broadcast his mind-speech and explain his logic multiple times. They had to return to Talon Keep. Even if they couldn't help, he had to know what had happened to them.

Without the coven bond, they were strangers who couldn't read each other and had conflicting goals. Dragons needed to be connected. Being coven-less was wearing away at his confidence.

"You have to do something." Ronin's voice begged him to take charge.

At thirty-four, Zanthor wasn't the eldest. Peyton had that honor by a decade, but neither of them were old enough to lead a coven.

Ronin leaned in. *"We're lost without the bond. Even I feel off. We've traveled together long enough that we can communicate easily, bond or not. I must admit, that steadies me. The others don't have that. They don't know you like I do."*

Zanthor didn't want to be responsible for five dragons. He still held out hope that his coven had adjusted. That a new leader had taken over when Kruzen died, and they'd found a way to beat the curse. But Gregor needed a coven bond now or he might not make it. He'd given up, lost in his despondency. And the others were lost, adrift in their fear.

Peyton shot to the sky.

"Stop, Peyton. We must stay together." Zanthor didn't want to use his influence again. But flying in different directions wouldn't solve anything.

"There's no point. They're dead. You know it. I know it. The only way we'll survive is to hide until this curse fizzles out." The belligerence in Peyton's tone incited Zanthor's ire.

Ronin was right. Zanthor had to do something. He couldn't remember ever being this angry and anxious. Without the coven bond, even he couldn't control his emotions. He'd never realized how much strength and acceptance his family gave him.

Only Ronin was calm. Unflinching.

"Why aren't you affected by this?"

Sadness seeped into Zanthor's mind as Ronin replied, *"I've never belonged. Not like the rest of you. I like and admire you. That hasn't changed."* He chuckled. *"I'm also used to suppressing my anger."*

Zanthor wanted to ask more, but now wasn't the time. Ronin's acceptance somehow solidified Zanthor's resolve. There was a solution. He just had to be brave enough to enact it.

"We need to work together if we hope to survive this."

Peyton circled overhead, still unwilling to return.

Zanthor concentrated on projecting the calm he felt from Ronin. *"We're struggling without a coven bond, Gregor most of all.*

It's not a weakness. Our bond is our strength. With this plague curse killing our family, we have to adapt. We must become a coven. And if we meet any other dragons who are lost, they can join us."

Fallyn shifted her tail but didn't say anything.

Morgan huffed. *"It's to be you?"*

"Doesn't have to be me. But certainly can't be the youngling."

Ronin snorted, then stood tall and spread his wings. *"I vote for Zanthor."*

Morgan and Fallyn bowed their heads.

"Peyton, do you concede?" Pleasure at their acceptance warmed Zanthor, but it should be unanimous.

"I do not. You do whatever you want. But covens are dying. The only way to survive is to be alone. You're a fool to take the risk." The dragon flew above the clouds, shutting his mind to any rebuttals.

Zanthor's wings drooped, but the others looked to him to lead. He wouldn't use his power to convince anyone. Peyton might be right. He didn't know.

He walked over to Gregor. *"Do you concede?"*

Gregor's eyes whirled his distress. *"I don't want you to die too."*

Zanthor's heart clenched. *"I'll try my best not to."*

If anything, Gregor's eyes whirled faster. *"Yes. I concede."*

Zanthor hoped he could help the youngling. There was something so broken about him. But first he must create a coven bond.

He dug deep into his minds, past the conscious and subconscious, to the depths of ancestral memory. It was there, at the core of what makes a dragon a dragon. Deep in his soul.

He concentrated on that core, and it pulsed, slowly, then faster. Until his entire self was suffused with light. He closed his eyes to better guide his thoughts.

Then Zanthor reached for the other dragons.

Ronin first, as he glowed in Zanthor's mind, a familiar presence. Then Gregor, because he felt his anguish as if it were his own. And then the other two, Morgan and Fallyn. A thread connected him to Peyton, but Zanthor severed it. That dragon had made his choice.

Zanthor gathered the dragons' energy into his core. He held it within his heart, and he whispered his own conviction into the bond.

A blast of energy transmitted to all the dragons, binding them as one coven. The connection felt new, but solid. They were family. They were home.

And one by one, he felt his coven ease into acceptance, their anger soothed, and their fears embraced. They would face this challenge together.

The flight to Talon Keep took longer than Zanthor expected. It wasn't Gregor's fault that he didn't have the strength to maintain altitude for long. They had stopped twice already to allow him to rest, but he was falling behind again.

"Land. Ronin, find something to feed Gregor."

"I'm not hungry." Even Gregor's protests lacked strength. They all felt his fatigue, so he should be gaining strength from them as well. But he was weaker than when they'd left the boys behind.

In the deepest part of his mind, where no one could hear, Zanthor worried that he might have to let the youngling go. Dragons cherished their young. They were full of life and potential. Gregor was none of this. His will to live had been shattered. Zanthor didn't know how to help him.

They landed next to a river that was a two-hour flight from the keep. Gregor collapsed, his mind closed in sleep.

They were close enough to make plans. Zanthor replayed the images from Gregor's memory of his furious flight and what he'd seen at Dawn's Keep. Ronin was intent on analyzing the timing of the curse.

"It might not spread via mind-speech. Humans breathe in the infection. It could be in the air currents." Morgan had a point.

"True. But then Ronin would have been infected when he flew over Dawn's Keep. And he's definitely not sick." If anything, Ronin had glowed with restrained energy since Zanthor formed the coven.

"I'm not sick. Mind-speech is the only thing that makes sense. Wind currents are too variable for humans to understand." Ronin rubbed his snout. *"Though those mages are getting more adventurous with their spells. They can influence the wind. Wonder if that's what trapped Karyn?"*

That's right. She'd lost consciousness long enough for the sorcerer to restrain her. *"She didn't fall from the sky. She'd already landed. Only a lack of oxygen could make her lose consciousness. It's a possibility."*

In order for dragons to beat this curse they needed to consider every scenario.

"Assuming that the spell had dissipated by the time Ronin flew over Dawn's Keep, we can add wind as a vector for spreading the plague." Zanthor wasn't sure how they could protect themselves from the wind. Mind-speech could be blocked.

"Can't spells simply exist? Does it need something to transport it?" Fallyn tapped his talon against a rock. *"What do we know about human magic, anyway? It's not like ours."*

Zanthor frowned. He didn't know that much about human magic, but he did know about dragon powers. They enhanced natural abilities.

"Magic affects every creature on Drakkoia, but only some have a way to access that magic. Our magical abilities are enhancements. Humans are the same. Some have abilities. They use words and potions to harness the magic within themselves to create spells that are related to their abilities. You all saw what Jason could do with

a natural affinity to temperature. As far as I know, a dragon can't draw heat to create fire, but it isn't too difficult to imagine one could if they had the right ability. The only difference I can see between human and dragon powers is that ours didn't exist until after the Great Wars started. Also, we can't manipulate our ability into a spell. Though I'm not sure a dragon would even try to do such a thing."

Gregor groaned and sat up. *"I'm ready."*

With leaps and hope in their hearts, the dragons headed for the sky, hopping thermals until they found a strong current leading home.

Zanthor flew in the front, deep in thought. There was too much that dragons didn't know. They'd become complacent in their superior strength and intellect. They'd ignored the wars, assured that human politics couldn't affect dragons. It was a shortsightedness that had sent him and Ronin to the keeps to change traditions. Human magic had killed their riders, transformed their hatchlings, and now it was killing dragons.

Dragons would have to acknowledge that human affairs impacted dragon life. If nothing else, this curse would show those clinging to tradition that the world was changing. It was time for dragons to adapt.

Talon Keep was in sight when Gregor sneezed violently, dropping down a thermal from the group.

"Are you all right?" Zanthor spoke to the youngling privately. The others didn't need to hear the conversation.

Distress wound through Gregor's mind. *"No. We must turn away."*

"Is it your power?" Zanthor inhaled deeply, but couldn't smell anything unusual.

"I smell mold. Something decaying or festering?" Gregor's uncertainty reminded Zanthor that his power was new. The youngling wouldn't know how to invoke it or what it meant. His

own power had taken him months to understand. He'd simply assumed he was right, and that everyone agreed with him.

Zanthor snorted at his naivety and the damage he'd done during those early months.

Unfortunately, Gregor didn't have time to figure out what these unusual scents meant. He reacted to the emotions they evoked.

"We'll proceed with caution." He already suspected that the curse had infiltrated the keep so had planned to be careful. But Gregor's power was warning them. So, Zanthor intended to be even more cautious.

He led the coven to a lower current, slipping through the clouds. The setting sun highlighted the treetops and hid the ground in shadows. He blocked the coven from using mind-speech to communicate with the dragons in Talon Keep. But as they neared the mountain bowl, the air thickened. Heaviness weakened his wing beats.

Gregor dropped lower in the sky, barely skimming the treetops. Suddenly, he backwinged and dove for a small clearing. *"I can't. It's too strong."*

Zanthor tried to fly higher, but it felt as if he carried two bears through a windstorm. He tilted his wings and dropped lower. The others weren't coping either. It was no use. They couldn't get any closer to the keep.

"Land."

Fallyn smirked. *"That's why we couldn't get close enough."*

Someone must still be alive to erect this shield. That gave Zanthor hope. But there was no way they could breach it to see.

"Stay here. I will fly to Crystalvale. The riders will have to be our voices and eyes."

Zanthor would inform the riders in the village, and they could use mind-speech to find out what had happened to the coven. He'd been on a mission to convince dragons to help riders defend their villages. Now it was time for riders to help dragons defeat this curse.

DRAGON RIDER QUEST
JASON

The next morning, Jason woke with no memory of the rest of the day after his conversation with Zanthor. Hunger gnawed at his stomach, but a sense of urgency drove him to wake Charlie. "Pack up. Time to go."

They loaded Warhog's saddlebags and strapped on their bedrolls. After mounting the horse, they headed into the forest.

The dragons had left at some point. They didn't need his help anymore. Thinking about them made Jason's head fuzzy, so he focused on covering as much ground as possible.

An hour later, Jason blinked, suddenly aware of his surroundings and his growling stomach. The sun was high, and he was traveling along an animal trail through the forest. He snorted, tightening his hands on the reins.

There was only one way he would be heading to nowhere with such vigor. Zanthor had manipulated him.

The dragon's magic might not be identical to a war mage's, but the effect was the same. He'd been pretty sure that dragons could use magic. This proved it.

He shook his head to clear any remnants of influence.

"Charlie? You with me?" Jason shook his brother's shoulder. Even the fact that they both rode the horse should've cued him into the strangeness of their actions.

Charlie groaned and rubbed his head.

"Head hurt?" Jason pulled Warhog to a stop and slid off.

Charlie grunted as he dismounted. "What happened? How did we get here?"

Yes. Zanthor had definitely messed with their minds.

Jason didn't know if he was horrified or impressed. A little of both. At least his own magic didn't seem to care. He hadn't felt this calm since before his parents left.

"I'm pretty sure Zanthor used magic. Maybe not a Manipulator's touch, but he convinced us that we needed to leave."

"Dragons have magic too? That can't be fair. Great Healer, my head is killing me."

Charlie's face did look a little green.

"Drink some water and eat something. That should help."

Jason scanned the overcast sky above the trees. He should remember which direction they'd traveled, but he couldn't. He had no idea where they were. Not that it mattered, since he didn't know where they could go.

The war mages were still on the lookout for people with magical abilities, and until Jason could control his power, he couldn't risk sauntering into any village.

The line of mountains peeking through the trees seemed familiar, like a memory. But not his. Jason frowned. Karyn's? Their connection during her illness had been filled with visions.

He climbed a tree to see the mountains better.

"What are you doing?"

Jason paused, looking down at his brother's upturned face. It was difficult to explain that parts of Karyn's memories were in his head without sounding like he was hallucinating. "Karyn's rider lived in a village near some mountains. If I get high enough, I might see some smoke or a road. We couldn't have traveled far, and we camped on our way to Dawn's Keep."

Charlie grinned. "Well, hurry up. I'm tired of sleeping on the ground."

His relief that Jason had given up his dragon quest battered Jason's conscience. His reason for wanting to find the village wasn't to find them a home. Dragon riders lived there.

They would know more about dragons and magic. They could help warn the dragons about the curse.

Because no matter what Zanther had made him believe, Jason was certain that Bloodstar's curse was more dangerous than dragons could handle.

Jason's dragon heart thumped loudly, and his magic pulsed in agreement. A dragon rider village was perfect for the next phase of his quest.

Clangs of a blacksmith's hammer, voices, dog barks, and the everyday sounds of people living broke the silence of the forest as they approached the village. The warm scent of baking bread drifted from a small cabin nestled in the trees. Laundry flapped above a woodpile, but no one seemed to be home.

The narrow trail wound past the cabin and joined a dirt road. Jason quickened his pace, his mouth watering at the scents. He wasn't sure how, but he would figure out a way to earn food and shelter for them. It had been too long since he and Charlie had eaten bread.

Warhog snorted and stopped. Charlie clucked and tugged on the reins, but the horse refused to budge.

"What's wrong with him?" Jason scanned the road ahead and the trail behind them, lingering on the cabin. The village wasn't visible yet, and there was nothing on the road that should bother the stalwart horse.

"I don't know." Charlie murmured in Warhog's ear. The horse's ear twitched, but he didn't move.

Over the course of the day, Jason had watched his brother's interactions with the horse.

"Can't you make him move?"

Charlie snorted. "How? He's twice our size and a lot stronger than either of us."

"Ask him nicely?"

Charlie's glare increased Jason's certainty that Charlie had a magical ability.

"I don't." Charlie's response to Jason's implication only confirmed it.

His brother could speak to animals. Or read their minds. Or something. It wasn't just Warhog. Odd that he had so much trouble with dragons. Or maybe not. Jason had to admit they were not animals.

Jason couldn't help smirking. Charlie's face turned red, and he kicked a loose stone. With a huff he rubbed Warhog's neck and murmured in his ear.

With a wet snort, Warhog proceeded down the road, pausing and snuffling the whole way. He obviously disagreed.

Charlie's expression was set. He wouldn't admit anything. Not yet. But they'd have to talk about it, and soon. He'd have to hide it, just like Jason. But at least his ability wouldn't destroy anything or be obvious. Plenty of people talked to animals. The animals just didn't listen.

The trees thinned, revealing the village. It wasn't large, but still, after so long away from people, it was loud. Scents and noise assaulted Jason, a chaotic mess of life. Three dogs ran up and sniffed them thoroughly before running off again. For some reason, Warhog relaxed, no longer hesitating or snorting.

Charlie pointed out a stable to the side. "Warhog will be more comfortable there."

Jason wasn't sure how they'd pay for it, but followed Charlie anyway. The stable consisted of four stalls, two with horses and two empty. Warhog dove in and munched on the hay. He seemed content.

"Hey there. You folks here to visit?" The woman's voice was jovial but there was a warning in her eyes. The rifle in the crook of her arm made Jason aware they still wore green uniforms.

His power coiled in his chest, and his face flushed with heat. For once Charlie spoke first.

"No. We're looking for a place to stay and some work. Hoping this might be home." Charlie was his most polite.

The older woman looked them both up and down. Jason didn't know what she saw, but her gaze softened.

"You're just kids. Come along. I bet you're both hungry. My daughter could feed an army, so I'm sure she has something for you." She grabbed Charlie's arm and dragged him behind the stable.

Jason blinked at the way she'd slipped in the army reference. He rubbed his dirty hands over the emblem on his right pocket, obscuring it as much as possible, and followed.

"I'm Eleanor." Her tone indicated they should supply their names.

"Jason, and this is my brother, Charlie."

They entered a sprawling two-level house made of stone and wood. Immediately, Jason felt at home. A woman was washing dishes at the sink.

"Melanie, we have guests."

Jason was willing to go along with whatever Eleanor said until he knew what was going on. Charlie sniffed loudly.

Just then, the salty scent of soup made Jason's stomach growl.

Eleanor laughed. "Thought so." She propped the rifle behind the door and turned the latch.

Melanie was short and round with a smile that crinkled her entire face. Her hair was pulled back, and a large apron covered her brown dress.

"Oh my. Where did you find these wee ones?"

"They wandered in from the forest. Dogs checked them out."

So, Eleanor had watched them. Jason rubbed his chest, happy they'd passed her test. He imagined they might've had a different greeting if they'd been older and well fed. Weeks of illness and living in the wild had probably helped him and Charlie look more pathetic than dangerous.

"Sit. Sit. You boys are skin and bones. Where did you come from?" Melanie waved them to a long table with twelve chairs.

Jason sat and a bowl of soup, along with a healthy chunk of bread, appeared in front of him. Charlie grabbed a spoon, and Jason elbowed him in the ribs. It didn't matter how good it smelled, they should answer questions first.

"No. Eat. I can wait." Eleanor sat down across from them and grinned.

Jason dug in. The flavors burst on his tongue—chicken, onion, celery, and spices he couldn't identify. The bread was hard, but when he dipped it into the soup and ate it, he almost moaned. Fish, mushrooms, and the occasional rabbit had been great, but this was stellar.

As he wiped the last bit of soup from the bowl with his bread, he sighed.

"Now that your bellies are full, we can talk. I wouldn't have heard anything over the growls of your stomachs. So ... Where's home and what are you doing all the way out here?"

Now that he'd had time to think, Jason didn't want to blurt out his story. He needed to tread carefully. Eleanor may have decided they weren't a threat, but he and Charlie had worked for the enemy. Brian had shot arrows at the soldiers from their camp.

"We grew up in Cromwell. Charlie's thirteen and I'm sixteen."

Melanie frowned. "You're pretty young to be out on your own."

Eleanor sniffed loudly, her gaze not as friendly as before. "They are. Which begs the question. What are you doing here?" The firmness in her voice brought Charlie's head up.

"Our parents died. Jason did everything he could. Yes. We joined the army. But we don't care about the war. We needed to eat." Charlie's outburst made Jason cringe. He could've eased into it.

"No need to get belligerent. I can see you're too young to fight. And from the look of you both, the army didn't treat you well. But that doesn't mean you haven't been forced to spy on us. There's more than one way to fight a war."

Jason couldn't help his snort. "We're not spies."

"Maybe not. State your business and be on your way."

Jason dove into the tale of the plague, Karyn, and his desire to find her dragon rider. He left out his interactions with the dragons. "Karyn wanted to know if Brian survived his injuries. And I wanted to tell him about her death."

Eleanor had been silent through the whole story. Now she stood. "Come with me."

Jason followed her outside, leaving Charlie behind with a distraught Melanie.

They didn't go far. She led him into a small healing center, an open platform with rooms made of movable curtains on one side and a large bath built into the wooden floor in the center. He walked past a child with a broken arm sitting next to a man with a cough.

Eleanor opened a door at the back of the receiving area and the familiar stench of sweat greeted him. Twelve people lay on cots, their eyes closed. A boy, not much older than Jason, looked up from laying a cloth on a woman's forehead.

"No change." His weariness settled in Jason's chest, a weight of despair.

"Do they have the plague?" It didn't feel the same, but why else would they be unconscious?

Eleanor raised an eyebrow. "What do you think?"

Jason shook his head. "No." They weren't wasting away. There was no coughing or moaning. Instead, the victims lay deathly still, their chests barely rising with each slow breath.

"Who's this?" The boy frowned at Jason.

Eleanor poked her finger at Jason. "This one survived the plague. Though you wouldn't think it to look at him."

Jason knew he'd lost weight, but she kept talking as if he were a walking skeleton.

"What's wrong with them?" Jason needed to know why she'd dragged him here. They would've known these people didn't have the plague. They weren't quarantined. Of course, this village might not know how to handle a plague.

"They have fever brain but haven't developed any other symptoms. I give them fever weed to help, but they've been like this for over two weeks."

Bloodstar had cast his spell three weeks ago. Karyn's coven died two weeks ago. Dread skittered up Jason's neck.

"Are they dragon riders?"

The Healer gasped, and Eleanor grimaced. "How did you know?"

It couldn't be. The curse shouldn't affect the riders too. But dragons communicated with their riders via mind-speech.

The curse affected people too.

Dragon riders couldn't help their dragon companions. No one could.

Jason swallowed. "I should've told you about the rest. The curse."

At Eleanor's nod, he recounted meeting Gregor and Zanthor, and about the curse and mind-speech. When he finished, there was silence.

Eleanor nodded, as if something had fallen into place. "Well, that explains a lot. They don't have fever brain. They're trapped in their minds. Richard, try to break the connection." She pursed her lips and sniffed loudly. "That's why the dragons didn't answer. Dead. All of them?"

Jason nodded. Nothing he said could soften the truth.

Her grief was in the tears she blinked to hide and the defeated bow of her head. But she didn't sink into her despair.

"Come with me. You must tell the dragon riders this tale. Hopefully, they'll know what to do next. This curse must be stopped." She grabbed his arm.

Hope bloomed in his chest. He could still help the dragons.

SILVERSTREAM

JASON

After Eleanor had dunked Jason and Charlie under cold water, clothes and all, she'd tossed two large brown tunics at them and whisked away their identifying uniforms. Once she deemed him decent enough, despite the fact that his legs were bare, she'd marched Jason into the village meeting hall, leaving Charlie with Melanie.

Jason tugged at the belt again, the tightness around his waist grounding him and making him feel a little less like a toddler wearing his dad's clothes. At least she'd let him keep his boots. Bare feet would've been mortifying. He shifted his weight from one foot to the other, wishing he could go back to the forest. Angry villagers shot questions at him that he couldn't answer.

Eleanor held up her hand. "That's enough. Going over it one more time won't change the facts. If the dragons are dead, we need to deal with their bodies before decomposition contaminates our water supply. We don't know if this curse killed Brian or if he died from his injuries, so there's no sense in fearing the worst. Melanie will work with the Healing Center on a counterspell for our comatose riders."

She pointed to an older man who hadn't spoken during the meeting. "David knows more about dragons than the rest of us. He will lead the expedition to the keep, and if any dragons have survived, his healing skills may be of benefit."

Three people stepped forward, and she glared. "Dragon riders will stay here and stop trying to communicate with dragons. If the boy is right, mind-speech could put you in a coma."

Eleanor pursed her lips, her narrowed gaze settling on Jason for a moment.

He gulped, suddenly certain she knew he'd left out details in his story. He'd purposely ended at Karyn's death and his recovery, jumping forward to their escape to avoid any hint that he had power, but Eleanor was a shrewd leader. Though it sounded like Melanie and David might have magical abilities, and they hadn't been turned into the war mages.

People dashed off to their tasks, and the tension holding Jason upright dissipated. He wilted. "Can I see Charlie now?"

Eleanor turned from giving David his instructions. "You have other things to do. I'm sending you to the keep." She winked, even though her voice was gruff. "I've a feeling you can *help*."

Jason didn't know what she thought he could do, but he wanted to see Karyn's home. Someone else could take care of Charlie for a while. Shame at his weakness made him clench his teeth. Charlie was his responsibility. He wasn't supposed to resent it.

"Go with David. Listen to him. He's worked with dragons all his life. And get some sleep. You're swaying on your feet."

She squeezed David's arm, worry in her posture. "Be careful. I'm trusting you not to use mind-speech at all. I don't think anyone survived. But the curse may lurk in their bodies. A sorcerer's curse doesn't follow normal rules."

Obviously, Eleanor knew a lot about magic. Jason wished he had time to question her, but David pushed him out the door and muttered a gruff, "Follow me."

They strode through the small village, past the stables, and continued down a dirt road to a small house next to a farmyard. Chickens and goats rushed to the fence, trilling and bleating. Obviously alerted by their cries, moos erupted from the barn.

David led Jason inside the house. "You can sleep on the couch." He disappeared into a room and returned with clothing. "These should fit. Boots are by the door. Change and meet me out back."

David turned away, but not before Jason caught the despair in the man's eyes.

The soft worn britches and thick brown tunic were special. He hadn't thought he'd miss the strange ability to know things, but ever since Zanthor had manipulated him, he'd been back to normal. David was old enough to be a grandfather, but these clothes were for someone younger and smaller. A grandson, perhaps.

Jason changed and shoved his feet into the tall boots, enjoying the soft cloth against his skin. His uniform had been stiff. Wearing clothes that fit boosted his confidence.

He strode after David, wondering what the older man wanted him to do to earn his supper.

Long reins and straps lay over a tall rail. David looked up and grunted. "They fit."

"Yes. Thanks. I've been wearing the same clothes for weeks and the tunic Eleanor gave me was a little big." An understatement, but at least only the Healer, Melanie, and Eleanor had seen his uniform. She'd been elusive about where the sorcerer had performed his spell, focusing on the plague and Charlie's desperation to save Jason. The deadly illness hadn't reached this village, but there'd been enough stories that people understood wanting to do anything to cure their family.

David's chuckle was sympathetic. "Her father was a big man. Guessing your clothes hadn't been presentable." His head tilted, but if Eleanor thought it best to keep it a secret, Jason wasn't going to say anything. He shrugged instead.

David gripped a strap of leather. "You can help me check these over."

"What are they?" The straps were too long for a horse.

"Dragon rider straps. This one is ... was for Rayvn. My dragon friend." He pointed to the longest straps, looped three times over the rail.

Of course. David was a dragon rider, and his dragon was dead.

Jason looked away. Nothing anyone said had made it easier when his parents died, but he had to say something.

"Sorry."

David rubbed his chest, staring over Jason's head. "I guess it's a good thing she didn't try to contact me before she died. I knew she was gone. I just didn't know how."

Nothing would ease David's loss.

Jason's magic pooled in his chest, growing with each breath. Needing a distraction, he reached for the thick leather strap. The leather was as wide as his palm and twice as thick as horse straps, but still supple.

A memory of Brian putting the straps on Karyn held him spellbound. She'd been excited to share the sky with him. Her emotions flowed through Jason, even though it wasn't happening now. He could imagine Brian's eagerness. His fear.

"What's it like to fly on a dragon?"

"Amazing. The world is a different place when you're on a dragon's back." The awe in David's voice made Jason ache to experience it himself.

At least David didn't seem as sad now, and Jason wanted to know more about being a dragon rider. Karyn's memories were all about being a dragon.

"How many dragon riders live here?"

David sat on a stool and dipped a cloth into a container. "Rub this on the straps, and check for any cuts or weaknesses in the leather. We had twenty at one point, but there's only nine of us left."

The balsam darkened the leather to a rich brown. He handed the cloth to Jason and pulled down another strap for himself.

"The set you're working on was for Sharyl. Larry flew with her two seasons ago, before an arrow caught him in the chest. She brought him here, but it was too late."

Jason ran his fingers along the strap, stopping at the intricate fastenings. Not buckles or snaps, but something made of wood. Like a button.

"Dragon hide is tough, but metal irritates over time. Smooth driftwood fasteners work just as well and prevent chafing. Dragons only wear the harness when we fly together, so we store them here." David waved to another rail to the left.

Jason had been too focused on what was in front of him. Under cover of a large lean-to were three more rails, each holding straps of various lengths.

"This rail is for checking them out. Those are for storage. And back there ..." David waved to the field beyond the barn. "That's where we trained."

At the end of the field lay a dense forest, but there were large gaps between the trees, tunnels covered in broken branches and strange mounds. "Dragons train here?"

David laughed. "Dragons don't need to train. We do. Riding a dragon isn't like riding a horse. They're big. Only young dragons could be compared to a horse. When an adult dragon chooses a rider, that person must learn to balance on something as big as a shed, or a house, or sometimes, if they're honored enough, a dragon as big as a three-story building."

"Wow. How big was Rayvn?"

"He was one of the smaller ones. Just twenty-one years old when he chose me. I was honored to be his first rider. We've flown together ten years. Ah. Now there's real magic for you. Nothing beats soaring through the sky, the wind in your hair, and the world below you."

David talked about fighting in the wars for five years before he'd been shot, nearly died, and survived with a constant ache in his back. Since then, he taught new riders and rehabilitated the old ones. But he'd spent the past year helping dragons with wartime injuries, from gunshot wounds to holes in their wings. The hills and tunnels allowed him to tend an injured dragon.

"They have their own healers, but this war has created new weapons that do more damage. Our hands and potions can get into places where talons can't." David sighed. "I worried when the others brought Brian in. His back had become infected where the arrow had been, so we knew he'd been separated from Karyn for a while. But then dragon riders fell to fever brain. Their screams filled the air, day and night, until they suddenly stopped. I knew then that something terrible had happened. Rayvn never answered my call, but I knew he was gone. I felt it in my soul."

Jason bent his head to his task. He was to blame. Those dragons were gone and only stories remained. His heart ached.

For the dragons.

For the world.

And for what David would see when they reached the keep. Jason wasn't sure this resilient man would survive.

He wasn't sure he would survive.

SCENT OF MAGIC
GREGOR

Gregor shoved his snout into his arms. Despite sleeping more than a hatchling, his body still ached from his frantic flight nineteen days ago. The rain didn't help. He couldn't get warm.

His stomach rumbled, though it felt less hollow than before. Ronin might bring back something to eat from his hunt, and then he would badger Gregor to bathe.

As soon as Zanthor had bonded all five dragons into a coven, Gregor had felt safe, loved.

Even though their coven was small, it worked. Hearing thoughts and feeling other emotions helped get him out of his own head. He wasn't alone with just his grief. Everyone had lost their family. They understood and helped one another when the emotions swelled out of control.

He wasn't drawn to the boy anymore. That had been strange. He'd never interacted with the humans who rode dragons, so he had nothing to compare it to. But Jason's emotions had been chaotic, intertwining with Gregor's and adding to his confusion and loss. Now that they'd left the humans behind, he was positive his desire to lay down and never get up hadn't been real. The plague curse must've affected him, even though he'd escaped death.

Today, he felt more like himself. Strong and adventurous. A thrill tingled through his body. All the dragons in his coven had powers. That hadn't been the case before.

Pain struck his chest, dulling his excitement. No. He couldn't remember them. Not yet.

His stomach rumbled again, eliciting a chuckle in the coven mind.

"Better deal with that, youngling. Before you make us all hungry." Zanthor's mirth pushed him upright. There was no judgment. If anything, Zanthor seemed pleased.

They'd settled in a forest near the human village, but far enough away that it would take humans days to reach them. Zanthor had left to enlist the help of dragon riders, while Ronin had spent the morning trying to break through the shield around the keep. Even thinking about the coven there brought back the musty, moldy scent.

Fortunately, Ronin sent an image of a group of deer grazing not far away.

"On my way." Gregor leapt for the sky, pleased that his wings unfolded easily. He flew leisurely to Ronin's perch downwind of the deer, his mouth watering at the sight. Hunting would be good.

Ronin nudged Gregor's shoulder. *"Follow close. As soon as I capture one, they'll scatter, so you have to be quick."*

Gregor's muscles tightened in anticipation. Hunting with adult dragons was more exhilarating than with other younglings. These animals weren't penned in to counter his clumsy attempts.

He followed Ronin closely, catching the buck in his talons as it veered away from the pack. The life drained from his meal, spilling blood on the field below and wasting delicious protein. Gregor loosened his grip.

"You'll do better next time. But that was a great catch. See, the herd is already regrouping. You were quick enough that they're not frightened, only wary. Deer expect to lose some of their herd. They won't travel too far, and we can hunt again."

Gregor glowed under Ronin's praise as he chewed on the fresh meat. Today was a grand day to be a dragon.

After a quick dunk in the river to clean off the blood, Gregor felt like his old self.

They flew back to the others, and the spicy scent of magic flowed through the air. He'd always been sensitive to odors, but with his new power he could detect more. Undertones and even the quantity. Magic was thin here, but there was more in the clouds to his left, spicier than the magic flowing with the wind.

Suddenly, a floral scent wafted through his nostrils. He sniffed, trying to pull more into his snout and identify the flower, but it wasn't familiar.

It pulled at him, unlike the scent of decay or the mold that forced him away from a keep. This one enticed him to follow, to find the source. He veered left, and it grew bolder, like buds bursting open.

Ronin's chuckle made the connection dissipate. *"Wrong way, youngling. Camp is south of us."*

"I know. It's just ..." Gregor couldn't really explain. He barely understood his power. *"I smell something, and I know it's important."*

Ronin sniffed loudly. *"Nothing but fresh air and musk from the deer."*

Frustration snapped Gregor's emotional shields into place. He didn't want Ronin to sense his struggle with associating emotions to an odor that wasn't really there. *"I can smell things that others can't. It's my power. For example, these clouds are filled with magic, but those aren't."* Maybe if he eased into the way it affected him, Ronin could understand.

"My power is like that. I can see through things, and if I concentrate, I can choose whether I see beyond the object or inside the object." Ronin huffed. *"It wasn't easy to control at first."*

His empathy soothed Gregor. Maybe Ronin's experience could help him now.

"The first time, I was overwhelmed. Zanthor thinks I have an overly sensitive sense of smell, but it's more than that. Like the keep.

The moldy odor makes me wary. And now ... I smell a flower that can't possibly be nearby. It's coming from the west, and I need to follow it." He tried to shield just how much it pulled at him. Every fiber of his being wanted to follow the scent that had only grown stronger while they flew.

"*You want to find a flower? I can smell the trees, the fish in the river, the various creatures hiding from our shadow, and grass. But even a bear wouldn't entice me to change directions, unless I was hungry.*" At least Ronin was trying.

Gregor veered again. It was getting harder to focus on their conversation. This time Ronin didn't correct him.

"*It's like a tug in my chest. Or a tightness. If I go toward the scent, it lessens, and I can breathe. If I try to fly away from it, my body tenses.*" He rolled his tongue along the inside of his teeth, hoping Ronin didn't make fun of him.

"*I've contacted Zanthor. Follow your instinct. Together, we'll see where it leads. It's good to explore your power and discover its limits or purpose. I've always been able to turn mine on and off, but I hatched with this sight. Your power is new. Just be cautious. We don't know which keeps are infected with the curse. Don't communicate with anyone outside of the coven until we know it's safe.*"

His warning sent a chill down Gregor's spine. The curse. He'd forgotten. Guilt clutched his throat, but that only made the floral scent stronger. Maybe his power was leading him to something that would ease his pain.

Gregor flew for hours, until the forests gave way to fields of green, yellow, and brown. Hills and streams gently wound through the farms. Humans looked up and pointed. He felt exposed.

He flapped his wings, gaining speed.

"*Slow down, little one. You'll burn all the energy from your meal.*" Ronin's voice was faint, far away.

Leading. Pulling. Gregor frowned. Yes. His power was leading him to something important. Something dragons needed? The scent grew so strong, he sneezed violently.

Yes. That was it. The intensity indicated an answer. He dipped a wing, gliding on the wind current. This flower wasn't something to be feared. It was leading him to something good.

"That's better. I didn't think you had the energy to fly that fast." Caution oozed from Ronin. *"We're flying across human territories. It's best if we stick close together from now on."*

Anger coursed through Gregor. He wasn't a hatchling. His power was new, but he wouldn't do anything stupid. Realizing Ronin could hear his thoughts, Gregor put up his shields.

This power had saved him. Warned him about the plague curse so he could survive. He had to figure out how it worked, so he could use it to protect his new coven.

These scents were the key to saving dragons.

DRAGON LIBRARY
SERI

Seri carefully turned the pages of the ancient human book. With the librarian watching her every move, she didn't want to accidentally rip the thick paper with her talon. He'd offered to read it to her, but she'd studied human language and would get more from reading the text herself.

Human emotions often colored the reading and changed the meaning.

The room wasn't large enough for a full-grown dragon, but Seri was a youngling, only seventeen, so she fit as well as a horse would fit in a room filled floor to ceiling with books. At least the ceiling was high. The tables were a little low, but not too bad.

She leaned over the book and skimmed the writing, searching for the author's reference to the source of magic. Dragon lore told of an ancient dragon gifting the humans with magic once they could communicate, but human lore started with a quest. This book was the earliest she could find that mentioned the quest.

Unfortunately, it was shrouded in philosophical questions about human's purpose and their adulation of gods. She was fairly certain some of those gods had been actual dragons, but it was never stated outright.

The word *power* caught her eye, and she pressed a little too hard on the page. The tear was tiny, audible only to her. There was no way a human could hear it, but guilt flooded her, anyway.

The human was sent to a land of ice fields and mountains, the sky filled with pink and green pillars. The rest went on about the trials of the journey and the final glory of the granted vision. Though sparse on concrete details, this was the best clue she'd found so far. The source had to be on the north end of the continent, past the snow-covered Dragon Mountain Range.

Seri's back ached from hunching over the books. She stretched, and her wings automatically unfolded, knocking books from the tables on either side of her. The librarian's outrage was instantaneous.

Her mentor, Crysta, sent a mental smirk. Seri responded with a sheepish shrug. It was hard to keep her wings tucked all the time.

Before the librarian could snatch the book away, Seri laid a talon on his arm.

"I'm almost done." She kept her mind-speech to a whisper. He did not have the mental fortitude of riders, and her communication gave him a headache, so she'd tried not to speak to him at all.

He fell back, clutching his ears. As if that would keep her out of his head. She tried not to pity him, but wasn't really impressed with this keeper of knowledge.

The dragon way was so much better. They stored their memories and lessons in archive stones so they could be accessed by generations of dragons. Nothing could destroy an archive stone. The Dragon Library on the hill behind the university contained knowledge that spanned thousands of years. These books, even with thick paper, would soon disintegrate. The newer books had thinner paper that no dragon could touch.

It took her another thirty minutes to scan the text for more clues. The human climbed a mountain at the end of the Dragon Tail Trail. Good. That gave her a direction.

They searched for a long lake that never froze, even though it wove through mountains of ice. The water was supposed to grant the human eternal life. Seri was absolutely certain that even vast amounts of pure magic couldn't extend a human's lifespan. But a lot of magic, localized in a lake, could elicit illusions, which is probably what really happened.

Only witches could direct magic by focusing their intention. She'd seen it. Her ability to see magical threads allowed her to witness the winding of those threads as humans performed their spells. Magic was everywhere. But if this lake did exist and it contained the true source of magic, it could affect humans and generate this story of the elixir of longevity. There must be accounts of humans selling or trading such a potion.

She closed the book and sent the librarian a request to find books on life potions.

"I'm done." She hoped Crysta was close. Despite being blessed with the ability to see magic, Seri's dragon skills were barely better than a hatchling's. She knew dragons were near, but she couldn't tell how close or far.

"Good. I'm hungry, so I know you must be starving. At least I ate yesterday." The image of a fat cow made Seri's mouth water. It had been a while since she'd eaten.

Her coven mates waited outside in the garden. Garianna slept next to a large hedge that had been trimmed into the shape of a rabbit. Crysta tapped her elegantly spiraled horn. *"Let's leave this intellectual quagmire."*

Garianna leapt up. *"About time. I don't understand why the Seer thinks Seri will find anything helpful in human records."* Her stomach grumbled. *"And I'm hungry."*

Seri grinned. Garianna was always grumpy when they had to interact with humans. Not that Seri blamed her. With so many humans roaming Cromwell University, there was a constant hum of anxiety and self-importance. It was enough to irritate even the most serene dragon, and Garianna had never been calm.

Devoted to Seri, yes, but neither patient nor quiet.

"Come, youngling. Let's get you fed, and then we can analyze your findings." As usual, Crysta took charge and laid out the most practical course of action.

But the magic around Seri shifted, fluttering at the edge of her sight like a slight breeze shifting debris on the ground. She blinked to refocus her vision and opened her mind to the magic around her. She'd always been able to see it, threads of color that flowed in the air, twining around dragons and spinning through nature.

Multiple colored threads formed a corridor into the sky. That was strange. Usually, magic ebbed and flowed like the wind. But this was a pattern. She stretched out her awareness, attempting to locate something to explain this behavior.

"Be still." Crysta laid her talon on Seri's shoulder. *"Two dragons approach."*

It was frustrating that Seri was lauded as the Oracle, and yet her own draconic abilities were less than they should be at her age. She couldn't sense them at all.

Garianna immediately stepped in front of Seri, her size easily concealing her. Only ten years older, Garianna had a presence that made most dragons wary. Her power was subtle, a controlled menace that made her the perfect bodyguard for Seri.

Crysta frowned. *"I don't believe they're a threat. The youngling is filled with urgency, and the other dragon protects him. Be still, and do as I say."*

Seri trusted Crysta and Garianna to keep her safe. Although just once she'd like to go on an adventure and discover the world on her own. But that was not her life.

Three Seers had proclaimed that her ability to see magic as a hatchling fulfilled a prophecy. From that moment, the coven had sequestered her. She had a guard and a mentor. At least now that she was older, she was allowed to leave Sunspire Keep. This trip to the university was the farthest she'd ever been from home, far enough that she couldn't call the coven for help, if she needed it.

Crysta and Garianna were protection enough from humans, but dragons were another matter.

The approaching youngling was younger than her. Usually, a dragon transmitted their name and coven, but this one was heading to them with a single-minded purpose. The other dragon was easier to sense. Ronin from Talon Keep was about Garianna's age, and he had important news to impart. He also had a fierce protectiveness for the youngling, stronger than Garianna's for Seri.

"You may land at the far end of the gardens. We wouldn't want to agitate the humans." Crysta's words held a cautious welcome. She positioned herself in front of Garianna, ensuring Seri wasn't visible at all. Crysta didn't have a power, but she had forty-four years of experience. Her copper scales glimmered in the sun, making her more imposing than her size.

Ronin landed, folding his wings and settling to the ground, giving the appearance he was about to take a nap. Gregor landed beside him, thin for a youngling of sixteen, though his emerald-green hide glowed.

Seri blinked. Her own turquoise hide was bright, as is normal for younglings, but his was brighter. Then she realized he was encased in green magical threads.

His mind was shielded, but his eyes whirled, and the magic threads shifted, winding around his head, slipping in and out of his nostrils. It must be his power. But she couldn't imagine what that would be.

The new dragons didn't bow or offer a greeting. Tension grew as the silence stretched.

"Well, what brings you to us?" Crysta's tone scolded Ronin for his breach in etiquette.

Magic wove a net around the dragons, as if protecting them from something or someone. Their public minds were shielded.

"Shield your minds." Crysta sent the sharp command, and Seri felt their coven bond tighten.

Suddenly, Crysta's mental presence disappeared. Seri hadn't known she could do that.

"What do you think is happening?" Seri leaned into Garianna's back, seeking a physical connection to ease her uncertainty.

"I don't know. I've never been shut out like this. Crysta is talking to the older one. She'll let us know when we need to." Of course Garianna was fine with letting Crysta deal with things. She couldn't see the odd way the magical threads dove through Gregor's nostrils. It was disconcerting.

Suddenly, the threads shot away, joining others in the wind. Gregor wilted, and Ronin wrapped his wing over the young dragon.

Crysta returned, no longer blocked from Seri's mind.

"You can stay. There's a hollow for dragons not far from here. Let the youngling rest until I return."

After her public invitation, Crysta leapt for the sky, flying swiftly toward their keep. *"Garianna, protect Seri mentally and physically from any other dragons. Ronin will fill you in on the danger. Stay here, until I tell you it's safe to leave. Seri must not be compromised. The prophecy demands it."*

Her emotions were hidden, but Seri still felt her urgency. Whatever Ronin had said was important.

"Shouldn't we follow her?" Seri wanted to stay together, not wait with strangers, especially ones who didn't follow protocol.

"No." Garianna pushed Seri back from the others. *"You do as I say, Seri. No arguing this time."*

"Do you know where she's going or what's wrong?"

"Sunspire Keep, but you're safer here." Garianna's answer only added to Seri's unease. Dragons were safest with their coven in their keep, not surrounded by humans and strange dragons who blocked their thoughts and emotions.

The other dragons left for the hollow, Gregor leaping weakly to the sky. Whatever had driven him here had taken a lot of strength. He was exhausted. What could affect a youngling so much?

Garianna rocked back on her tail, her emotions finally spilling over. *"This is a disaster."* Her distress brought tears to Seri's eyes. *"Tell me what's going on. Now."*

The story was more terrifying than Seri could've imagined. A human sorcerer had created a curse that transformed a human plague into one that killed dragons.

She wanted to dismiss it as impossible, but Gregor's weakness and Ronin's protective demeanor told her some of the story had to be true.

Resolve straightened her tail. She had to keep her coven safe from the curse. If humans could survive the plague, then so could dragons.

Everything she'd read whirled through her mind, but the unusual behavior of the magical threads around Gregor bothered her. Her quest for the source of magic was more important now than before. If dragons couldn't protect themselves from the curse, then magic would be the only way to stop it. They would need a lot of magic, and maybe a sorcerer of their own.

She didn't know the whole prophecy, but this must be why she had this power. Magic was the key to surviving this crisis.

Seri strode back into the university library. *"Find me every reference to your plague."* She broke into every human mind in the building, not caring if it hurt their delicate brains. Humans had warped magic to create this curse. The least they could do was help by gathering books for her.

DAWN'S KEEP

JASON

Two days later, they started the trek to Dawn's Keep late in the afternoon. Jason had followed David around the village as they collected tents and supplies, in between tending the straps and the animals. Stories of dragon riders and their duties had filled Jason's dreams with the wonder of dragon flight.

Charlie sidled up beside him, already healthier, his cheeks rosy, a vigor to his steps that had been missing. He was still thin. It would take more than a couple of days of food and rest before Charlie was healthy, but village life suited him.

"Melanie is a fabulous cook. Here." He handed Jason a warm bun.

The scent of cooked meat and spices made Jason's mouth water. He bit into the warm bun and groaned at the burst of flavors. Nothing beat a bun filled with meat, carrots, and spicy sauce.

"Thanks. You better get back." Jason pushed Charlie's shoulder, glad that he got to see him before the trip. He didn't know how long he'd be away.

"I'm coming with you. Melanie put me in charge of camp food."

Jason wanted to protest. His brother would be safer with Melanie. She'd taken him under her wing, treating him like one of her own children. This trip was something Jason needed to do, and it would be easier without the pressure of taking care of Charlie.

But Charlie's obstinate pout stopped him. He'd promised not to fight anymore and to treat Charlie as an equal. So he ruffled his brother's unruly hair instead. "Couldn't think of a better person to watch over our meals. Make sure you sample everything."

"Stop it." Charlie ducked away, but his grin was relieved.

Oddly, Jason's heart was lighter with his brother near. They'd done everything together so far. Maybe part of his dread had been that he'd have to see the dragons alone.

A well-worn path wound through the forest and up a shallow incline, making for an easy hike. Before the sun set, they set up camp. Too tired to stay awake, Jason climbed into David's tent, and the fireside murmurs sent him into a deep sleep.

He woke the next morning with Charlie curled next to him.

David popped his head into the tent. "Time to get up, boys."

He didn't say anything about sleeping in, so Jason assumed they'd been left on purpose.

He nudged Charlie awake, and as soon as they exited, the tent collapsed, and someone grabbed the bedrolls and tied them to a horse. Warhog wasn't with them, and for the first time, Jason wondered how the horse was faring.

As if Charlie read his thoughts, he rubbed the horse's neck. "Hope Warhog's doing all right. The stable hand wrapped his legs and said he needed to rest for a week."

Once again, Jason was certain his brother's connection to Warhog was magical in nature. But they had another long day ahead, so he ran to find David, knowing there'd be something for him to do.

"Do dragons always live on mountains?" The question had niggled at Jason for a while. He knew the continent was large, but there were thousands of dragons and until he'd joined the army camp, he'd never really seen one.

"No. They prefer heights and often settle on mountains. But some live on the cliffs over the eastern and western seas, while others have burrowed into the ground, creating immense tunnels. There's even a keep nestled in the dense Nightwood Forest."

Jason tilted his head. "And dragon riders come from nearby villages?"

"Mostly. Every keep has at least one village nearby. But not too close. Dragons discourage people from building anywhere that could affect their food supply. But that works to our advantage. Valleys and lowlands are best suited for farming, as long as we have a clean water supply. So it really doesn't make sense to build our villages and towns in more rugged terrain. But sometimes there's a conflict. Villages can't expand up the mountain or into any boundary set by the dragons. Even Cromwell can't expand southward. Dragon keeps were established there long before the sprawling town was built."

Jason had never thought about dragons defending territory, but he'd seen marks on General Riley's maps where the army couldn't travel. Now he wondered if those had been dragon zones.

"What would they do if someone settled too close to a keep?"

"That's one of the tasks of a dragon rider. Twice I had to speak with the homesteader, but since Rayvn had already located a suitable alternative, they weren't too upset about moving. All the terrain is visible from the sky, and dragons know of our needs. Generally, people are grateful for a better location. Most people respect dragons. But sometimes a dragon encourages the people to leave. You've spoken with them. They can be intimidating."

True. The fact that dragons hadn't used their superior strength to harm people during the wars had been a source of pride for Karyn. For a moment, Jason was transported into a memory of her flying over Silverstream with her rider.

He blinked it away. He preferred to stick to his own memories, but one day he might see the world from the sky.

By late afternoon, the stench hit, rancid and cloying. Jason swallowed more than once to keep from gagging. It was more pungent than an animal carcass, filling his mouth with bile and burning his lungs. His heart intermittently squeezed and then thumped hard, unable to settle on a rhythm.

Karyn's heart.

Sometimes he forgot. But right now, it wasn't reacting in a way any human heart would.

Many villagers wrapped cloth over their noses and mouths. No one spoke. But their fear, disgust, and sadness seeped into Jason. And his power, that had settled uneasily in his mental box since the dragons left them days ago, pulsed in his head, as if preparing for battle. He clenched his fists and breathed through his mouth, hoping to stop the stench from making it worse.

"Something bothering you?" The concern in David's expression almost prodded Jason to share his struggle and the odd effect their emotions were having on him. But exposing his ability was dangerous. Despite the obvious respect for Melanie's magical powers in the village, he still didn't know who to trust.

"Just the smell."

David pressed his lips together, handing Jason a blue cloth.

"It's more than that. I've been around dragons all my life. There's something about you." He sighed. "We all have secrets, son. The burden is eased with sharing. But you're new to us. Just know, I've seen a lot of unusual things. When you're ready, maybe I can help."

And with that odd statement, he strode ahead to talk to another person.

Although David had been kinder than anyone else he'd met since his parents' death, Jason didn't think the old dragon rider could help. The odor obliterated his other senses, and the cloth over his nose did nothing to stop it, because the smell didn't just come from the air.

It was inside his head. In his heart. In his soul.

He feared he was about to face something worse than watching Karyn die. So much worse.

Dread slowed Jason's steps as he neared Dawn's Keep. He'd wanted to see Karyn's home, but Gregor's memories haunted him. He coughed at the unbearable stench and followed David, setting his gaze on the dragon rider's back.

Jason hadn't been prepared enough.

The shock, the grief, and the disgust that emanated from the others almost sent him fleeing back down the mountain. He gritted his teeth and took that final step forward so he could see for himself.

At first it was chaos. Mounds of red, green, gold, and blue. Some taller than a tower. Others no bigger than a dog. Then they came into focus.

Dragon heads at odd angles. Wings bent in a way that formed sails in the sky. Dragons on top of dragons. Some alone in sleeping alcoves carved into the mountain. Eyes open. Eyes closed. And yellow phlegm everywhere. Flies buzzed happily, wafting up in clouds when anything shifted.

Jason's heart stopped. His vision narrowed, and all he could see was the baby dragon, the size of a chicken, at his feet.

"Breathe!" David smacked Jason between his shoulders, and the world rushed back into focus.

The contents of Jason's stomach rushed to his mouth, and he vomited, heaving long after there was nothing left. He wasn't the only one.

Piles of vomit only added to the stench.

So many dragons. Dead.

He couldn't even see the rest of the keep past the wall formed by two huge dragons in front of him, but it was easy to imagine.

More of this horror.

"Let's set up here. Grab the axes and saws. Build the pyres. The sooner we cremate these corpses, the better." David's voice rang with authority. None of his anguish leaked through, but Jason felt it.

Jason swallowed one last time and joined the villagers setting up the fire. Cremating Karyn as soon as she'd died had been a blessing for both of them. Without Bloodstar's magic to draw on, there was nothing Jason could do for these dragons, and he wasn't ready to walk through the carnage.

Hours later, the stench from burning dragon flesh was worse.

Charlie was helping with the food preparation, but Jason wasn't sure anyone would be able to eat. Even his saliva tasted of death.

Almost three hundred dragon bodies spread across a keep that David said normally took thirty minutes to walk across. They'd barely cleared an area the size of a small garden. The dragons were huge. Even lying down, their bellies stretched up like grotesque leathery mountains. Flies buzzed everywhere, feasting and replicating.

Dragons didn't deserve to be reduced to this.

Guilt tore through Jason. He'd been the catalyst for Bloodstar's curse. It didn't matter that another plague-stricken person would've been chosen, or that the sorcerer couldn't have foreseen this consequence. Jason was alive because of the spell that had killed all these dragons.

As he threw the logs onto the fire, heat wrapped around him, sinking into his skin, shifting his emotions.

He should've died. Then none of this would've happened. These dragons would still be alive, and the curse wouldn't even exist. His survival caused this.

The fire fed his magic, and his emotions shifted. Anger burned through his soul, pulsing through his heart and heating his face.

Anger at Bloodstar and at the devastation he'd caused. Anger at himself for surviving.

Jason clenched his fists as power surged from his head and filled his body. The heat grew. Too big for his head. Too big for his body.

Each emotion that battered his soul, from within, from Karyn's memories, and from the villagers around him, only fueled his power more.

Jason sucked in a desperate breath, but there was no relief. No fresh air to clear his mind. His hands ached as if they burned from the inside. If he didn't release this heat, he would explode.

But there was nowhere to hide from the villagers. No escape.

Jason ran past the fire, searching desperately for a gap in the wall of dragon corpses. But even though they'd spent the day cutting limbs, there was no passage through, only more bodies. More death.

His power pulsed through him in waves of agony and heat.

Someone would see, and he'd have to flee with Charlie. The last thing they needed was to be turned into the war mages. But he had no choice.

Jason thrust his hands onto the giant torso in front of him, the dragon hide still supple, untouched by decay. He whispered the spell he'd created with his father so long ago. A spell meant to ease the pressure of his magic.

But nothing could ease this pain.

Magic poured from his hands, his chest, and his head. Jason closed his eyes against the brightness and gave in to the heat.

Flashes of Karyn as she died, of his parents before they left, and of Charlie covered in bruises at the farm, rushed through him. All the emotions collided in his belly and flowed through the magic, strengthening it, shattering it, until he was nothing but white-hot fire.

Shouts assaulted his ears, but he couldn't stop. He couldn't see. All he could do was feel.

Anger, pain, grief. Fear.

Charlie's voice broke through, though Jason couldn't hear the words.

He had to stop, before his magic consumed everything in sight. He had to protect his brother.

Concentration took effort. Waves of heat and light defined him, and he struggled to sense his own body.

"It's OK, Jason. Let it go." Charlie's voice. Calm. Steady. The way he spoke to the horse.

Jason didn't know what he meant, but focusing on Charlie snapped him back to his body. The searing heat dissipated, and he blinked, suddenly drained, a dragon's talon clutched in his hand.

The ground in front of him was bare, except for a pillar of green ash swirling in a vortex. Jason looked up and gasped.

He'd gouged a giant path through the decaying bodies. Colorful ash piles, some as tall as him, lay between towering walls of charred body parts stretching to the far end of the keep.

Voices rushed in, and Jason collapsed, giving in to the sudden darkness, clinging to his brother's whisper. "Rest. I've got you."

MAGIC EXPOSED
CHARLIE

Charlie grabbed Jason's hand, suddenly afraid of his pallor. Pain shot through Charlie's palm and up his arm, as if fire burned through to his bones.

Charlie gasped and let go, clutching his hand, terrified at what he'd see. His hand was uninjured, though a searing tingle shot up his neck and into his skull.

David lifted Charlie's unconscious brother into his arms.

A thick fog rolled over the devastation, hiding it from view and obscuring anything more than a few feet around them. Charlie couldn't see or hear the other villagers, only Melanie and David.

"Follow me." Melanie clutched his forearm and pulled him after David's retreating figure.

He struggled to understand what had just happened. His brother had lost control. That was obvious. He'd burned a tunnel through the dragons and turned them into sparkling ash. But where had all that power come from?

Charlie stumbled, and Melanie steadied him.

The fog was unnatural, heavy and dense, possibly created from the intense heat of Jason's spell interacting with the air. Charlie couldn't hear anything from the camp. Even his own breathing was muffled.

Jason's head lolled back as David leaned to open the tent flap. Fear that Jason was trapped in fever brain like the dragon riders in the village made Charlie light-headed.

He stepped into the tent, hoping his brother wasn't cursed, that he was merely drained from expending so much magic. There was no need to fear the worst. Not yet.

After David lowered Jason to the cot, Charlie stared at Jason's prone figure, the tightness in his throat releasing when Jason's chest rose. His breathing was clear. There was no rasp. His brother wasn't dying.

David rolled Jason to his side and tied his hands behind his back. "Well, that was unexpected."

Charlie turned to face them slowly, wondering if they were going to restrain him too.

Melanie frowned for an agonizingly long moment, weighing his fate, before sighing, her feelings shifting from fear to anger to resignation so quickly, Charlie wasn't certain he'd caught everything.

The band around his chest loosened. Jason was all right, and Melanie had come to some sort of acceptance. David was harder to read.

Sounds rushed in, the rest of camp going about their day, while the tension grew inside the tent. Charlie was the first to break.

"You already suspected he had powers." The secret was out, and there was no point denying it.

Melanie sat, gesturing for Charlie to take the other chair while David stood beside her, blocking the exit. "Yes. It was obvious you weren't telling the whole story. Was Bloodstar even involved or just a famous mage to blame?"

Shock shot through Charlie at her accusation. She thought Jason had enough power to kill dragons. "Everything we told was the truth. Bloodstar created the curse that killed these dragons. We only kept Jason's ability a secret."

David scoffed. "You expect us to believe that your brother's magic had no part in destroying our dragons? He's so full of guilt, anyone can see it."

"No. He was dying, and Bloodstar needed someone infected with the plague. That's all." Charlie couldn't keep the panic from his voice. Had Bloodstar known of Jason's power? He couldn't have. "And Jason's magic changed *after* the spell. He's been trying to control it. He didn't mean to ..." How could he even say what Jason had done? He'd burned through dragon bodies as if they were made of wax.

"Your brother just happened to use enough magic to destroy an entire village because he lost control?" Caution emanated from Melanie.

David's disbelief pulsed against Charlie, making it hard to focus. He didn't know how he could sense their emotions so clearly, each one a separate entity. His hand and arm still burned from touching Jason, and his head pounded. Maybe Jason's magic had affected his empathy.

Charlie swallowed, wishing his brother would wake up and explain everything. But Jason wasn't moving, and it was up to Charlie to convince Melanie they weren't dangerous and to stop her from turning them both over to the war mages.

The pressure of keeping Jason's secret, of watching him lose control and collapse, and of sensing the emotional turmoil rolling through Melanie and David burst a dam inside Charlie. He told them about their parents being taken by the war mages without a chance to say goodbye. How Jason had to care for them both in the orphanage. About Jason pulling away and becoming more of a loner than he'd been before. Charlie's own struggle to fit in, to make friends, and then having to start all over. And lastly, about his brother almost dying, his desperation to save him, and the brutality of Bloodstar's solution.

"Jason changed after that. All he cares about is dragons. He can't control his power. Nobody has taught him anything about harnessing an ability. Before our parents died, he could light fires easily and cast simple spells, but now the heat overwhelms him.

Please don't turn him over to the war mages. He's a good person, my favorite person, my brother."

Charlie stopped, stunned he'd shared so much of his hopes and fears. But he felt cleansed. Holding it in had made him moldy. He released a shaking breath, suddenly aware that the tension in the tent had shifted to compassion.

"We don't conscript witches here." David's voice was gruff, his sadness somehow easing Charlie's fear more than any assurances could.

Melanie huffed. "No. We don't. That's one of the reasons this war started. But I guess they don't tell you about that history. We can choose to use our abilities however we wish. This is how it's always been. But then one day, some of the witches on the council decided that power should be monitored. We have sorcerers, mages, witches, and everyone else, all determined by their level of magical ability. I don't know what specifically started the Great Wars, but I do know that our side has the choice to fight or stay home and protect our families."

Charlie shook his head. That couldn't be right. The Great Wars had gone on for decades. There must be an equal amount of magic on both sides. Otherwise, one side would've won a long time ago. "People volunteer their essence to fuel the war mages?"

"Some do. But there's enough magic in nature." Her confusion didn't make sense. Maybe he wasn't reading her emotions correctly. For the first time, he wished his ability worked on people instead of animals. Then he could touch her to understand.

"My parents died from the extraction. Why would anyone choose that?"

Their shock rocked him back in his chair.

David's face twisted, his eyes shiny. "War mages killed your parents by draining their essence?"

Charlie nodded, a new anger rolling in his chest. It was obvious that the mages on this side of the war didn't do this. If he'd grown up here, his parents would still be alive.

With an inarticulate cry, Melanie wrapped her arms around Charlie. "I'm sorry. That's not how we do things. You're both safe now. You've borne this burden for too long."

Charlie leaned into her hug, feeling like a ten-year-old again, when his mother could make everything better. "You'll help Jason with his power?"

It was more than he'd hoped for, more than he expected. Really, he just wanted them to untie Jason and let them go. But deep down, he knew his brother wouldn't have left. He didn't know how to help Jason or how to make him accept that the dragons weren't his problem anymore.

"Yes, but your brother will have to work hard. With this much magic, he will only grow more dangerous if he can't learn to control it."

Charlie nodded. "He will."

"And you too. Your ability will consume you if you don't learn to protect yourself from it."

He wasn't even surprised that Melanie knew he had powers. All that mattered was that he and Jason were safe from the war mages.

Charlie pressed his lips together and nodded, even though she was wrong about him. His ability was simply a part of him, empathy enhanced by magic to include animals. There was no way to turn it off, and he couldn't hurt anyone, including himself.

"Now, get something to eat. After expending so much energy, Jason will be starving when he wakes. I'll send a message to the village. Until then, it would be best for everyone if he stays in this tent. Understood?"

Melanie didn't completely trust them, after all. Charlie glanced at David but couldn't discern the man's feelings. Whatever enhancement he'd absorbed from Jason was gone, or they knew how to keep their emotions hidden.

Charlie strode through the camp, suddenly ravenous. The fog had cleared but still shrouded the dragons, making them appear as colorful hills. The selective nature of the fog made him wonder if he'd been wrong about it being a side effect of Jason's outburst.

Someone was hiding the dragons. Someone with a great deal of magic. Someone who might be able to help Jason learn to control his power.

Hope lightened Charlie's steps. Jason had insisted they stick together and keep everyone else out. He'd always preferred books and solitary walks to friends and games, but Charlie was different. He missed playing ball with his friends. He missed going to shows.

Ever since their parents died, he'd let Jason dictate their life. Partly because he was sad and partly because he'd been lost. Life had changed in an instant, his home gone and his friends out of reach. He'd struggled to embrace his new normal, feeling like he was disappearing from the world, from life. His childhood was over.

Talking to others at the orphanage had helped. They'd all suffered the same abrupt shift after being ripped from their old lives. But then Jason decided a farm would be better, and they left. Charlie had to make new friends to keep the loneliness at bay. He'd convinced some of the boys to play ball after dinner, but Jason had stopped their game, saying they were too loud and would get in trouble. His brother didn't understand that Charlie needed to do something fun, to remind himself that life would get better.

Then Jason moved them to the army camp, and Charlie had joined the soldiers' card games when he should've been sleeping, basking in the laughter and talk of the future. Returning to his tent, to Jason, who would badger him to eat more or turn over whenever Charlie tried to talk, had become harder each night.

Eventually, Charlie would slip into his bunk long after Jason fell asleep.

And then Jason got sick. Caring for the plague-stricken had given Charlie a purpose. He was part of a team, making decisions and providing suggestions. At least until his brother tried to die.

Anger still wove through those memories. He didn't want to imagine what his life would've been like if Jason had died. Even surrounded by dead dragons, Charlie was still grateful to Bloodstar for saving his brother. But he was also angry at Jason for giving up, for leaving him.

Jason had survived, but instead of finding a home far from the war and the plague, they'd embarked on this quest. It didn't matter that the dragons would already know that Karyn had died. Jason had to tell them exactly what had happened.

Charlie had gone along with every choice, happy that his brother was alive, even though it felt like he didn't matter. But when the dragons arrived, Jason's quest changed. His connection to the dragons consumed him. He cared more about them than anything else, more than his own brother.

After the dragons left, Charlie had hoped to finally get his brother back. The quest was done, and the dragons didn't need his help. But then it turned out that Jason had chosen Silverstream because of its proximity to the dragon keep.

Again, Charlie didn't matter.

It was all about the dragons.

Charlie was done with lonely journeys of self-discovery and following dragons. Jason's way hadn't worked. As a matter of fact, his power had gotten worse and now it was out of control. It was time to try something new.

Sharing his story with Melanie had energized Charlie. She hadn't cast them out, even though he'd sensed her fear of Jason's magic. No war mage would take them away. These people wanted to help.

This was something Jason never understood. He needed isolation, but Charlie believed in community.

Obviously, his brother couldn't control his magic without guidance. Jason's fear that he would hurt Charlie made sense now. He would have to see that the only way to learn control was from other witches. He couldn't figure it out on his own.

Charlie ladled soup into two bowls and returned to the tent. The future didn't have to be a life of loneliness. These villagers would help, his brother would learn to trust others, and he would have a home.

QUEST FOR CONTROL

JASON

For the next two hours, Jason was sequestered in David's tent. Melanie glared, while Jason held his temper. At least he wasn't tied up anymore.

"I can't tell you what I don't know." He rubbed his hand through his hair wearily. His power had settled, no longer a danger. But if she kept badgering him, it might decide to grow again.

Just like after he'd incinerated Karyn, his thoughts flowed easier. The constant battle with his magic, even when it wasn't trying to burst free of his mental box, wore down his logic. But sensing emotions and knowing what was behind it hadn't gone away.

Melanie was afraid. He had to convince her that he would never have anything to do with war mages.

"You have too much power for it to *just* be an accident." She huffed, but at least she sounded more resigned.

Jason suspected his growing power, and the abilities he hadn't told her about, came from Karyn. Convincing Melanie that he'd lost control because he'd been overwhelmed by all the death was hard enough.

"I know you have secrets. If they hurt anyone, I'll hunt you down myself."

He believed her. Melanie had taken care of Charlie, but the iron in her voice reminded him that she had a magical ability too.

She untied his hands. "But I do believe that you didn't mean to lose control. Until you master your emotions, you're a danger to everyone." She pointed at Charlie. "You get back to your duties."

As Charlie scurried past her, she sighed. "At least you were smart enough to run to the far side of the corpses before your outburst. Only a few people saw what happened. David told everyone the intense light was from a bizarre lightning blast. For your training it would be best for you to set up camp at the other end of the keep. By nightfall, Heather will be here. She's the one to help, I think. And there's more than enough corpses to practice on. Listen to her, and you might be of use to us."

Jason nodded his response. Nothing irritated Melanie more than his questions. But he was burning to know who Heather was, and why she could help and not Melanie.

Jason strode through the tunnel he'd created, weaving through mounds of sparkling ash. They no longer swirled in vortexes, but some piles were taller than him.

The corpses were huge, taller than any building he'd ever seen. There was no blood. Just a wall of charred flesh with gaps where a wing or limb had been sheared off with his blast. He didn't know how he had wielded so much fire and remained unharmed. Or how he'd managed not to obliterate Charlie when his brother touched him.

Jason stretched his fingers, trying to sense the heat rushing to the tips. But there was nothing. Just like before, his emotions were subdued, as if releasing his magic had cleansed him too. He wasn't angry at the villagers for being afraid, and he wasn't upset at being restrained. Sadness was the only emotion that rolled through him now. Even that was muted.

So many dead. Magic shouldn't be so powerful. Spells required intention. Bloodstar had intended to make the enemy dragons ill. So how had his spell twisted into this curse?

Jason's intention had been to release the tension. He'd chanted the spell, but something had gone wrong. His emotions had been overwhelming, but it was more than that.

Death and fear defined his life.

His power had been growing ever since his parents died and he turned sixteen. Control had been easy at first, burning words into wood. Saying the spell. And each time he'd been able to cool the heat.

This time his emotion had been stronger than his intention. Maybe that was the problem. But how was he supposed to control his emotions? Life wasn't easy. He and Charlie were struggling to survive with no family, no home, and no way of changing that.

Karyn's quest had helped. His goal had been clear. Tell her family about her death. He hadn't thought beyond that task. He didn't know what was in his future.

The wall of charred flesh mocked him. This was what happened when he lost control. He wielded more magic than should be possible without draining his essence. Even when he'd destroyed rocks, there hadn't been enough heat to do this. Magic had to come from somewhere.

Jason stopped, his heart stumbling a beat. Siphons could draw magic from outside of themselves. But the evidence was there. Even if Jason drew magic from every part of his body, he shouldn't have been able to burn a small dragon. Trees were one thing, but dense dragon bodies required a lot more energy. And he'd cut through at least fifty corpses.

Siphons were the worst type of the war mages. They'd killed his parents.

Jason's power coiled inside his chest, a fearful mass of heat, and sweat erupted over his entire body. He clenched his fists, vowing he'd never become one of them.

His magic subsided, but his emotions were no longer muted. Everything stood out in stark detail. He'd drawn magic from somewhere.

Not the dead.

That would be impossible. Wouldn't it?

He gulped, suddenly terrified he was becoming more of a monster than the sorcerer who'd cursed the dragons and the war mages who'd killed his parents.

Heather was not at all what Jason expected. She was only fifteen years old and short, the top of her head barely reaching his chest. Though slightly built, with an innocent face framed by curly red hair, something about her commanded attention.

She stood in front of him, her hands on her hips, and tilted her head. "You don't look big enough to hold this much power. If I hadn't walked through the damage, I wouldn't believe it."

Jason shrugged. He wasn't about to confirm or deny his own suspicions. If he was a monster, he'd never learn control and the world would be better off if he disappeared. But Charlie needed him, so he had to try.

She crouched and touched the ground. A green tendril grew, unfurling and twisting, until a nightberry bloom burst free.

"I grow. You destroy." She unfurled her bedroll and sat on it, continuing to hold his gaze. "Tell me all you know about magic."

Jason stared at the flower. Possibly a seed had been below the surface, but he doubted it. The keep was bare of any plant life.

Heather's magic was powerful, and she was in full control of it. She might be able to help him.

He sat across from her and told her everything he'd learned from his parents. She listened without interrupting, her red hair shifting in the light breeze. He couldn't read her expression, but he could sense her calmness.

"Good. You have the basics. But you may not grasp just how much our intention guides magic. Without it, magic can do what it wants."

She spoke as if magic had a mind of its own.

"Now, tell me about the sorcerer's spell. Every detail you remember. What you felt. How Karyn's death affected you. And how it changed you."

This was going to be a lot harder to explain. Plus, Jason didn't want to expose everything. His doubts and fears. The enhancing of his senses. These were confusing but had nothing to do with his magic. So he focused on the facts. On the growing heat and how he'd cremated Karyn. How his power had settled until the first camp. Burning trees and rocks when he was overwhelmed. He didn't mention his suspicion that Zanthor had manipulated him, or how his power had been dormant afterwards, until he arrived at Silverstream.

When he was done, she smiled. "Good. Emotions drive your power. You've been angry since your parents died. You've been worried about your brother, and about being homeless. The war didn't help, amplifying your fear, and then the plague made you completely helpless. The spell and Karyn's death must've been shocking, but you also have survivors guilt from it. I can see that you care for your brother. We might be able to use that, but there's guilt wrapped in there too. You blame yourself for a lot of things you couldn't possibly change and that's affecting your magic."

She stood and held out her hand. "Come."

Jason let her tug him to a dark green dragon. Everything she said only confirmed what he'd already guessed. Emotions messed with his ability, but it wasn't like he could shut them down.

"Touch the wingtip."

He started to release her hand, but she tightened her grip. "Use the other hand."

Jason slid his fingers along the membrane, the texture of leather, but thinner. For a moment, awe held him still. He was touching a dragon wing.

"Now, focus on the core of your magic. You said it was in your head?"

Jason nodded, pulling his attention back to his task. Sometimes the heat coiled in his chest, but that was harder to control. Right now his magic was safely contained within his mental box.

"Is it big or small? Does it pulse or is it quiescent?"

"It fills my head and pulses."

She squeezed his hand. "That box you built is a good start. So, imagine opening a tiny door in it and allowing just a smidge of energy out."

Sucking in a deep breath, Jason allowed the tiniest amount of magic out of the box.

"How does it feel?"

He looked down into her curious gaze. "Strong."

She blinked. "Interesting. I want you to burn a hole in this wing. Focus on your intent, not your emotions. Breathe in, then out, and release only the heat you need. Don't think about anything other than burning the smallest hole you can."

He nodded and tried once again to release their hands.

"Trust me."

He tried not to let his fear of sending his power to the wrong hand be his focus. He sucked in a breath and released it.

Just a tiny hole. He could do this. He'd burned rocks, but he'd been trying to ease the pressure of his power. Now he had a tiny spark. The rest of his power pulsed in his mind, pulling the coil loose in his chest. He breathed in again. This wasn't going to work. He could feel his whole body tense.

"Stop." Her voice was gentle, encouraging. "Relax. Magic wants a way out. But you are in control. You know how to do this. Empty your mind of fear. Just focus on sending that energy down your left arm to your finger and into the wing. You can do this."

For a moment, he wondered if she could hear his thoughts. But she wasn't a dragon.

He tried again, setting his intention on burning the wing.

The rush was instant, like water cascading over a waterfall after a rainstorm. Power surged out of the box, down his neck, and up from his chest, shooting along his arm to his fingertips. Light blazed so brightly, he had to close his eyes.

He felt a cooling swell in his right hand. It surged up his arm and engulfed his chest, then shot to his brain.

Jason opened his eyes, his power somehow nullified. "What did you just do?" He turned, but Heather stared beyond him, her eyes wide.

The whole dragon had been reduced to a pile of green sparkling ash.

He'd failed.

"What did *you* do?" Her response was dazed, but she wasn't afraid. Her eyes shone as she gazed at him.

He snorted. "I lost control, obviously."

She grinned, a dimple forming in her cheek. "No. You didn't. Look. Only the dragon attached to the wing is gone. The others are intact."

Maybe she was right. But he was supposed to burn a hole, not obliterate the whole dragon. If she hadn't countered his magic, he wasn't sure he would've been able to stop the destruction. His intention had done nothing to slow down his power.

"You cooled my heat. How did you do that?"

"That's my power. Opposing energy. Mom says because I'm contrary." She pursed her lips and raised an eyebrow.

He laughed, a short burst of surprise. His mother had called him that on more than one occasion.

"So, you didn't actually grow the nightberry from nothing." She'd told him her power was growing. Like Melanie, Heather gave him half-truths.

"In a way I did. The ground was fallow, so I made it fertile, allowing the seed I planted to grow. The opposite to your heat is cold, so I was trying to freeze you. But I don't have as much power as you, so the result was cooling."

The possibilities of her power swirled through his mind. Hot and cold. Life and death. Her power could create or destroy, and she wasn't afraid of it. He felt her acceptance of her ability, her peace with it. He wasn't sure he'd ever feel that way about his magic, but if she could control it, then he could too.

Heather scooped a handful of the green ash and poured it from one hand to another. "This is beautiful. Do all dragons transform into sparkling ash when they're cremated?"

He frowned. "No. They turn into normal ash on the pyres." It took a minute to sink in, and he wasn't sure he believed it. "I did this with my magic?"

She laughed, a sound of hope and delight. "Yes. You turned a corpse into the essence of a dragon with your power. See? It isn't a curse. You've created beauty."

Maybe she was right, but until he could control his magic, he was a danger to everyone.

Resolve stiffened Jason's spine. He would learn everything she could teach him. Of course, he had other powers he hadn't told her about, enhancements from Karyn. But once he was no longer at the mercy of his ability, he could master them too. For the first time since his world fell apart, hope wrapped around Jason's heart.

TEST OF POWER
GREGOR

Gregor sniffed the flower Seri held out. It had been three days since Crysta left, and Seri had turned from searching human books to exploring his power. They'd wandered into the university gardens to see if certain scents elicited a reaction. So far he could identify the scents of fifteen flowers, and he didn't see the point. It wasn't like knowing the name of a scent could tell him what it meant.

"Nothing?"

He shook his head. The sweet woody smell of the purple flower didn't evoke his power.

"I don't think this is how it works." The path narrowed, and Gregor had to step around an overgrown rose bush. There really wasn't enough room for dragons in this human space.

Seri gently lifted a bright coral rose.

Gregor closed his eyes and huffed, refusing to sniff. He could smell the entire garden and didn't need to focus on any flower to know that none of them affected him. And he was getting a headache.

She glared. *"Fine. Let's go to the orchard then."*

At least she couldn't hear his thoughts. If they'd belonged to the same coven, she'd know exactly what he thought of her experiment. But because their coven bonds kept their emotions private, she had to trust what he said. It was freeing. They'd been able to get to know each other in a manner he'd never experienced with the younglings in his coven.

He shied away from the days he'd been alone, with only Jason's mind to center him. It didn't seem real anymore. That time was blurry.

Zanthor was his center now. Gregor could sense his presence, even though the leader was too far for mind-speech. But Zanthor still hadn't arrived. He'd left for Crystalvale five days ago to enlist the help of the dragon riders. Anxiety gnawed at Gregor's gut.

"Don't worry until you have to, youngling. You'll find it less stressful." Ronin's voice rumbled in his head, dispersing his fears. There was something so steadfast and comforting about the big blue dragon.

Seri hummed and crossed her eyes. The colored part of her eyes whirled, making Gregor dizzy.

Ronin's laughter rang through Gregor's mind. *"She looks like a hatchling who hasn't figured out how to make their eyes work."*

Since Ronin was resting on a hill on the other side of the university, Gregor didn't know how he could see Seri's eyes.

Ronin's sigh held a wealth of emotions, but he buffered them before Gregor was engulfed. *"I see through you. Our coven bond ... With so few in our coven, we can connect easily. In a large coven, you'd have to focus on one dragon to be able to see and hear what they sense. But with us, it's easier. You can do it too."*

Seri spun in a circle. *"There was something. For a moment. What were you thinking about? Maybe your power is tied to your thoughts."*

They'd reached the orchard now and new smells, sweet and fruity, bombarded Gregor. But one stood out, familiar. He dashed over to a tree filled with shiny green orbs.

"What's this?"

"Hang on." Seri uncrossed her eyes and breathed deeply. Gregor could sense her confusion and felt remorse at running off.

Obviously, using her power took some effort and wasn't as simple as blinking to reset.

She leaned into his shoulder as she pulled one of the fruit from a branch. *"These are apples. Try one."* Her grin dared him to be adventurous.

Not one to back down, Gregor grabbed an apple. It burst, sweet juice running over his talons and dripping on his feet.

Seri's glee bubbled in his chest, and he grinned, delighted at her response to his blunder.

The apples were softer than he'd expected. This time he carefully twisted one off of the branch, his talons puncturing the outer skin, but the apple was intact. He popped it in his mouth.

Sweet and tart. They tasted like they smelled.

This was the odor that had led him to Jason.

"Wait. I saw it. A thread of green. Was it the apple? Did it invoke your power?"

Gregor shook his head. He could sniff apples all day and nothing would happen. *"I was remembering what happened when I followed this scent."*

"There was magic. For a moment. Maybe attached to the memory. Let's find another one that you remember." She clapped her talons together, her excitement contagious.

That would be lilac. Even thinking about it made Gregor tense. He didn't want to remember his flight deep into the snow-covered mountains or the scent of decay that had driven him from his home.

Seri's frustrated growl snapped him back to the present. *"It's like looking at an afterimage of magic. There was a flash of purple and yellow, but they faded so quickly, I couldn't trace them. So, it's not your thoughts. Though your memories are still linked to magic in some way. But earlier, when we left the garden, the magic was stronger. What were you feeling then?"*

He tried to recall. He'd been worried about Zanthor.

"There."

Gregor felt warmth rush to his face. He didn't want to share his concerns with her. *"Can you stop accessing your power and look at me normally?"* Anger was better. This was confusing enough, and he didn't think that exposing his fears was the key.

Seri stepped back. *"I was only trying to help."*

He hadn't meant to hurt her feelings, but he wanted her to stop analyzing him. *"I know. But I can't evoke my power. The odors I detected weren't actually there. So smelling all this won't make it show up."*

Seri knew a lot about magic. She was the Oracle of a prophecy carved into a special archive stone centuries ago. Gregor didn't know anything about it, but Seri's life had been dedicated to magic. So she understood how magic worked for all the powered dragons in her coven. She believed that all dragons hatched during the Great Wars had powers, though she hadn't figured out why.

But Gregor wasn't as certain. Until this curse, he hadn't had powers. Ronin hatched with his. Zanthor discovered his later in life. Many dragons in Gregor's former coven didn't even believe in magical enhancements.

"Some dragons turn their magic on and off, like me. But for others, it's a part of them, present all the time, enhancing their abilities. But some are like yours. Initiated by a trauma. Understanding the triggers will help you control it."

He knew what she meant, but he didn't want to remember his experiences, nor dwell on them. But there was something she might be able to help with.

"When I get a scent, I found that flying in a certain direction changed the intensity. And asking questions affected it too."

"Interesting. What sort of questions?"

That would mean remembering. *"Things like, will this help me? Is there danger?"* Those were generic enough that he didn't have to state the specifics or the answers.

Fortunately, she didn't access her power again. Instead, she walked back to Garianna and Ronin, deep in thought.

Gregor was fine with silence. He'd spent enough time talking about his power and the curse. Too much looking at the past. If he was going to figure out his power, he needed to think about the future.

A whisper of lilac made his nostrils twitch. The scent was different from the one emitting from the lilac bush in the garden. This was interlaced with hope.

"Wait. Whenever I smelled something, I also felt something, like the scent had an emotion." He wasn't going to tell her it had just happened.

"Have you tried asking questions and seeing if that evokes your power?"

Gregor snorted, although something about her question felt right. Unfortunately, his response embarrassed Seri, and she turned away with a huff.

"I'll try that. Thanks." And to show her that he meant what he said and wasn't simply humoring her, he tested the theory.

What do I need right now to keep us safe?

Gregor wasn't expecting a reply, but the briny scent of ocean water wafted through his snout. He sniffed and turned in a circle. It came from the north. He moved toward it repeated the question. Kelp wound through the salty scent, and a feeling of satisfaction.

Following it proved more difficult on land.

"Where are you off to, youngling?" Ronin's voice cut through Gregor's concentration.

He stopped. Seri bumped into him, her eyes uncrossing. *"Don't stop. Your power's working."*

Communicating with Ronin was as easy as a thought. No mind-speech was necessary.

"I'll follow from the air." Gregor sensed Ronin leaping for the sky, and comfort rolled through him. This time he wouldn't be alone.

But this scent didn't frighten him. It was simply an answer.

Gregor and Seri followed a path around the university and down a hill. The salty odor led him up the next hill to a broad clearing filled with archive stones. The tall stones made of granite, shale, and quartz glowed with the etchings of dragon memories.

Having only touched the coven's black volcanic archive stone, Gregor was amazed at the variety. *"These are all archive stones?"*

Seri nodded. *"This is Dragon Library, and these are Learning Stones."* She dragged him to a pillar at least three times his height. *"This is the keystone, where covens share meetings and announcements. It's my favorite, since it contains centuries of events."*

He touched the pillar with his talon. Images and words spun through his mind. He backed away and shook his head.

"It's overwhelming the first time. There's a technique to accessing it. Unlike an archive stone with the most recent memories stored on the surface, this stone reveals information according to your needs. You have to focus on what you want before you touch it."

Gregor would have to examine it later. Right now, the scent was pulling him away. Though he felt they'd found part of the answer.

As he strode through the Learning Stones, some tall and straight, others leaning over and covered in moss, the scent grew.

"We should be able to use the keystone to warn the other covens about the curse." Gregor sent the thought to both Seri and Ronin.

Ronin landed. *"Yes. I'll scribe what we know, but it will get lost among the scouting updates. Zanthor will have to add a formal report. A coven leader's message is always given priority, but this will help."*

Gregor nodded and continued sniffing his way through the stones until he found a pile of smooth lava rocks. The scent disappeared.

"Wow. That was amazing." Seri's awe yanked Gregor's gaze up. She waved at the pile. *"What did you ask?"*

He shrugged, embarrassed at her reaction when his power had failed. Rocks weren't an answer. He must've misunderstood. The keystone made sense.

"I asked what we needed right now to be safe from the curse."

Her frown was adorable, adding a squiggle to her snout. He tried to anticipate her question.

"I know. It doesn't make sense." His failure to using his power made him squirm.

But Seri bounced on her tail. *"This is perfect."*

He couldn't contain his confusion.

Seri rolled three rocks between her talons. *"These are pieces from archive stones. The ones known to hold the most memories are made of lava. There's even a cool story about a dragon crafting one from hot lava."* She shook her head, as if even she couldn't believe the story was true. *"It's fascinating. But humans use these to create art."* An image of shapes and bowls flashed through Gregor's mind.

Ronin had finished updating the keystone and now stood beside them. He picked up one of the larger lava stones and hummed as he scraped his talon across the surface. The etching glowed before it settled into the surface. *"These will work."*

"I don't understand. How? For what?"

Ronin ducked his head and sent soothing mint to Gregor's mind. *"Sorry. I forget how young you are."*

Which only fueled Gregor's ire. He wasn't a hatchling.

"That wasn't what I meant. Younglings rarely have experiences to etch into the archive, so there's no way you could know. These are miniature archive stones. We need to communicate without mind-speech and without interacting physically with other covens. These are small enough to transport easily. Any dragon can etch messages into them."

Gregor frowned. His power had led him here, but there weren't enough stones to give to every dragon. *"Wouldn't they fill up?"*

Ronin nodded. *"Yes. They're much more limited compared to these archive stones, which store years, even generations, of information. But ..."* He wiped his palm over the surface and the etching disappeared. *"We don't need permanence. These can be reused for normal communications, at least until they eventually crumble. Think of how water can cut through cliffs over time. Our thoughts will do the same. So we'll need to gather more stones, but this will work."*

"You found exactly what we need." Seri's wonder filled Gregor's chest, and for a moment, he basked in it. She believed he'd done something amazing, when all he'd done was ask a question and followed a scent. But it did mean that maybe he could invoke his power.

Warmth rushed through Gregor, stiffening his spine, raising his head, and straightening his tail. His power *was* useful. He'd found a way to communicate without mind-speech.

MAGIC AND POWER
JASON

Jason flexed his fingers and growled. "This isn't working!"

Heather rubbed his shoulder. "We've made progress. You're only cremating one dragon at a time now."

"Yes. But my *intention* was to only burn a small hole."

Charlie snorted. "Seems like you *intended* more than that."

"Well, I didn't." Frustration only increased the heat coursing through Jason. With all his practice, his magic was in a constant state of readiness. He should've needed time to recover his energy, but he didn't.

"What if you're transforming dragons into ash instead of destroying them?" Heather stared at the sparkling piles from his efforts.

"It's the same thing." Jason stomped up to the next dragon corpse, determined to make his magic obey.

"Maybe. But a campfire converts wood into smoke and ash. The amount of ash left over is a small portion of the original piece of wood. But even a large building wouldn't leave this much ash behind."

That was one way of looking at it. But Jason couldn't figure out what difference it made. He still couldn't *convert* a small part of a dragon wing.

"Dragons are denser, so there's more residue. But I haven't seen any smoke." He was trying really hard not to snap at her. Heather was only trying to help.

"No. It's your power that makes a difference. The dragons on the pyres break down normally. Only you produce sparkle dust. Your power is driven by your emotions." Her eyes opened wide, and a gleeful smile lit up her face.

Her logical leap made his head spin. He already knew that emotions made it harder for him to contain his magic. But to jump from sparkling piles to his feelings being the cause didn't make any sense.

"That's not how magic works."

"Not usually. But I've heard of instances where people can cast spells they shouldn't be able to during times of emotional crisis. A woman who stopped a building from crushing her children. A man who parted water to save his dog from drowning."

Jason glanced at Charlie, who grimaced and shrugged his shoulders, just as dubious.

Heather circled a pile of ash that was taller than her. "Even when I use my ability, emotions are involved. Sure. I set my intention, but I have to want it. There's a reason for casting the spell. An emotion tied to the outcome."

She scooped a handful of purple ash. Considering each particle was the size of a fingernail, calling it sparkle dust was offensive.

"How do you feel when you see these dragons?"

Jason shrugged, uncomfortable with discussing the intense emotions that rolled through him every day. But he could see that she wouldn't let it go.

"Angry, sad."

She nodded. "That makes sense. But dig deeper. Are there any other emotions?"

"Helpless." He surprised himself. He'd thought his guilt was the strongest emotion in all the turmoil. Now he wished he could take it back.

"There. That won't help with control. But when you've used your ability around Charlie, you *do* have control. How do you feel about him?"

Jason snorted. "Annoyed."

Charlie stood up and punched Jason in the shoulder. "Brother's prerogative. It's my job."

"I'm serious, you two. I'm sure you feel more for each other. I love my sister, no matter how annoying she can be."

Heather was right, again, and maybe on to something. Jason sighed, knowing he'd have to dig into all his feelings. Of course he loved his brother. But ever since their parents died, he constantly worried about Charlie, especially when he'd lost weight and aggravated Barnaby. If his brother would just think before he blurted out his thoughts, he'd realize there was a better way to get people to do what he wanted. But Charlie was passionate and impulsive, and he stood up for others. No matter what it cost him.

"Protective." Somehow, Heather was pulling answers from Jason that he didn't consciously know.

Charlie grunted and looked away.

"Yes. That's a completely different emotion and equally powerful. So, what if you focus on protecting Charlie, and then try again? But also, don't think of using your magic to destroy. You're converting these corpses into something special."

Jason shrugged. He didn't think it would change anything. The next corpse was bigger than the ones he'd cremated before. He sucked in a deep breath, put his hand on the dry membrane, and focused on his feelings. How he couldn't bear to see his brother hurt, and how it was his responsibility to keep Charlie safe. He pushed away the resentment that rose at his parents for leaving, and at Charlie for making life harder. Jason remembered their laughter growing up, and how his parents had made him feel. Warm, happy, and full of hope.

With the next breath he pushed the heat to his fingers and allowed only a little escape. He was creating safety.

The surge of power was less than before, and when it tried to overflow, he pushed down the onslaught of fear and guilt that threatened to overwhelm him, refocusing on what he wanted for Charlie.

The magic receded, and Jason took another breath, his shoulders lowering for the first time.

It worked. There was a fist-size hole in the wing, edged with sparkling green.

Heather clapped. "You did it. How did that feel?"

Jason wished she'd stop asking him to shout his feelings. It wasn't like he could think of Charlie every time he wanted to burn a corpse. His power coiled, ready to be released again. The moment of calm evaporated, as if it had never existed.

"I think you've proven that emotions are the key to your power. Do dragons make you feel anything else, other than helpless?"

He understood what she meant. Helplessness wouldn't make his power burst from him. It had to be a more active emotion. Like protection. He knew what it was, but he didn't want to say it out loud.

"Stupid. Insignificant. Small." Charlie offered as he examined the hole.

"Shut up." But it worked. Jason distanced himself from his discomfort. Heather was helping. It didn't matter what she thought of his feelings. And Charlie was right too. Dragons were so much more intelligent than he'd expected. They made him feel young and inexperienced yet had treated him with respect. He was connected through Karyn. Through her heart. He was alive because of her.

"Guilt. I feel responsible. But also angry at the sorcerer, for what he did to Karyn. To me."

"That's it. Guilt and anger are strong emotions, but they're negative. They add to your sense of helplessness and prevent you from controlling your power. Don't you have any positive emotions when you think of dragons? Something that will help you gain control. Magic is sneaky. It wants to be set free, no matter the cost to you." She sounded like she spoke from experience. Not her own. But sadness flowed from her.

Jason blinked. He hadn't sensed emotions since his outburst. Probably imagining it. Her voice had changed, and he'd be callous if he couldn't see that she was sad. Maybe being around dragons had helped him notice other people's feelings. Dragon emotions were intense.

Gregor's pain and despair had been inside Jason's head. In his heart. He recalled how Zanthor had honored him by treating him as an adult, listening to him and working with him to figure out the curse. Dragons had treated him differently from any person he'd met. Like family.

"I've got it." Heather didn't need to know. This was his.

Jason focused on this sense of family. Of how he cared what happened to Charlie and Gregor, and how Zanthor had made him feel capable of keeping both of them alive and safe.

He set his intention and pushed the magic through his fingers, guiding and resetting whenever his focus wavered, or the negative emotions threatened to break free. It took more time, but when he was done, the hole was twice the size of the first one.

He could control his magic.

Heather clapped, and Charlie hooted. Their joy at his accomplishment made him blush. He'd done it, but it had taken a lot of effort. Holding only one emotion was harder than it sounded. Still, he felt more energized. Before, when he'd poured out all his power, he'd been drained. Maybe it was because burning a hole took less magic than transforming an entire dragon, but he worried there was something more going on. The heat rolled through his body, unabated and ready.

"Where am I getting all this magic from?" Jason didn't expect Heather to know, but she'd helped so far.

"What do you mean? We draw from our own energy."

"I'm not drained. I have as much magical energy as before. But when I cremated all those corpses, I used a lot more energy. More than should be possible. And even though I collapsed afterward, my power was replenished in a short time."

Charlie walked past him and stroked the dragon's wing. "That's right. So you must've drained your own energy. Bloodstar was exhausted after the spell too. But he still maintained the illusion hiding us."

Charlie hadn't mentioned the sorcerer's reaction before. But it reminded Jason of his fear that he was a siphon too.

"What if I'm siphoning magic from outside of myself?"

The others were silent, maybe trying to work it out. At sixteen he didn't have as much essence as an adult. Yet the amount he needed to cremate an entire dragon, never mind a mile-long row of dragons, was more than any person could hold.

Heather was the first to offer a solution. "Maybe you're not. But Bloodstar could've been. The spell must've changed your connection to magic. Changed *you* in some elemental way, other than the obvious." She pointed to his chest.

They hadn't really focused on the fact that the heart pumping his blood was a dragon heart. Maybe Karyn's heart was a factor in enabling him to access more magic.

"But even if I am a siphon, where am I getting the magic from?" A sudden thought sent shock waves of denial through Jason. "Crap. What if I'm draining both of you?"

"No. I don't feel anything missing. My core of energy is intact." Heather's hand now rested on his chest.

Charlie gasped. "What if you're siphoning the dragons? Zanthor had powers."

But Heather shook her head. She stepped away, dropping her hand to wave at the corpses. "They're dead. What energy could they have?"

Jason rubbed his chest, missing the warmth of her hand. He was connected to dragons with his heart. Charlie might be right. "What do we know about them? What if they're literally made of magic?"

Her face scrunched. "You can't siphon magic from the dead. Doesn't matter if they have powers or not."

"She's right. Otherwise, war mages wouldn't need to harvest magic from people with magical abilities. They could get it from anywhere. What if you're tapping into magic directly?"

"Don't be ridiculous, Charlie. That's impossible."

"Why not? Magic has been diminishing. We thought it was because of the war, but what if it's because the war mages can siphon magic directly?" Charlie's logic made terrible sense, but Jason didn't want to consider it.

"Then they wouldn't have needed Mom and Dad. They would still be alive." The unfairness of it all rose to Jason's throat, causing his power to grow. If the war mages could siphon magic from the air, then no one had to die for their battle spells.

"I'm not saying every mage can do it. But what if Bloodstar could? And somehow his spell gave you that ability."

Fear and anger rolled through Jason, too much to contain. He clenched his teeth and turned back to the dragon corpses. He had no intention of burning a pathetic hole. If he didn't release his rage, he'd hurt both Heather and Charlie. But he could feel his control slipping as all the injustices scrabbled at his mind.

His parents hadn't been given a choice, their essence cut short for the stupid war. Barnaby beating Charlie for protecting a younger boy. The plague almost killing him. And Karyn. She'd saved him, but for what?

"Run away." He hoped they heard him through the roar in his head. Thoughts kept spinning and every one increased his power.

He had to protect Charlie from the war, from starvation, and from himself. Jason cried out as he released his power, unable to contain it anymore.

The light wasn't as bright. The heat not as hot. But it still rushed through his body, cutting out the world around him, burning through the emotions he didn't want, the ones he longed to be free of. And then the magic was gone, and Jason drooped, spent.

"You did it." Amazement pulsed from Charlie.

Jason opened his eyes, expecting another tunnel of charred bodies. But only three dragons had been transformed into glittering piles of ash. There were no charred body parts. The other corpses were untouched.

He'd done it. Thinking about protecting Charlie had helped him control his outburst. Too bad the responsibility of taking care of him also caused his power to build to the point where he had to release it.

Three dragons were better than a tunnel of half-burnt corpses, but he'd used too much magic. Siphoning that much magic would have repercussions, a price. Who or what was paying it?

Jason dropped to the ground and let oblivion take him away from all his worry.

When he woke, Heather and Charlie were deep in discussion, their heads together as they examined the dragon ash.

"It has to come from somewhere." Charlie ran the glittering particles through his fingers.

Jason sat up, expecting his head to hurt, but he felt fine. Better than fine. His magic flowed through his body as if he hadn't just transformed three dragons and collapsed.

"I still think he must be drawing it from the air." Heather's voice held awe.

She didn't seem to realize how horrible that would be if true. He could siphon so much magic that people wouldn't be able to breathe. If that's what Bloodstar had done, then he'd turned Jason into a monster. He groaned.

"You're up. How do you feel?" Heather's concern wrapped around him, making his heart stumble a beat. She really did have a beautiful smile. Her kindness was soul deep.

Jason rubbed his hand through his hair and glanced away. "I'm good." He shrugged. "Where does magic come from—the air, grass, water, us?"

She pursed her lips. "I don't know. Magic is everywhere. War mages can siphon from things that contain magic—people, objects, nature. My mother told me it was in the air we breathe and the food and water we consume. As much a part of life as anything that makes us who we are."

That made sense. Jason's father had described it as a resource within himself, similar to a soul. Something so intertwined to life that you couldn't separate it. But Jason was able to contain his power in his mental box. Or at least he'd been able to before. Now he wasn't sure he could pull all the magic coursing through him into a single space. At least it only expelled through his fingers so far.

"But you said the sorcerer was able to maintain an illusion spell and cast this spell. It sounds like he drew on a lot more than nature."

Charlie frowned. "Yes. And the tent seemed to appear and disappear. He wasn't able to keep it completely hidden. But inside the magic was steady. The tent was big enough to hold the dragon and us. Yet on the outside, it looked no bigger than normal."

Jason nodded. "When I left, the tent was completely invisible. The guards couldn't see it at all. So Bloodstar was able to maintain the illusion even when he wasn't there."

"What if it wasn't Bloodstar who super-powered your magic? We have no idea what having a dragon heart is doing to you. Maybe her blood flows through you, and with it her magic."

Did Karyn have magic? Jason didn't know. She hadn't told him she did. It wasn't until he met Zanthor that Jason even suspected dragons had magic. Maybe they didn't. Maybe it was rare. But Gregor could smell things that weren't there.

Jason shook his head. There was so much he didn't know. "I don't think I'm drawing magic from the air. We would feel a difference." He sucked in a deep breath. "It seems the same to me. I consumed a lot of power. And I have a dragon heart, not dragon blood. So there's nothing special flowing through my veins."

Heather paced between them. "Technically, I'm a siphon. I draw from nature, or in the case of your fire, I draw from that energy and generate the opposite power. When you think about it, all of us with magical abilities are drawing energy from ourselves. We're all siphons. Why not from the air? We know magic is everywhere, that some people have enhanced abilities and that others can transfer magic from one form to another. Your ability is fire and that requires air."

"But my ability isn't just fire. I can freeze too. It's all about temperature. Right now I cast heat because it's still warm, even though it's fall. But during winter, I draw in the coldness and can freeze things."

"Yes. That proves my point even more. You're not hot. The air is hot. And when it's cold out, your power changes." She tilted her head. "Can you make fog or rain?"

Jason had never thought of trying. But if she was right, and he did draw from the air, he might be able to produce magic in between hot and cold.

"Maybe. I've never tried. But even if you're right, this amount of heat is more than the air temperature right now."

"Your emotions." Charlie stilled. "Even if you're drawing magic from the air, something is making you siphon heat to be able to burn this much. Could magic be a combination? You're drained after an explosion. Are your emotions subdued afterward too? Is it your energy, the air, and your emotions?"

The fact that Charlie could put all that together bemused Jason. His brother hadn't ever struck him as a deep thinker. But Charlie had done many things while Jason had been ill. He was growing into his own person.

"Maybe. I do feel calmer afterward. And the more I burn the better I feel."

But they were ignoring the most dangerous part. The air was limitless, constantly there. His power would have no end. Siphons drew from living things. Heather and Charlie claimed they were unaffected, but he wasn't so sure. If Jason was right, he couldn't use his power around them anymore.

FEVER

JASON

Three nights later, rain pelted the tent. Jason rolled over for the fifth time, trying to find a dry spot on his bedding but feared that was impossible. Though it was still dark, he could hear the camp waking on the other side of the keep.

Charlie slept through it, unmoving. Exhausted. He'd run back and forth to the main camp, bringing Jason and Heather food and water. Jason had often been frustrated by his brother's lack of initiative growing up, even though his dad kept saying that Charlie was doing more than Jason did at the same age. But now, a warm glow of pride swept through him. His brother had changed, more helpful than Jason could've imagined.

Jason groaned as he sat. Water ran under the tent, soaking through. No wonder he hadn't slept well. A faint glow in the sky hinted that it must be dawn.

"Wake up, Charlie. We have to get going." Jason shook his brother's shoulder, then wrung the sopping bedding to remove the excess water before rolling it. He wasn't sure where they'd stay once they got back to the village.

With the onset of the rainy season, it would be difficult to keep the pyres burning. He could still use his powers, but staying would defeat the purpose of keeping his abilities secret. Melanie wanted him to learn control, not to expose his magic. He hoped. That's if he was even allowed to stay in the village. Eleanor might decide he was too much trouble.

"Come on. You can't really be sleeping in that puddle." He nudged Charlie with his foot.

But Charlie didn't move.

Fear swept away Jason's annoyance at packing up by himself. He touched Charlie's head. It was hot. Too hot.

Jason swallowed. Charlie had been healthy through everything that had happened. What if he'd caught the plague? Or worse, what if Jason's magic had done this? He couldn't remember how many times his brother had appeared, talking him down from a surge of power, completely ignoring Jason's demand that he stay away.

What if he'd siphoned Charlie's essence, weakening him? He didn't know how siphoning had killed his parents. Maybe it looked exactly like this.

Charlie needed a Healer.

Jason rolled Charlie off of his bedding. Then he packed up the rest of their belongings and shoved them under a dragon wing. Heather could collect them later. He wished she was here now, instead of at the main camp. But every evening she'd left to sleep in Melanie's tent.

With a grunt of effort, he lifted his brother. He was heavier than Jason expected, but then he'd never carried someone before. Charlie's head lolled backward, and Jason winced at the pain that must be causing his neck. He shifted his grip to support Charlie's head with his shoulder, but then his grip was insecure.

A sob caught in Jason's throat. He couldn't even carry his brother.

"Charlie, wake up!" Shouting wouldn't make a difference if he had fever brain.

Charlie didn't respond.

Jason crumpled, holding his brother in his lap. This was hopeless. He'd been focused on what he needed, on his magic, and now his brother was sick, and he couldn't even help him. His power was useless when it came to anything that mattered.

Or was it?

If he could push heat out, maybe he could draw it in. Jason's heart beat faster. He'd only used his power on wood, stones, and corpses. Nothing alive. Except trees, and he'd destroyed them. He was in control now. Thanks to Heather and Charlie.

But they couldn't help him now. He was alone.

The rain was cold. A long time ago, with his father's help, he'd cooled a cup of water, back when his power was still new and took effort. But now his power was so much stronger. He didn't want to freeze Charlie.

He needed to draw in the fever. Charlie's forehead was blazingly hot under Jason's palm.

Jason breathed in deeply, then blew it out slowly. He could do this. Only a little at a time.

He set his intention to draw heat and wake his brother.

Another breath, in and out.

Jason closed his eyes and imagined the heat rising from Charlie's body and flowing into his hand, like mist. Not a flood. Light. Slow.

At first there was nothing. Only his brother's breathing and the raindrops bouncing. Jason's breathing matched Charlie's. Slowly, his hand grew warmer, while his magic stayed in his body.

This was softer, more connected. He opened his eyes and focused on his love for Charlie, on his desire to reduce the fever, to help his body heal. Not that Jason was a Healer, but the fever was there for a reason, and adding that to his intention couldn't hurt.

He didn't want to hurt Charlie. No burning. Just absorbing heat.

Charlie's eyes flew open. "What?"

Jason instantly dropped his hand and wrapped his arms around Charlie. He'd done it. Warmth rushed through him, though he was uncertain whether it was simply his magic reacting to his emotions or Charlie's fever combining with his power. It didn't matter. With the cold rain pouring down, his magic wouldn't grow out of control.

"Hey. You're all right. We have to get going." He wasn't ready to tell Charlie what he'd done. Hopefully, it lasted. But in case it didn't, he needed to get his brother to the Healer as quickly as possible.

"Why are you hugging me so tight, and where is our tent?" Charlie stood, confusion in his voice.

Jason forced out a laugh. "Just trying to get you to wake up. You must've overdone it yesterday. Let's go."

As Charlie walked ahead of him, Jason watched him closely. So far, his brother seemed fine, but he worried he'd only delayed whatever was wrong with him.

He couldn't lose Charlie after everything that had happened. He just couldn't.

Heat grew in his chest, flowing through his body. He stopped, hoping the rain would hide his movements. Jason reached for the nearest corpse and released his magic. It flowed, rather than bursting from him. From his heart to his hand and into the dragon's body.

Easier than before. But different too.

Jason felt more centered. More focused. He drew the coolness from the air and controlled the flow of fire. This time he saw his magic engulf the dragon and leave the others untouched. It was slower, but he felt the rightness of it.

Not just control, but a way of honoring the dragon, transforming it into a blue-black ash that glowed for a moment. The rain scattered the pile of ash into rivulets that wound under his feet.

A peace settled over Jason. This was control. Both giving and taking. Balance.

Somehow, his brother had saved him again.

Once they reached the village, Jason would make a deal with Eleanor. As long as she took care of Charlie, Jason would spend his time cremating the decaying dragons. At least until the snow came. Either she could come up with a story or keep the other villagers away from the keep. Or he could leave, if that's what she wanted. He didn't care as long as Charlie was safe.

ZANTHOR'S QUEST
JASON

The trip down the mountain was a blur. Jason watched Charlie the whole time, offering a hand when his brother stumbled or swayed. By the time they reached the village, his brother's eyes were glassy, and the fever had returned. Not as hot as before, but obviously he was fighting something.

Jason pulled Charlie to the Healing Center. Eleanor could wait.

Fortunately, Richard wasn't busy. He took one look at Charlie and ushered them to a cot.

"When did this start?"

Jason rolled his shoulder, trying to ease the tightness. "Last night, I guess. He was hotter this morning and wouldn't wake up."

The Healer checked Charlie's temperature, and then slowly swept his hands over his body. Healers used magic differently from witches. They didn't cast spells. They sensed fluctuations. Somehow this informed them of anything that needed curing.

Jason held his breath as Richard lifted the leg of Charlie's britches. His calf was red and swollen, a small cut oozing pus. Relief wilted Jason. His brother had an infection. Not fever brain and not drained of his essence by Jason's magic.

Richard nodded. "Must've become infected from the dragons. Normally, corpses aren't a problem. But the dragons died from an infection."

"Does that mean he has the plague?" Jason's mouth went dry. He'd assumed the curse couldn't transfer to people through physical contact. What if he'd been wrong?

"I don't think so. His symptoms don't match, and it's only his leg that appears to be affected. My guess is that this Dragon Plague actually caused dragons to become infected in some way. From what I've been told, it's faster and more violent than our plague, involving a lot more discharge of bodily fluids. Charlie's cut probably became infected from any number of things at the keep."

He looked up at Jason. "Don't worry. The fever is killing it off. I'll apply a poultice to draw out the infection and as long as he keeps it covered and rests, he should improve in a day or two."

Jason wasn't as confident in Richard's theory. The curse was created from the plague. Richard hadn't been at the keep. He would've seen it was more than a bad infection that killed the dragons. Charlie might not have the curse, but his infection came from contact with the dragon corpses, or from the putrid discharge that had covered the keep. Even the Healer couldn't know that he'd survive.

Charlie sat up. "See? I'll be fine. Stop mothering." And that did more to ease Jason's worry than the Healer's assurances.

Heather ran up as soon as they left the Healing Center. "Hurry. You're needed at David's place."

Jason ran ahead, leaving Charlie to follow.

David stood by the pen, his animals begging for his attention. But his eyes were glazed over.

Jason touched his shoulder. "Is everything all right?"

David shook his head and sighed. "Zanthor's here. I didn't mean to let him in, but he says he's not infected."

The rain obscured the field behind David's house. Jason peered through the gloom but couldn't see Zanthor. Of course, the dragon could change his appearance to blend in, something he'd never explained.

"He didn't have any symptoms when I met him." Jason hoped that was still the case. He didn't want the man to get fever brain.

"He's come for help. Villagers have shot at him." Anger vibrated through David's voice. "He's hidden himself, worried that we would attack him too. I've told him about our riders falling to fever brain. He thinks that's why he felt so much fear and hostility when he tried to land at Crystalvale."

So the curse was affecting other villages. "But why would dragon riders attack dragons? Aren't you bonded?"

"It wasn't riders who attacked him. They're probably comatose like ours, so the villagers must fear they'll be infected too, especially if they found out that dragons are sick. But I suspect mind-speech is only dangerous if the dragon has the curse."

Jason jogged to keep up with David's long stride. "But Zanthor doesn't, so you're fine." Although David hadn't known that when he allowed Zanthor into his mind.

Zanthor could've spoken to Jason. He tried not to let that slight disappoint him. David was a real dragon rider and Jason wasn't anything. Of course, the dragon spoke with him. But still, Jason rubbed at the ache in his chest. Rejection hurt.

"I'm not rejecting you. I didn't know you were here." Zanthor's voice filled Jason's mind with warmth, the connection tapping into a part of Jason he'd forgotten somehow.

His heart beat a happy rhythm, and his senses opened. The fragrance of rain and grass strengthened. The patter of raindrops on leaves and the smack of drops hitting the dirt road became louder. Jason could identify the animals in David's barn shuffling and bleating. Even the distant hum of voices from the village was audible.

"You manipulated us into forgetting about you." Not entirely accurate, but with this rush of scents and sounds, Jason knew

it had been more than convincing them to get on with their lives without dragons. He felt more alive now than he'd felt since Zanthor and the other dragons left.

But he'd forgotten how mind-speech exposed his thoughts and feelings.

"I'm sorry you felt betrayed. You'd told us about the curse. There was nothing more you could do. But I need your help, again, and you're probably the only one who can do it."

Purpose lightened Jason's steps as he followed David to the house. There was something about being with dragons, being in their minds, which completed him. He forgot about his worry over Charlie. He forgot about his troubles with his powers. He just wanted to be with Zanthor.

"There is something odd about your mind. You're human. I'm a dragon. You can't be me." Zanthor's words didn't make sense, but Jason drew away mentally, becoming more aware of his body, his brother following, and David in the lead.

He wasn't a dragon. He didn't even want to be one. But something inside of Jason had changed with Zanthor near.

David would help him understand this odd connection. Maybe speaking with a dragon heightened his senses. Maybe that meant he could become a dragon rider too.

David swung open the door to his cabin and ushered them inside.

"You can share the room at the end on the left." David's tone was gruff as he abruptly turned around. "I have to tend the animals."

Charlie wilted, settling on the couch with a groan, looking far too pale.

"You OK?" Jason placed his hand on Charlie's forehead.

"Stop it." Charlie pushed Jason's hand away.

Since his head wasn't too hot, Jason didn't argue. Charlie didn't need to know that Jason had used magic, and that he worried he'd made the infection worse.

"You should rest. Let's check out the room." Jason straightened and left Charlie on the couch.

"See, told you I was fine." Charlie's relief settled into Jason's chest, letting him know Charlie hadn't been sure.

Jason clenched his teeth. This strange power was back. He didn't want to know how everyone else felt. The only logical reason for sensing emotions again was Zanthor's return.

The room contained two narrow beds, a small window, and a chest against the wall with the door. Identical dragon quilts covered the beds, one green and one blue. Jason fingered the worn fabric and scanned the room for clues, but the walls were bare. Inside the wooden chest was a matching set to the clothes he wore, along with two other sets in a lighter beige fabric. David had lost twin boys at some point. His sons likely, given the care that had been taken to preserve the room.

With a curse at the unfairness of death, Jason tore off his wet clothes and put on the other set. Charlie could wear the lighter ones. Jason had a feeling his brother would sleep for the rest of the day.

It took a lot of badgering to get Charlie out of his wet things, into the fresh clothing, and under the quilt. But soon, he was sleeping soundly and looking better. And so young. Sometimes it was easy to forget he was only thirteen.

The memory of how their mother cared for him when he'd been sick prompted Jason to lean over and kiss Charlie's forehead. "Rest and heal. Wake up to a new day full of possibilities."

Jason straightened, glad his brother hadn't heard him.

David was in the kitchen. "You should eat."

Jason dug into the fresh hot bread, wondering where it had come from. David had just returned from the keep, same as him.

"Eleanor knew we'd be back once the rain started. Heather dropped this off while you were settling Charlie down." There was a question in David's eyes.

Jason looked away. "This is fantastic. Charlie has an infection, but I thought it was fever brain this morning." He surprised himself by blurting the truth, but David had earned his trust. "I'm glad it isn't."

David closed his eyes and grunted. Jason bit into the bread, wondering if he'd said something wrong. But when David opened his eyes, he nodded. "Sometimes a fever is just a fever. I'll take care of him while you're gone."

"Where am I going?" Fear that Eleanor had told David to feed him and send him away ran through Jason's veins. Of course they were afraid of him. He'd been stupid to think he could just stay after revealing his power. At least they'd take care of Charlie. Maybe it was a blessing that Charlie was too tired to follow him. These were good people. Melanie and Heather would ensure Charlie was happy.

"I have to warn the covens and the villagers about the curse. Mind-speech with an infected dragon makes riders ill. I can't risk taking David. You're the only one I know who's spoken with a cursed dragon and didn't lose your mind to fever brain. This is why I need your help." Zanthor's voice was carefully factual with no emotion clouding the words.

And Jason knew that Zanthor was showing him there was no power behind his request. Not that it was a question. Zanthor was right. Dragon riders couldn't risk it. David had been spared because his dragon hadn't spoken to him before she died and because Zanthor wasn't sick.

Excitement and fear churned through Jason. This was it. A quest to help the dragons. It felt right. But Charlie needed him.

His heart ached. Dragons needed him too.

He'd made a promise to Karyn. Not to care for them, but ... He'd given them the curse. And now that curse hurt dragon riders. Heroes. Legends. He had to save as many as he could.

David grasped Jason's hands. "It's a big task for someone so young. There's risk. People are shooting at dragons. Villagers don't trust strangers. There are too many people greedy for war mage coin. Your magic is hard to hide. And then there's the war. You'd have to fly over the front lines and army camps to get to the southern keeps."

Anticipation soared through Jason's soul. He could see the world from the sky. He could touch the clouds. And he could ride Zanthor. Be a real dragon rider.

Jason loved his brother. He really did. But this connection to dragons was his. Something special, granted with Karyn's heart. He had to help. To save them from this curse. And then he could get back to his responsibility to Charlie.

"Yes. I'll do it." He answered David and Zanthor at the same time.

Charlie would be cared for while Jason saved the dragons and the dragon riders.

DRAGON RIDER
JASON

Fortunately, the rain stopped, but everything was soaked. Putting the riding straps on Zanthor required more than the combined effort of Jason, David, and Heather. She'd shown up to say goodbye.

Zanthor was still the whole time, but Jason could feel his impatience to get moving.

David rubbed Heather's back before sending her to tighten the strap at Zanthor's neck. Their easy familiarity made Jason wonder at their relationship.

"She's related. I don't always understand human connections, but his sister was her grandmother."

Having Zanthor in his head again was disconcerting. Jason didn't know how to hide his thoughts and emotions from their mental connection. At least Zanthor knew how to put on the straps.

"Tighten that one more notch."

The buttons were easy enough to get into the holes, but holding a strap tight against Zanthor's body and then getting the button in required more strength than a malnourished sixteen-year-old could handle. David reached over Jason and wrenched the leather together, allowing the button to pop in.

"Zanthor doesn't want you falling off." David grinned before bounding to the other side of the dragon.

That was good, because Jason didn't want to fall off either. He was both excited and terrified to fly.

Even though it was late, Charlie still slept. Jason still hadn't figured out how to say goodbye. Zanthor didn't know how long their quest would take. The distances involved and the fact that Jason would have to travel on foot to the villages and keeps meant he could be gone for months. The rains had just started, but some of the areas they needed to reach would have snow, making travel treacherous. But Zanthor needed to stay out of range of mind-speech. And he didn't trust villagers to treat him with respect.

David slapped Zanthor's side. *"All set. Wish I could go too."*

"You can help by warning the nearby villages. No one should try to speak to a dragon. And don't worry. I'll take care of the boy." Zanthor's ability to allow Jason to hear his mind-speech with David still surprised him. He'd experienced it among dragons, but hadn't expected to be able to hear people communicate with dragons. *"Remember to keep your mental shield up. After this is over, we will need experienced dragon riders."*

Zanthor expected this to end one day soon. Hope burned in Jason's chest. There must be a way for dragons to protect themselves from spreading the curse.

"Time to go." David handed Jason a dark green cloak. "You'll need this. It gets mighty cold above the clouds. It's waterproof too." His voice was gruff.

Jason swung the cloak over his shoulders, the leather weighing him down more than physically. "Was this yours?" The cloak was long, reaching down to his knees.

David's laugh was hollow. "No. It belonged to one of my grandsons."

The twin beds. Jason bit his lip. He didn't want to pry. "Thanks."

"You'll grow into it. When you get back, I'll tell you about them." David turned away and grabbed a backpack from the lean-to next to the rails. "Take this. It's got everything you need. I replaced a few things. It's been a while since anyone used it, but you should be fine."

He positioned the backpack over Jason's shoulders, then turned to shove a narrow bedroll under one of the straps at Zanthor's shoulders. Jason had wondered why the strap split into two behind the spot where he would sit.

"Acts as a bit of a backrest when you need it." David's grin was slight, his eyes filled with worry. "You do what Zanthor says, even if you don't understand why. He has the experience."

Jason barely knew David, but this man would take care of Charlie as if he were his own son. He knew that. "Tell Charlie that I'll be back for him."

He was a coward, but he couldn't tell Charlie he was leaving. It would be too hard. His brother would be fine with this man. And it wasn't the same as when their parents left. Jason had known he wouldn't see them again. He wouldn't do that to Charlie. He was coming back.

Heather touched Jason's arm and leaned in to kiss his cheek. "We'll take care of him. But you be careful."

Jason blinked as he blushed. The warmth of her lips was gone, but for a moment he'd felt her admiration. Her patience in helping him with his power had impressed him, but her laughter and intelligence had stolen his breath. He thought she hadn't noticed him at all. He was just a task. But it seemed she might be interested in more.

He'd had no time to think of a future. Too busy trying to survive with Charlie. But when he was done with this, maybe he would have time to get to know her better.

"I will." He couldn't think of what else to say. It wasn't like he'd had a chance to flirt with a girl before. "Um. Thanks." Jason fiddled with the riding straps until he heard her leave.

"Ready?"

Jason nodded. David had already explained how to mount. So, ignoring the pang at not saying goodbye to his brother, Jason slipped his foot into the lowest loop and heaved himself up. He settled into the space in front of Zanthor's wings, along his shoulders, and gripped the strap in front of him with both hands. The bedroll was a comfort at the base of his spine. Without it he'd feel like he would slip off.

"You'll be fine. I won't let you fall. Now, hold on. The first time is the hardest."

Zanthor rose, and Jason grasped the strap tighter as he fell backward. Clouds filled his vision, the ground now at his back. His stomach knotted. This was not like riding a horse.

Without another word, Zanthor leapt, his wings snapping open. Jason turned his head to watch the ground, but he was jolted forward as Zanthor flapped, rising farther into the sky. After several mighty flaps, they leveled out, and Jason was once again upright.

His neck hurt, but he was too afraid to let go of his death grip to rub it.

"You can look now." Zanthor's body vibrated under Jason as he spoke, surprising because Jason thought mind-speech was all mental.

"Yes and no. Our communication is mental, but our bodies are involved, just like yours when you speak."

But Jason needed air to speak, so his chest moved, and his throat vibrated.

"Think of it like your throat. Our speech vibrates through our bodies, but it's transmitted through our minds instead of our mouths."

It kind of made sense. Jason shrugged, discovering that the conversation had relaxed him. He loosened one hand and rubbed his neck, easing the ache.

"Sorry." Remorse flowed through Zanthor's words. *"I'd forgotten what it's like for a first-timer. I was Ariel's second match."*

Jason wasn't sure how he could ever get comfortable with takeoff, but they glided through the clouds now. *"It's OK. I should've asked for more details about how to ride."*

"Next time, lean forward when I launch to prevent your neck from whipping back and forth."

Is that what had happened? Jason bent his neck forward and back, then twisted, wincing at the pain of each motion. He was about to ask more but then the view caught his breath.

Dawn's Keep lay to his right, the mounds of corpses rising over the trees surrounding the keep. The village at the base of the mountain was tiny, just a bunch of rooftops with glimpses of road in between. He could make out shapes moving, but not who they were. The treetops below him whipped past, little spires of green, with fuzzy branches hiding anything beneath them.

He shifted to look ahead and spotted a huge gray cloud. Zanthor flapped his wings again and they dove through it. Rain slammed into Jason, forcing his eyes shut. And suddenly, it was gone.

They flew above the clouds, the bright sunlight making Jason blink. He wiped the water from his face. His legs were soaked through, but the cloak had kept most of his body dry, except for his head. Next time, he'd put on his hood before they dove through a rain cloud.

The ground was hidden now. There was just him, Zanthor, and the sky. As far as he could see were clouds of various shades of white and gray. A mountaintop peeked through in the distance, but otherwise they were alone. Silence wrapped around his soul. The wind shifted and Zanthor tilted causing the wind to whisper in Jason's ear. With a powerful wing flap, they rose, capturing a thermal and gliding through the brilliant blue sky.

Joy bubbled through Jason in a way that wasn't possible on land, a wondrous sensation that could only be felt on the back of a dragon.

As the sun's heat dried his hair, Jason sighed, his heart finally at ease, his mind clear of doubt and regret. Here, in the sky with Zanthor, anything was possible.

ARCHIVE STONES
GREGOR

Gregor sniffed deeply. Since he'd found the stones, his power had been dormant. Not a single unusual scent. Seri was off with the humans again, researching their diseases and cures. He wasn't sure that anything humans did would help dragons beat a curse. Magic and diseases were completely different, even if that sorcerer had combined them.

Snores interrupted Gregor's quest to elicit answers from his power. Ronin was sleeping again, which was why Gregor was trying to smell something unusual now. When Ronin was awake, he teased Gregor for trying to evoke his power, calling him Sniffer.

At first it had bothered Gregor, but there was no malice behind Ronin's thoughts. It was a term of endearment. Acceptance.

Their small coven was very different. Gregor could sense more from Ronin than he'd ever been able to from anyone in his old coven. The sharp pain in his chest made him stuff his memories into the deepest part of his subconscious mind. He was getting better at blocking thoughts that caused his body to ache. He refused to dwell on the past. On what he'd done.

Only the future mattered. Without the hum of hundreds of dragons in his mind, Gregor could easily hear the thoughts of the other dragons.

Ronin had been worried yesterday. Zanthor, Fallyn, and Morgan should've joined them by now. But Gregor sensed only determination and boredom from his coven mates. There had been one moment of panic three days earlier, but it was gone before he could wake Ronin to ask about it.

There was nothing for Gregor to do, and he didn't want to sleep all day like Ronin. That wasn't entirely fair. Ronin had revealed that he hadn't been treated well in his old coven. Something about his size not matching his age. It made the dragon tired all the time, and some older dragons had decided he was lazy and needed to be forced into activity. Considering dragons could sense each other's emotions, Gregor didn't know how they could've hurt him, but Ronin was adept at hiding his feelings.

Ronin found their time at Dragon Library peaceful, telling Gregor to rest while he could. But Gregor wondered if sleeping was Ronin's way of hiding. Gregor had slept to numb the pain when ... No. He couldn't change the past. Only the future mattered.

Gregor wandered to the pile of archive stones they'd gathered and picked one up. The messages Garianna and Ronin had etched into them were simple.

There was a plague curse that affected dragons. Isolating and avoiding mind-speech was the best way to survive.

But he didn't think it would be enough. Besides the fact that they only had fifteen stones, they weren't as durable as the standing archives.

Gregor laid his talon on the tall gray pillar beside him, amazed at the tiny vibrations and the hum that filled his head. The stone contained years of information. He didn't know how to focus his mind to access it properly. Only the most recent message filtered into his mind.

The scout's memory unfolded. Gunshots split the air as the scout wove through the dragons with riders. Bows twanged as arrows rained down on the battle below. Dragons veered to avoid being shot and one had to land to remove an arrow from their rider. When the battle was done, the scout had flown over the ruined ground and counted the human casualties. He'd added a mental line over the battlefield to show that his side had moved forward, forcing the other side to retreat half a dragon length.

Gregor hadn't realized that dragons kept track of the war. Karyn had fought. So had others, but as a youngling he'd never heard anything about it.

Seri insisted the war was about magic, but from this report it looked more like humans fought over some invisible line. He couldn't figure out why this spot of land meant anything to those fighting.

Dragons would never waste so much life. It was unnecessary. Magic didn't belong to anyone.

Ronin hadn't shown him how to guide the archive to answer questions, but Gregor had touched every stone on the hill, gathering an assortment of reports that only added to his confusion. He found one where Zanthor was begging dragons to become involved. To help their riders' families.

Bored, Gregor arranged the small stones into the shape of a human. He needed two more to get the feet right. A smell fluttered through his snout. Sharp. Almost like the scent of a broken pine branch after a storm, but with an additional bite.

Excitement raced through his chest. He'd evoked his power!

But how? He hadn't been asking a question. He circled Dragon Library twice, before returning to his incomplete figure. There. It was a little stronger.

He'd been thinking about the war. Humans. The scent dissipated.

He hummed. So far his ability helped him find what he needed or avoid something dangerous. This wasn't a warning. The scent didn't frighten him. So it must be about something dragons needed.

The portable archive stones? The scent pierced his skull, filling his snout and obliterating all other scents.

To build a bigger picture?

The scent wavered.

More stones. The scent pulsed.

But they already had enough to warn each keep. The pine scent grew.

The message?

Gregor sneezed at the onslaught of fragrances, too many to separate. He must be doing this wrong. The scent disappeared. He sniffed deeply, turning in a circle in an attempt to recapture it.

He growled with frustration. It was gone.

"What are you doing, Sniffer?" Ronin's laughter startled Gregor.

His first reaction was to deny he'd been doing anything, but Ronin had powers too. If the older dragon would stop making fun of him, then maybe he could help Gregor.

"Your power is special. Even though it's unusual. I didn't mean to belittle you. What's the problem?" The contrition in Ronin's words mollified Gregor. Dragons knew where they stood with each other. And Ronin hadn't meant to ridicule him.

Ronin didn't deserve Gregor's belligerence either. Older dragons weren't always patient with younglings. It wasn't personal.

"I smelled something when I was handling these stones. I tried asking questions, and sometimes the scent grew, but now it's gone."

Ronin deepened their mental connection, searching through Gregor's memory. *"I think you were on the right track. We do need more stones. If we had hundreds, we could drop them over each keep and then the covens could use them to communicate without mind-speech. But I don't know where we could find so many. It's not like any rock will do. It has to be the right composition to hold messages."*

Pine, sharp and tangy, returned, stronger than before. From the west.

"That's it. We need more, and there's some in that direction."

Ronin laughed. *"I don't see how magic can tell you where to find them."*

Heat rushed to Gregor's cheeks, and his tail drooped. But then he thought of Seri's power. Maybe she could see where the magical scent came from. Ronin would believe her. This time Gregor kept his thoughts tucked in his private mind.

But a certainty settled in him. His power was a guide. It could lead him to what they needed. And right now they needed more than a warning. Dragons needed a way to communicate safely within their covens too.

The scent of crushed pine needles narrowed, no longer a mass coming from one direction. It was a trail, as easy to follow as the scent of one specific deer. Gregor's body tingled.

"Seri, I think I found more stones. Can you help? You should be able to see the magic leading me."

"Be right there."

Her easy acceptance of his request stiffened his tail. Ronin could make fun all he wanted. As long as Gregor believed in his power, that was all that mattered. And Seri's confidence in him meant more than Ronin's, but he wasn't going to admit that where Ronin could hear.

Seri flew over and landed, Garianna her shadow.

"If you're going on a quest, Ronin and I will tag along." Garianna nudged Seri's shoulder, but her eyes swirled with excitement.

Seri clapped her talons, and her delight washed over Gregor. He wondered if she'd ever been allowed to explore with other younglings. She'd told him this was the first time she'd left the keep, and he got the impression she'd been protected all her life.

Seri flashed a toothy grin. *"I love quests."*

Her turquoise hide glowed with energy. Gregor blinked. He was pretty sure he'd never glowed.

"Which way?" Ronin's eagerness filled Gregor. He wasn't the only one who'd been bored waiting for Zanthor.

He turned to the west and leapt for the sky. The others followed. The scent was steady and clear.

Seri occasionally crossed her eyes, sending encouragement. She could see the magic trail he followed.

Out of curiosity he veered off the path.

"What happened? It's gone." Her disappointment crashed through him, making him sorry he'd taken away her enjoyment. But it did confirm that she couldn't see the scent trail unless he was connected to it.

Pride filled his chest. His power couldn't be replaced. It was his. Gregor veered back, inhaling the tangy pine that filled his snout. A spicy sweetness wove through it occasionally. He really needed to identify more fragrances, so he knew what he was smelling.

Seri had shown him all the flowers and plants in the garden, but this was different. Almost like the scent of magic and dragons mixed together.

After flying for three hours, they reached the Thoran Sea. Waves crashed against a long rocky outcrop. The scent pulled him along the water to a cliff unlike any he'd ever seen. Tall black hexagonal pillars spilled from the bluff, falling into the sea.

The beach was an organized platform of tall and short hexagons, some three times as long as Ronin. Gregor landed on the surprisingly smooth rock on the beach. Interlocking blocks of black and gray, interspersed with sand-filled pools, stretched to the trees bowing at the edge of the forest. Gregor gazed around, amazed.

Even the cliffside was composed of tall black pillars. He'd never seen rocks this solid or big.

The tide rushed in and crashed, pulling away with a loud sucking. Barnacles, anemone, and starfish covered the first four feet of basalt, but the rest gleamed in the weak sunlight.

Ronin laid his talon on the nearest pillar protruding from the strange shore. *"Raw archive stones. They must've been harvested centuries ago and placed in each keep. Look, there's not a single mark on them."* His awe washed through Gregor, who had never considered that the archive stone at the center of his keep had been placed there by dragons. It made sense. The stone, where dragons etched their memories, didn't match the surrounding granite or shale rocks.

Ronin stepped back and stared up at the cliff. *"Volcanic activity must've formed these thousands of years ago."* He shook his head. *"I don't know how you smelled your way to them, but that sniffer of yours is something special."*

Seri leaned against Gregor, her tone reverent. *"There's a lot of magic here. More than normal, and so many colors."*

Pride filled Gregor. He'd done something right. They needed archive stones and he'd found them.

Garianna picked up one of the loose stones that had chipped off the rock they stood on. *"We can't possibly cut those pillars. But we can gather the pieces and use them for message stones. They'll last forever. I suggest we take as many as we can back to Dragon Library. We can tell others where to get more."*

The scent hadn't faded, though it had changed. A hint of lilac mixed with the tangy scent of pine. Even the rotting kelp clinging to the outermost rocks couldn't disguise the smell.

Gregor wandered while the others searched for loose rocks. The scent was strongest by the pillars, leaning over the sea from the cliff. The tide was rushing in, crashing against the cliff and spraying him with salt water. He couldn't go any farther. Even as a dragon, he had to be wary of the power of the sea. And he was still a youngling.

The scent shifted with the wind. As the water sprayed the air, Gregor spotted an opening at the base of one of the pillars.

Seri came up beside him.

"I felt your excitement. What is it?"

He pointed out the gap. *"There. Can you see a depression, maybe a cave?"*

She sucked in a breath. *"Yes. Maybe not a cave, but there is a hole. And magic is coming from it."*

That was all he needed to hear. As the tide pulled back, Gregor rushed forward, fighting the current to get a better look.

"Wait." Seri's shout came too late.

Water rushed under Gregor and swept his feet from beneath him. He lunged for the lowest pillar, twice his height, his wings outspread as he scrambled to climb before the next wave sucked him down into the jagged rocks.

Talons grabbed his shoulders, yanking him into the air.

"Foolish youngling." Ronin's censure rumbled in his chest as they flew out of reach of the grasping water.

Salt spray covered Gregor. But before he could respond, the lilac fragrance shot through his snout to his brain.

Halfway up the cliff there was an opening between two pillars, high above the water's reach.

Ronin dropped Gregor on top of the moss-covered cliff.

Seri flew over and clasped Gregor's talons, her enthusiasm matching his own. *"Did you see it? There's magic leaking from higher up."*

Her touch made his heartbeat falter. He'd never felt this way around other younglings. Seri was special in so many more ways than her magical ability.

He coughed and pulled his talons free. *"Yes. I think that's where we need to go. The scent was stronger as Ronin flew past."*

"Good thing he did." Disapproval oozed from Garianna.

Gregor wilted under her glare.

"Thanks for the assist, Ronin." He bowed to the older dragon. If Ronin hadn't caught him in time, the sharp edges and powerful water could've ripped his wings or worse, injured his limbs. His skin wasn't as tough as that of an adult dragon. But even Ronin could've been hurt if he hadn't timed it just right.

Ronin snorted. *"I was a youngling once, you know. Now let's take a look at this cave you're both so excited about."* His humor was back. Gregor was glad.

But Garianna still glared while she checked Seri for any sign of injury.

"I'm fine. I wasn't even close to the water. Stop fussing, Garianna." It felt like a longstanding argument between them.

Gregor pretended to examine the storm clouds on the horizon.

Ronin gripped Gregor's shoulder. *"Stay away from the rocks. They look smooth, but it's sharp enough to cut through your hide."*

Gregor followed Ronin carefully, allowing the older dragon to find the best perch for them on a pillar halfway down the cliff. Seri and Garianna joined them after a while, resentment pulsing from Seri.

They'd obviously argued.

The ominous clouds that had been whisking across the sky blew over them. The rain was a drizzle at first and then heavier, soaking them in minutes.

"I see it, but it's too small for any of us to explore. This rain is making the rocks slippery. Let's gather our stones and head back." Ronin flew to the shore, expecting Gregor to follow.

Seri leaned in. *"It's not that small. I've been searching the university library for the source of magic. This could be it. There's certainly more magic coming from that hole than anywhere else I've ever been. But the stories are so vague. Most mention snow."* She laughed, a charming sound that warmed Gregor's chest. *"One story did mention steps as big as a castle."*

If he found this magic source, she would clap her talons. Gregor really wanted to make Seri happy. So, he pushed his snout into the opening and sniffed. The scent of lilac filled his nostrils. Not a hint of pine or that strange spice.

He pushed his head in farther. He could keep his wings tight against his torso and he might fit. He twisted his shoulder and slipped a little deeper into the gap. Now he was committed. The basalt scraped his wings and he winced, but it wasn't that bad.

"Gregor. Don't be foolish." Ronin's warning came too late.

The rain had made the rock slippery, and once Gregor's wings were through, he tumbled forward. He hit something solid, and pain shot through his skull. At least he'd stopped falling.

"Gregor! Answer me." Seri's voice vibrated through his entire body.

"Ugh. Stop yelling." He rubbed his head and yelped when he encountered a tender bump. He tried to stand, but the walls spun. He must've hit his head harder than he thought. Gregor steadied himself against one of the pillars. The one beneath him was sloped at a precarious angle, and if he slipped, he would fall farther.

Ronin snuck into his mind. *"Are you all right?"* His tone was gentle.

"I think so. But this is going to sound strange. The rock is warm." Actually, it was hot and beginning to make Gregor uncomfortable. There was also a whooshing sound, like water rushing.

The others left him alone with his thoughts while Gregor looked up at the opening above him. There was no room to spread his wings, so he couldn't fly out. And the pillars were too smooth to climb. He was stuck.

Embarrassment wrapped around him. All he'd wanted to do was impress Seri, and now he was trapped in a cave.

Spotting a break in the pillar he clung to, Gregor attempted to climb. If he was higher, the others might be able to pull him out. But pain shot through his shoulder and his side as soon as he moved.

He must've bruised his side when he landed. His wing was tender, but he should be able to fly. Gregor checked himself for any cuts, but his hide was intact.

Lilac shot down his snout, yanking his gaze to his feet. His power sensed something here, but he couldn't see through the darkness below him.

Suddenly, there was a rush of hot air and boiling water shot over his feet. Gregor jumped out of the way, and rocks tumbled over him, dislodged by his movement.

"What happened? Are you hurt?" Ronin's questions steadied him.

"No. But there's hot water here."

"Sounds like a volcanic vent. Try to find a cool spot. It might get hotter down there. We're breaking trees to get you out."

The walls shook and a rumble filled the air. Rocks fell, and Gregor danced on the slippery slope to avoid getting hit. The dim light of the opening seemed dimmer.

"Hurry. This cave is filling up with rocks."

Suddenly, Gregor wasn't so sure his power had been leading them to something dragons needed. Plenty of broken stones lay along the beach. There was nothing inside this cave that couldn't be found outside. The source of magic would be vast and wouldn't fit in a cave. He'd misunderstood his power, and now the scent was gone.

With each tremor, Gregor clung to the side trying to avoid the rocks tumbling down, while lifting his feet as hot water threatened to boil his toes. When he got out of here, he'd be more cautious about following his snout.

COVEN BOND

ZANTHOR

Zanthor's plan was simple. He would fly over each keep, his mind safely blocked from mind-speech, and have Jason shout a warning about the curse. But he wasn't sure it would be enough.

Dragons weren't likely to listen to a human, and certainly not a boy.

He wished he could push his power through Jason to convince dragons of the severity of the situation. But not only was he unsure of how that would affect Jason, he didn't even know if it would work. His power was based on his own belief. And right now, Zanthor didn't know if dragons would survive this curse.

The connection to his small coven gave him hope. He felt their emotional state across the distance, even though he couldn't reach Gregor and Ronin with mind-speech. Fallyn and Morgan were closer, camped next to Talon Keep. Their presence grew in his inner mind, a part of his subconscious that hadn't existed until he created the coven bond.

Though Zanthor was certain his old coven knew of the danger, or they wouldn't be surrounded by an invisible shield, flying over the keep would test Jason's reach with mind-speech. They might hear a human. Plus it was good practice and would distract Jason from the worry that filled his thoughts.

"Should I explain the curse?" Jason sounded small, uncertainty filling his mind. He wanted to help, but he doubted dragons would listen to him.

"No. Keep it brief. To the speech we've worked out." Zanthor infused confidence into his words, exerting his power as slightly as possible. The last time he'd convinced Jason that everything was fine, the boy had lost half a day in a trance.

"What if they have questions?"

A fierce protectiveness for his coven prevented him from offering to listen through Jason. Even that might be too much of a risk. Jason would have to deal with questions on his own. *"Tell them we don't know more. The important thing is to stop the spread by staying in their keep."*

It was the best Zanthor could do, though he ached to know what had happened to his family.

As he flew closer to Talon Keep, Morgan and Fallyn entered his consciousness. *"I'm on my way with the boy. Any news?"*

Morgan's voice was thin, taking effort to communicate over the distance. *"The villager you sent ... unable ..."*

Even though her message was weak, her sadness transmitted easily. When he'd landed in Crystalvale three days ago, he hadn't known that mind-speech caused fever brain in dragon riders who spoke with infected dragons. He'd suspected something was wrong when the villagers had shot at him. That's why he'd hidden at Silverstream.

Zanthor had flown to David's fields many times in the ten years he'd bonded with Ariel and had even watched the training sessions. He'd hoped that David would tell him why the villagers had attacked.

Discovering that the dragon riders were comatose was a shock. Fortunately, Jason had shown up. Otherwise, Zanthor would've had to fly to another village, until he found a human who could warn the dragons.

At least David's relationship with Ariel had prevented him from shooting Zanthor. The old dragon rider had trusted Zanthor because Jason had said he wasn't infected. Still, he'd expected David to help.

But no dragon rider wanted to risk fever brain, leaving their family to watch them wither away unable to wake, eat, or speak. David's thoughts had made that clear, as well as his desire to send Jason away. Zanthor couldn't imagine what Jason had done to cause the unease.

"... *closer?*" Morgan's voice was still faint.

"*I'll fly over Talon Keep, then meet you.*" Zanthor hoped they got his message. If he couldn't hear them, they might not hear him that well either. Though he did remember Kruzen recalling him from missions when he was out of range. A coven leader may have more reach.

An hour later, Zanthor flew higher into the sky. The air thinned and Jason struggled to breathe, but the barrier held. No dragon in the coven had this power. But the curse had invoked Gregor's power, so perhaps it was a new ability, ignited by fear.

An invisible shield should be impossible for a dragon. Dragon powers were enhancements to natural abilities. Zanthor flapped his wings to fly one more dragon length, but then Jason passed out.

He couldn't go any higher without injuring the boy. Zanthor dove, giving up his quest to fly over Talon Keep.

"*What the hell?*" Anger pushed away Jason's fear and confusion. That was good. He was tougher than he looked.

"*You were in no danger. I know the limits of humans.*" Zanthor pushed a little. The boy's emotions needed to settle before he transmitted his warning with mind-speech. No one would believe a frantic child.

Jason relaxed. "*Warn me next time.*"

Zanthor kept his chuckle to himself. Nothing would've changed the outcome, but Jason could believe he was in control if it helped him focus.

"This is as close as I can get. Concentrate on projecting your message, like an announcer." He'd picked up the word from Jason's mind when they'd discussed broadcasting a message. It was a way of being heard without shouting. For their purposes, the analogy would work.

Jason sucked in a huge breath, already ignoring Zanthor's advice, but then he let it out. Calmness settled over him, and Zanthor felt the boy shift inward mentally.

"Warning. Dragons have been infected by a plague curse. Isolate to protect the coven. The curse is spread through mind-speech. Many dragons have died."

Jason's voice was clear and confident. There were no emotions, only intent to get the message through. Still, Jason was only a human. His voice didn't have the reach of a dragon, not even a hatchling.

Zanthor flew around the barrier so that Jason could transmit the message three times. They'd done what they could. Jason had done well, but Zanthor needed to know his coven was safe. It was time join the others.

As he prepared to land, pain stabbed his head. Moments later, his wings ached. Zanthor wavered, then flapped his perfectly working wings to gain height and flee. He gasped when the sensation disappeared as quickly as it came.

Zanthor landed next to Fallyn and Morgan. They were unharmed, and a quick evaluation cleared Zanthor of any injuries. Suddenly, he was hit by several sharp jabs all over his body, as if trapped in a rock slide.

Zanthor stretched his awareness along the coven bond, searching for the source. Gregor's pain pulsed, farther west than where he should be. Ronin seemed unharmed, but whatever they were up to was too dangerous for Gregor.

"Fly with me. The others need us." Morgan and Fallyn would follow. They had no choice. Too bad he didn't have the same control over Gregor and Ronin.

"What's going on?" Jason's repeated demand finally penetrated.

"Change of plans. Gregor is hurt and we must go to his aid." The boy would be in for a long, uncomfortable flight through the rest of the day and night.

Zanthor wondered what had driven them from Dragon Library. They were to the west. A shorter flight, but still two days away. He hoped Jason could sleep in the straps, because an urgency filled him, and he would only stop to allow the boy to void in the bushes.

The coven was all that mattered now. He must protect them. Even if it was from their own foolhardiness.

NIGHT FLIGHT

JASON

Jason's teeth chattered as he pulled the riding cloak tighter around his ears. Everything hurt. His thighs burned from clutching a moving dragon. He'd tried bending his knees and setting his feet against Zanthor's neck but had found it too unstable.

They'd been flying for hours. He shifted, attempting to find a spot that didn't stab his butt. Zanthor was all muscle. Unfortunately, every time he flapped his wings, those muscles rippled under Jason, hard as rocks. When he'd mounted the dragon he'd assumed it would be like sitting astride a horse, but he'd been dreadfully unprepared. There was no soft curve of back to settle into. And despite the straps, he shifted with each wingbeat. Gliding was blissful, the only time Jason could relax.

He was probably doing it all wrong. But the straps left him little leeway in places to sit, and he wasn't confident enough to move without the thick leather around his waist.

As soon as the other dragons had joined them, Zanthor had barely spoken, leaving Jason to his thoughts. They only stopped once for Jason to relieve himself and eat. Gregor was hurt, possibly trapped, and a sense of urgency hung in the air. Zanthor had warned Jason they needed to fly through the night. But as the sun dipped below the horizon, the temperature dropped, Jason gazed at the sliver of sunlight, begging it to stay a little longer. Of course, his wishes didn't matter. No magic could halt the sun.

The sudden darkness took him by surprise, but before terror could take over, the stars appeared, blanketing the sky in a round, upside-down bowl. More than he thought possible, each twinkling light so close he felt as if he could touch it.

A fierce shiver shook his entire body and his hand slipped, allowing the freezing wind to whip under the hood of his riding cloak. Jason lunged for Zanthor's neck, attempting to block the wind and grab some warmth from the dragon. Desperately he reached for his magic. But the heat that had coiled in his chest and battered his mind was gone. Instead, the freezing air slowed his heartbeat and his thoughts.

He'd always known he could draw cold as well as heat, but he'd never experienced this much in his life. Ice spread through his veins, shaking his body and numbing his face, with no intention of leaving no matter how hard he tried.

"I'm sorry. Night rides are hard on experienced riders."

Jason buried his face into Zanthor's unyielding neck. He wanted to be strong. To help. But if they didn't land soon, his magic would be the death of him. He didn't even have the energy to explain the problem to Zanthor.

Lassitude stole Jason's stamina. He closed his eyes, focusing on protecting the last bit of warmth left in his body as his limb froze.

"Hang on. There's a village thirty minutes away. You can tell them what's happening so they can inform the dragons at Sunspire Keep. I sense dragons outside of the keep, so it's possible the curse hasn't reached them yet."

Jason felt Zanthor's cautious hope. If distance from Dawn's Keep made a difference, then maybe dragons could survive the curse. *"I'll try, but my hands are frozen, and I can't feel my legs. The only thing holding me on are the straps."*

Zanthor chuckled. *"Those are training straps. You won't fall, even if you sleep."*

That was reassuring, but soon it wouldn't matter. Jason couldn't feel anything. The icy numbness consumed him. Even mind-speech took too much effort.

He hoped Charlie would be all right without him. He was sorry he hadn't said goodbye or told his brother how much he loved him. Charlie would have to embrace his power and learn to hide from the war mages. Heather would help.

"Rest. I got you." Zanthor's voice was far away, a faint rumble, and the last thing Jason heard before hands pulled him from the dragon's back.

Two men held Jason upright, which was a good thing, since his legs and feet were frozen blocks incapable of supporting his weight.

Zanthor leapt for the sky, and a whoosh of cold air set Jason's teeth back to their chattering. He would never be warm again.

"You'll be all right, lad. Come sit by the fire. It's a cold night, and the rains aren't far off. Some dry clothes and a good night's sleep will do you a world of good." The voice was kind and gruff.

Jason wanted to tell the man about the dragons, the curse, the pyres, but all he could do was clench his jaw as his body shook. His explanation would have to wait until he was warm again.

The next morning Jason woke to the sounds of people talking. He stretched and discovered he lay in a huge bed, covered in blankets and furs. He moaned, snuggling into the warmth, something he'd never take for granted again.

Hard to believe he'd ridden a dragon and almost frozen to death. Now it seemed like a plague-induced hallucination. But none of those had felt so hopeful.

With a last blissful sigh, Jason forced himself out of his warm cocoon. There were people to talk to and dragons to warn.

The door led to an open room with long tables. His stomach growled as the scent of bacon and eggs cooking hit him. The tables were half full, maybe twenty people at first glance. His legs took him to the grill, his mouth watering.

Zanthor probably didn't realize Jason needed to eat more often than a dragon. Or he did, but their mission had been too important. Jason hoped his message had gotten through to the dragons at Talon Keep.

"You're looking better. Got some pink in those cheeks. Here. Have a double. Welcome to Goldfield." The cook grinned as she plopped four eggs and four slabs of bacon on a plate and handed it to him.

Jason blushed, embarrassed that everyone knew his first flight had been a disaster. He turned and encountered many curious stares. The plate tipped, and Jason gripped it tightly. Dropping his food would only make them notice him more.

"Come. Sit here and eat up. Zanthor told us something of this curse, but said you'd have more information." It was a command.

Jason exhaled. Army life had taught him to eat when offered, so he sat and dug in, while the rest of the room lost interest and went back to their conversations.

Far too soon, he licked the last of the salty bacon fat that had dripped down the side of his palm. He examined the man who'd sat across from him. He was older than Jason's father, but not as old as David, with a restrained energy that hinted he was rarely still. Jason couldn't tell if he was the village leader, but something made him think the man was a dragon rider. Maybe it was the familiarity in how he'd said Zanthor's name. Maybe it was the way he swayed slightly as he spoke to the others. As if riding a dragon was more comfortable than walking on the ground.

Jason told the man about the curse and Zanthor's plan for warning the dragons. The man nodded at certain moments, but his gaze remained steady and open.

"That matches some of what Crysta told us, but we didn't know about the fever brain." The man turned to the woman beside him. "Explains much. Tell the Healer, and warn the other riders to avoid mind-speech until we know it's safe."

She rose and rested her hand on the man's shoulder. "Careful, Mark. You're at risk too." Then she hustled away, dragging five others in her wake.

They must have some sick dragon riders, and that would mean the curse had infected the dragons in the nearby keep. But these villagers weren't fearful, not like the ones near Zanthor's home. They hadn't attacked and they still spoke with their dragons.

"We have two riders with fever brain. They've been isolated, since we assumed it was the plague. So far they're the only ones affected. We didn't think it had anything to do with the illness spreading through the dragons. I've been up to Sunspire Keep twice with supplies." Mark shook his head. "Darn dragons wouldn't believe they were sick. Dragons don't get sick." He imitated their mantra and laughed, but it wasn't a happy sound. "Seems they can. Maybe now, they'll listen to us."

Jason wasn't so sure about that. Dragons didn't believe in rest and soup to cure illness. "You mentioned Crysta. Is she a rider?"

"No. She's a dragon. Two dragons at Cromwell University warned her of the sickness. She showed up a few days ago, but only one dragon was showing any signs of distress. They thought he'd eaten something rotten. But since then, more have fallen. Some just sleep, while others attack and need to be restrained, and one has been transmitting bizarre images. We've all been shielding our minds since. Didn't know about the coven at Talon Keep, though. Or the connection to fever brain."

So the curse was spreading, but it had slowed. "How many dragons are affected?"

Mark shook his head and frowned. "That I don't know. Was only fifteen the last time I checked. But now that we know mind-speech is dangerous, I'll have to send a nonrider to check. Crysta and some dragons left with Zanthor. Something about a dragon in distress?"

"Gregor. He might be trapped in a cave-in. Zanthor wasn't sure."

"The emerald youngling. Those dragons are fiercely protective of their young. Not many survive. We have four at Sunspire Keep, but there were almost a dozen at Dawn's Keep." He shook his head sadly. "Are they really *all* dead?"

Jason nodded. He still had to tell him about the funeral pyres. If the curse kept spreading, these villagers would have to burn dragon corpses too.

Since there were still dragons unaffected at Sunspire Keep, there was hope. The curse could be running out of magic, or at least slowing enough to give the dragons time to find a cure.

SAFETY

SERI

Seri sat on the clifftop, her talons resting on the top of the basalt pillar. Two days had passed since Gregor fell into the cave. He slept, but she didn't want to leave him alone.

"You have to eat and sleep too. He's not going anywhere." Garianna's frustration swept over Seri. Her words didn't matter.

Gregor was only two years younger than Seri. He'd survived more than any youngling should have to endure. As a hatchling she'd been trapped in a cave. The loneliness had been the worst. She'd known her coven would rescue her.

But they'd tried to free Gregor, and he was still trapped. If this was where he would die, then she wanted him to know she cared.

"Fine." Garianna's huff was almost comical as she dropped two large fish in front of Seri. *"Eat, youngling, before I force you away."*

Garianna was her dearest friend, but she'd never spoken harshly, not even when Seri had made mistakes growing up. Seri didn't have the energy to console Garianna or to explain her connection to this young dragon from another coven.

Gregor was impulsive. He believed his ability was special, even though he didn't understand it. She wished she could be more like him. As the proclaimed Oracle, she was overprotected, her every action controlled. Gregor had experienced more life and loss than any dragon she knew. The older dragons had taught her much, but deep in her soul she suspected that Gregor could aid her in becoming what everyone else wanted.

He had to survive this challenge.

But she wasn't sure he could. They'd tried to break through the rock. Ronin's ability to see through solid masses had identified a thinner area in the rock above Gregor. But they'd barely scratched the surface. The pillars were massive.

Even though Ronin had tossed a fish into the hole every four hours, Gregor wasn't doing well. He'd been malnourished and exhausted when he'd arrived at the library, his spirit broken. Only exploring his power had filled him with purpose. She'd tried so hard to make him laugh.

Seri ate, despite her lack of hunger. Garianna was only trying to help. *"Gregor, are you there?"*

"Yes. I'm fine. You should eat. Go sleep for a bit." But he was lying. She could sense the apathy behind his words.

Ronin returned with two broken trees, and Garianna immediately began peeling the smaller branches off. The plan was to use logs to wedge the pillars apart enough that Gregor could get out. Neither dragon would let Seri help, so the only thing she could do was keep Gregor company until he escaped.

"Crysta is on her way with more dragons." Garianna's statement was a relief.

Seri had always struggled with sensing dragons at a distance. It was one of the reasons Garianna was her constant companion. But she could sense nearby dragons, especially if she cared for them. Every time the hot water burned Gregor's feet, she felt it. He struggled to conceal his emotions as much as she did.

She wished she were stronger or that her magic was something useful enough to free him. This proved that the Seer had been wrong. Seri wasn't the Oracle from the prophecy. If it wasn't for her ability to see magic, she'd be considered a liability to the coven. She couldn't hunt as well, see or hear as well, and her intermittent shielding prevented her from fully engaging with the coven.

"Stop with the doubt. The others will be here soon and sense it. Shield your mind, Seri." As usual, Garianna forced her to assume her role and hide her secrets.

Seri reinforced her mental shielding, pushing her doubts deep into her private mind. For other dragons, shielding was automatic. Seri had to work at it. But once her shields were up, they were impenetrable, enabling her to project the Oracle mantle the coven desired. Only Garianna and Crysta knew her true self, but lately, Garianna seemed to be losing patience with her.

Five dragons accompanied Crysta. Seri felt Gregor's excitement, before he shut his mind to her. They must be from his coven.

"Zanthor came. I'll be free soon." His admiration for his leader shone through.

Seri wished she could've given Gregor that hope. An Oracle should. But she was just a weak youngling, with useless magic.

Instead, she was shuffled to the beach for her safety while the other dragons pried the cliff apart.

An hour later, the pillar crashed into the sea, widening the gap. Unfortunately, the water rushed into the hole and swept Gregor off his perch above the lava vent. He panicked, suddenly submerged underwater.

"Oh, for the love of Torin, breathe." Ronin's mirth didn't help.

The older dragons took turns digging with their thick talons and prying apart the remaining pillars trapping Gregor. Finally, Ronin reached into the hole and pulled the soggy youngling out.

Gregor coughed up the sea and grinned. He was clearly exhausted and a little battered, but he wasn't embarrassed, as Seri would've been. No. He glowed with purpose and gratitude. Even more surprising, Gregor wobbled over to Zanthor and leaned against the older dragon's torso.

Zanthor's concern washed over Seri as he enfolded Gregor in his arms. *"Be more cautious next time."*

Seri blinked, shocked that he expected future adventures. Her minders would've reprimanded her and then sequestered her for weeks. There would be no next time, because she would've been smothered with protection.

Zanthor was a very different leader. Obviously, he was too young, and his coven was small, only five dragons. But there was a strength to him. He was a survivor.

"Come. You've done everything you could for the youngling. Let his coven deal with him now." Crysta's command was gentle and etched with pain.

Seri followed her to the tree line. *"What's wrong?"*

Crysta leaned her forehead against Seri's and interlaced their talons. *"Some of our coven have been infected. According to Zanthor, the curse has slowed, but we don't know how many more will fall. You can't return home."*

Shock held Seri still, her heart pounding in her ears. She'd known no other home. How could they send her away? Fears of being alone, of her coven dying, and of losing her connection to her family raced through her mind, but she was careful to keep them from slipping out with other dragons near. *"Where? How long?"*

"Remember that quest you've always wanted to do?"

Seri nodded. Through her ability she'd been able to trace connections between some dragons and their parents. Dragons didn't care about parentage. The coven was family from the moment a hatchling arrived. But she'd been exploring abilities in the younger dragons and had discovered a thread of magic joined some powered dragons to a specific dragon. Secretly, she hoped to find her own parents to see if they could explain her faulty senses. Other dragons must struggle. But this trip to Dragon Library had been the farthest she'd traveled away from Sunspire Keep. And she'd been with Crysta and Garianna.

"Zanthor has agreed to take you with him. After he warns the other covens, he will leave you with the coven at Whitecliff Keep. You will be safe there."

Sarcruze's coven was isolated. For good reason. She knew the history. The coven at Dawn's Keep had always been large. After some disagreement with the leader, Sarcruze had left with a contingent of dragons over fifty years ago. He'd formed his own coven on the northeast cliffs. Since then, two other covens had broken away and settled in the south. Many dragons speculated that covens comprised of more than two hundred were bound to splinter. Dawn's coven had grown to almost three hundred. Now they were dead.

Grief swept through Seri. She hadn't known any of them, but she still felt the loss. Drakkoia would not be the same.

She gave herself a moment to feel the pain, and then she pushed it down to focus on her future.

The only thing she knew about Sarcruze was that he had a mate, Fiona. Dragons rarely chose to mate with the same dragon more than once. One story was that Sarcruze had left when Fiona was told to mate with someone else. It was a love story shared among the younglings as a warning, but instead it filled them with forbidden excitement, to defy traditions enough to leave the coven and start anew. But in another story, Sarcruze was a renegade dragon with no scruples about killing anyone who disagreed with him.

Either story could be wrong, but Seri didn't want to leave her coven at all. *"I'll stay safe with you. At the library or somewhere else."*

Crysta tightened her grip. *"No, dear heart. You're too important. We mustn't lose the Oracle to this curse. You'll see. The Seer had a vision. Zanthor has already survived. He will lead you to safety. Once this is over, I'll come get you. It has been decided."* There was no room for disobedience.

Seri gazed longingly at Gregor. He would choose his own path, but she'd never had that luxury. She bowed her head. *"Yes. I will go with them."*

At least she'd be with Gregor, and she could research family links between keeps, if they allowed her close enough to see the magical threads. Seri set her teeth together as she pulled out of Crysta's grasp.

Her ability might be the key to finding a magical cure. Then the plague curse would end, and she could return to her coven. It was the only way.

Then her destiny as the Oracle would be fulfilled, and she could enjoy the normal life of a youngling.

SILVERSTREAM CONNECTIONS
CHARLIE

Warhog had escaped his stall again. Charlie strode across the dewy grass to the far end of the paddock. This was becoming a daily battle. The horse rubbed against the worn fence and the boards vibrated.

"Hey there. You need to stop running away." Charlie kept his voice soothing. Warhog had been content to graze near their campsite in the forest, but now, surrounded by other farm animals, the horse seemed unsettled. It didn't make sense. Horses generally craved companionship, and David had three horses. Warhog should be happier.

Charlie stroked Warhog's neck, bracing himself for the onslaught of emotions. Yesterday, the horse had been upset, and it had affected Charlie all day, augmenting his own frustrations.

Jason had left without saying goodbye, without promising to come back. Charlie thought he'd moved on and settled into life in Silverstream. But Warhog's emotions had shattered the illusion and shown him that his feelings were merely buried.

He'd been short with David, even though the man had taken care of him, providing shelter, clothing, and food. Slamming doors had been the only thing that soothed the anguish rolling through his mind. After everything he'd done to save his brother, Jason left him alone.

Dragons were more important than family. Jason would never see Charlie as anything more than a burden.

Warhog lifted his head and stared into the trees. His desire to break through the fence and investigate filled Charlie with a restlessness, a certainty that something important was out of reach. But then Warhog's back twitched, and he resumed his scratching, the urgency disappearing in a haze of relief.

Charlie's side itched from nonexistent bug bites, Warhog's discomfort, not his. "Come on. Back to your stall. A little of David's salve will make you feel better."

Warhog twisted his head to gaze into Charlie's eyes and then nudged him with his nose. Charlie could almost hear the horse's acceptance.

He grabbed the lead and headed for the barn, but Warhog snorted and dug his feet into the ground. His nostrils flared as he turned back to the forest.

Charlie had experienced Warhog's fear of something lurking in the trees when they'd first approached Silverstream. He'd seen Jason's smirk when Warhog decided to step onto the road. But Charlie hadn't done anything. The threat had simply disappeared.

This morning, Charlie felt more complexity from Warhog. The horse was hungry and itchy, but an enticing scent pulled him toward the forest. Charlie sniffed, but he couldn't smell anything different. Just the pungent pine of crushed needles, the musty odor of horse sweat, and the scent of freshly turned soil.

Still, his power was changing. Not just with Warhog. Each time he touched an animal, he understood more. Sometimes it felt like they were aware of his growing comprehension and wanted to communicate with him.

He dropped the lead and put his hand on Warhog's forehead. "What is it?"

For a moment the world spun. Charlie closed his eyes against the sensation of falling. A scent filled his nose, warm, earthy like Warhog, but also sweet. A longing to find the female and bring her back to the safety of the barn swept through Charlie, and he locked his legs, resisting the urge to leap over the fence.

He opened his eyes, his hand still on Warhog's forehead. "Probably a wild horse. But you can't just barge out there. Let her come to you."

Warhog shook his head, and his lips vibrated an impressive denial. "Thhppft."

Charlie laughed. "It doesn't matter if you agree or not. Let's head back to the barn."

He offered Warhog a carrot from his pocket. The carrots would last all year, but now it took three spell casters to maintain the cold storage when it used to take one.

Distracted, Warhog nibbled at the carrot and walked to the barn. Charlie placed his hand on the horse's flank. Warhog's focus was on the grain and water that would be available at the end of his walk, the scent forgotten.

Charlie shook his head, unease shifting through him. Had the carrot been enough to change the horse's mind, or had he convinced him with his power?

He'd ask Melanie at their next training session, but first, he needed to finish his chores. Warhog's escape had already made him late for school.

As Charlie dumped grain into the various bins and refilled the water, his thoughts wandered back to his brother.

He understood that Jason couldn't have taken him on his latest quest. It had been the dragon's decision. Dragons didn't allow untrained riders on their back, never mind two. But he still should've told Charlie he was leaving. Instead, Charlie had woken to find his brother gone, and no one could tell him when Jason would return.

Since then, Charlie's days had settled into an easy routine of school in the morning, and magic lessons with Heather and her younger sister, Sandra, in the late afternoon. Evenings were spent with David and Melanie and their extended family over the dinner table.

Everyone in Silverstream was related in some way. Melanie was David's niece, and the mother of Heather and Sandra. David had only one child, a son, who died in the war. His daughter-in-law and twin grandsons had lived with him until they'd perished in an avalanche.

They'd all made sure that Charlie felt like a part of their family, but still, he missed his brother.

The sun shone on the grassy field behind Melanie's sprawling stone house, the autumn wind chilly. Charlie pulled his cloak tighter around his neck as he listened to Melanie's instructions. Their magic lessons had shifted from minor spells to her preoccupation with his empathy.

"Build a bubble around yourself." Melanie formed a circle with her hands.

"With what?" So far, blocking other people's emotions had eluded Charlie. It wasn't really a problem he felt needed to be solved. It was simply who he was, and he couldn't turn off empathy.

Most of the time, he didn't even sense emotions. Melanie thought it depended on the person. Some transmitted emotions more than others did, which made sense, since David was one of the hardest people to read.

"Not an actual bubble. Imagine a soap bubble growing so big you can step inside."

Charlie snorted. A thin layer of soap wouldn't block anything.

Heather pushed his shoulder. "Just try it. She has a knack for finding ways around magic."

Sandra was too busy with her illusions to be of any help. Bunnies made of flower petals hopped around her feet. Her giggle broke into his thoughts, and he grinned. She seemed younger than the year between them. The wars hadn't stolen her childhood, and being around her had helped him regain some of his.

Her illusions were completely different from his mother's engulfing visions. But then, she was only twelve. She might become more powerful as she grew.

Charlie hoped his power didn't increase. It was fun understanding how animals felt and even what they might be thinking. But ever since his own emotions had been influenced by touching Warhog, Charlie had realized that Melanie might be right. He needed to control his empathy before it distorted his ability.

So far, the only time he'd understood the drive behind emotions with people had been after Jason had blasted a tunnel through the dragons. Charlie's ability was confined to animals, and he was content to keep it that way. But he worried that might change, so learning Melanie's protection spells couldn't hurt.

Melanie snapped her fingers. "Are you trying?"

She often lost patience with him, while Heather treated him as if he were younger than Sandra. They'd had years of training. He'd only started learning the simplest of spells. This was more complicated and didn't involve a spell. But everything related to magic involved intention.

Charlie frowned, trying to imagine a bubble of protection, but feared his own disbelief was getting in the way.

Flower balls rolled over his feet. One of Sandra's illusions. He caught her gaze and she grinned, daring him to say something. He scrunched his nose and stuck out his tongue.

Her giggles filled him with light. He could do anything. But then this was what he was trying to prevent. Her joy was affecting him.

He huffed. Fine, he would expand Sandra's illusion. With no effort at all, he pictured it wrapping around him.

The field disappeared and he was trapped inside a sphere of interlocking flower petals. Melanie spoke, her voice muffled. "What do you sense?"

He breathed in, the sound echoing in his ears. He was alone. His heart stuttered, and he gulped. His ears clicked with the pressure. The flower ball disappeared.

Charlie licked his parched lips. He'd never felt that alone, isolated and disconnected from the world.

"Well?"

"It worked too well. I could see anything and could barely hear you, Melanie." He wasn't about to tell her about the terrifying loneliness. It was bad enough that somehow an illusion had been real enough to block out the world.

She tilted her head. "You must've made your shield too dense. What did it look like?"

He squiggled his nose. That must've been it. "A huge flower ball."

Heather burst into laughter, but it wasn't malicious. She ruffled Sandra's hair. "Her illusions are pretty cute, but maybe you should try the soap bubble instead."

Melanie interrupted them. "More importantly, how did you feel when you were inside of it?" Her smile encouraged him to share his experience.

"Separate?"

"You're not sure?" Heather rolled her eyes.

Charlie was trying. He glanced at Sandra for help. She understood illusions.

She stood, wiping flower petals off her britches. "Anything you create inside your head is real to you. My magic creates objects that are visible, but not real. It disappears if you touch it. Everyone can use their imagination to create something. Your brain stores it in the same place as an image, a memory, or a story. So, the bubble in your mind was something apart from reality, but real too."

It made sense, but he'd never thought of his own imagination as being physical. Maybe that part didn't matter.

He repeated his answer with more confidence. "Yes. I was separate from the world."

"Good. But that's too much. You only want to block emotions. Try again." Melanie offered him a smile of encouragement.

It was easier this time. He didn't want to shut out the world. Melanie's original suggestion made more sense now. This time, he visualized a giant soap bubble and mentally stepped into it.

The walls were almost invisible, a slight sheen letting him know they existed. He could easily see everything around him.

Charlie waited for the surge of emotion, but it didn't come. He focused on Sandra, because her emotions had always been easy to read. "Transmit something."

She ran around him with her arms spread wide and squealed, "I'm a dragon!"

There was nothing different. He couldn't sense her obvious delight. Melanie had been right. The mental sphere didn't need to be solid to block his empathy.

Charlie popped the bubble and a pressure returned to his chest, making him aware that he could sense everyone around him to some degree all the time, but it felt normal.

"It worked!" He couldn't keep the shock from his voice. "How?"

"The mind is a powerful force. You decided the bubble would protect you, so it did." Melanie grinned, her pride bolstering his confidence.

"But why didn't I need a stone wall or something stronger?"

She shrugged. "That would've been my next suggestion. Dragon riders shield their minds to protect themselves from the pain of mind-speech. Some, like David, imagine a thin barrier, but others imagine cliff walls. The flower ball blocked too much for you, and you decided a thin barrier was enough."

He wasn't sure that he'd decided a bubble would work. But the reason didn't matter as much as the result.

Sandra's joy as she continued running around the field didn't bother him, but he had to ensure he could control this shield. He played with the opacity of the bubble, but as soon as the sphere became too solid, he felt trapped.

He popped his shield. "I can't keep imagining a bubble every time I'm overwhelmed. It takes too long."

Melanie raised an eyebrow. "Well, that's what practice is for. Eventually, it will always be there for you to step into whenever you're uncertain if your emotions are being influenced by someone else's. Now, run along to the stable and see if they need help."

Their training session was over. Heather tugged Sandra the other way as Charlie jogged along the road. He hadn't thought he needed to protect himself from empathy, but now that he'd experienced the difference, he wanted to be able to do it all the time. He would be able to focus on learning the limits of his ability with animals without worrying their emotions would make him do something he didn't actually want to do. His emotions would be his own, unless he wanted to sense someone else's.

He couldn't wait to tell Jason.

If his brother ever returned. He was still angry at him for leaving, but he wanted Jason back. They may have different ways of dealing with their grief and with connecting to the world, but they were family. Melanie had taught him so much about magic. Jason wouldn't need to hide from the world once he stopped being afraid of his ability.

Charlie's magic would never be as strong as Jason's, but he'd discovered he could access it to generate complicated spells. The type of ability didn't matter. He had more magic than people without abilities.

Jason needed to experience the acceptance this village had for magic. Being safe and unafraid had loosened a knot that had twisted in Charlie's stomach for so long. He wanted that for his brother.

Once Jason got back, Charlie would convince him to stay and learn to control his power. They could have a life away from the Great Wars, with people who appreciated magic, and with a new family. A future without fear.

DRAGON WARNING

JASON

Jason spent five days at Goldfield before Zanthor returned. *"Time to get back to our mission."*

Relief flooded through Jason. He was ready to leave.

The villagers had been eager for news about the curse. But once he'd told his story a couple of times, they'd left him alone. With nothing to do but eat and sleep, he'd soon turned to wandering the village. He had no trader coin to purchase food or clothes. The villagers were living their lives and helping the dragons at the keep.

At Silverstream, his focus had been on learning to control his power while cremating dragon corpses. During his time in the army, he'd been a runner and a tent steward. Even at the farm, he'd organized the younger boys and harvested crops. Through it all, Charlie had been there.

Ever since his parents were conscripted, Jason had taken care of his little brother. The only time he hadn't was when he'd battled the plague, trapped in fever brain visions and unaware of reality.

Jason had wanted time apart to see who he was when Charlie wasn't his responsibility. But he missed his brother's easy laugh. He missed sharing adventures. But mostly, he missed the way Charlie looked up to him and accepted him at the same time.

After Zanthor's summons, Jason packed his belongings and headed for the clearing. Several dragon riders gathered around Zanthor, their brows furrowed in concentration. Many villagers had promised to warn other riders about the danger of speaking with infected dragons. Jason hoped it would be enough, but travel by horse was slow, and the nonstop autumn rains had turned most of the roadways to mud. Soon snow would fall, preventing travel.

He straightened as he approached the cluster of riders. Because he rode Zanthor, they afforded him respect. At least when it came to dragons. He'd had to bite his tongue many times to stop himself from correcting their assumptions about the curse. Seemed few believed a sorcerer, even one as powerful as Bloodstar, could cast a spell that could harm a dragon. Never mind one that could endure for more than a day. They still believed that dragons had the same plague as humans. That a strict quarantine would be enough to stop the spread, along with rest, fluids, masks, and hoping some were immune. Maybe Zanthor could convince them of the speed and inevitable fatality of the curse.

Some villagers had more disturbing interpretations of the crises. Jason had overheard one man muttering that the plague had probably come from dragons in the first place, and the villagers were in danger because of dragons. Jason really hoped that rumor didn't spread. Dragons needed to be helped, not vilified.

Jason settled into the riding straps, tightening the safety belt around his waist. He leaned forward as Zanthor prepared for his mighty leap. This time his neck didn't snap as they took off. Those first wing flaps jolted Jason, but he gritted his teeth and held on tightly, determined to at least appear as if he knew how to ride.

"What troubles you?" Zanthor's calm voice drew Jason's attention away from the tiny villagers below.

Jason couldn't convince everyone that dragons weren't dangerous. He'd provided the facts. Still, he felt he should've done more.

"Nothing that matters right now." The sky was clear of clouds, the air crisp, and Jason wanted to enjoy the view before the rain came again. They were flying a short distance to Glowstone Keep so Jason could broadcast his warning.

"We have a solution to replace mind-speech." Zanthor told him about the message stones the others had found. His coven would follow them at a distance and drop the stones while Jason shouted his warning. This should keep the other dragons safely out of range of mind-speech.

Images flashed through Jason's mind of a tall monolith at the center of Zanthor's keep. Dragons etched symbols into the stone with their talons. Glowing lines then circled the pillar before sinking into the surface. This was how they stored their history, their stories, and their memories. Yet more proof that dragons used magic.

One day Jason hoped to see one of these archive stones. There should be one at Dawn's Keep. That reminded him of the reason Zanthor had left him at Goldfield.

"How's Gregor?" The young dragon hadn't been strong when Jason last saw him, and Zanthor had left so abruptly.

"He's bruised and embarrassed, but otherwise healthy." Then, as if Zanthor understood Jason's worry for the youngling, he launched into the story of how he and the other dragons had to dismantle a cliff of tall black pillars to get Gregor out of a lava tunnel.

Jason laughed at the troubles they had inserting branches and wedging the stone apart. Ronin and two others had taken turns pulling at the rock and digging their talons into any cracks. Meanwhile, others had gathered up all the broken rocks and etched messages into them. Even the sea decided to get in on the adventure, filling the cave with water so that Gregor had to swim for the last part of the rescue. Zanthor chuckled, revealing that dragons could breathe underwater, but in his fright, Gregor forgot. When they finally rescued him, the youngling was coughing up kelp. He wasn't impressed with their reaction to his distress.

Zanthor's concern wound through the story. He cared deeply for Gregor, even though they'd only met three weeks ago. Their coven bond was as strong as Jason's attachment to his brother, maybe stronger.

"How far apart is each keep?" He was already getting sore. Resting hadn't eased the ache in his muscles from his night flight. This time he would remind Zanthor of his need to eat and stretch his legs.

"The next two will take half a day each. Then I'll have to decide if we'll head north or south. The next keeps are a full day's flight away. But I want to reach the ones closest to Dawn's Keep first and work our way outward. Unfortunately, that means a two- or three-day flight to cross the continent to get to those on the western shore." Zanthor's tone held an apology.

Jason groaned. Hopefully, he adapted quickly because he was in for a lot of flying.

"I'm sorry. I did try to get one of the riders in Silverstream and Goldfield to take your place, but they refused."

Jason understood. The villagers had lost their strongest adults to the war. There was no reason to risk fever brain when he was already doing the job.

"I must admit, I'm not sure if any human would survive mind-speech with a cursed dragon. Even you. I'm honored by your courage."

It wasn't courage.

Jason shoved his shame down deep where Zanthor couldn't witness it. *"Many of the villagers don't believe there is a curse. They honestly think that dragons are sick. I guess I'm all you have."* And Jason vowed to do his best and not burden Zanthor with his aches and pains.

"I'll try to make it as easy as possible. You're no good to me broken. It may take longer, with rest stops for you to recover, but I will take care of you."

Jason wasn't sure how Zanthor could reduce the pain of flying, but he'd take whatever he could get. He stroked Zanthor's neck, feeling slight bumps under the warm leathery skin. *"I know."*

The dragon's emotions flowed through Jason. Zanthor meant every word. Jason had a duty to these survivors and to the remaining dragons. He would warn them, even if it took weeks. And then he'd return to his life with Charlie and hope that he'd done enough.

DRAGONMOON FESTIVAL
CHARLIE

Charlie followed Sandra into the forest behind David's training area. School had ended early for the autumn festival.

"Come on. Keep up." Her breathless excitement enticed him to forget his worries about Jason.

His brother hadn't returned from his dragon quest, and no one knew how much longer he'd be gone. Dragon keeps ranged from half a day's flight apart to a week's flight across the continent, and Jason would be stopping at the villages too. David assured him it was too early to worry. But Jason might get sick, or the curse might affect Zanthor, or the dragon could abandon Jason far away, and Charlie would never know.

Heather jogged past, sending him a quick grin. "You're never going to finish in time."

He raced down the narrow trail after her. Worrying could wait. Today was filled with sunshine and new experiences.

Both girls had been secretive about this part of the Dragonmoon Festival, and even the boys he'd befriended grinned and shook their heads when he asked. Today he'd finally learn what all the excitement was about.

Life was peaceful in Silverstream. People didn't obsess about the war. There was no fear of mages descending and conscripting anyone with magical abilities. Here, people used their magic how they wanted. It reminded him of home, before the war edicts stripped it of magic and joy.

When Charlie was six years old, his mother would perform star illusions at every great event. Sometimes she let him dress up and act out a scene on the stage below. His entire class once performed a play about a princess and a frog once.

He missed his brother every day, but the routine of school, helping Melanie with her baking for the weekly market, magic lessons with Heather and Sandra, and evening chats with David filled his days. It was only when something unusual happened, and he wanted to share it with Jason, that his fears resurfaced. Or late at night, when the stars reminded him of his family and all he'd lost.

Charlie burst into the small clearing where at least twenty kids waited, their anticipation filling him with energy.

Heather held up her hand, and everyone fell silent. "Hidden throughout these trees are eggs that reveal this year's story. You can work in teams or solo, but all the clues must be placed on the platform by three. We don't want a repeat of three years ago when the story was incomplete."

As the others dove into the underbrush, Charlie shifted uncomfortably. He didn't know the rules of this game.

Sandra grabbed his arm, her grin infectious. "I'll help you. Our parents hid dragon eggs this morning. We need to find all of them to create a dragon story."

"You have dragon eggs?" He'd seen some, of course, in the display case at school and sometimes in shops, but they were rare.

"Of course, silly. Dragons lay thousands of eggs!"

That couldn't be right. No creature could lay so many eggs. Sure, there were thousands of dragons, but they weren't all female and they wouldn't lay eggs at the same time. Maybe she meant over their lifespan. Still, that was a lot of eggs.

He patted her hand. When Sandra thought she knew something, there was no changing her mind. Besides, he didn't want to ruin her fun with his questions.

"Lead the way."

She pushed him forward. "No. I've done this many times. You have to find the right one." She made it sound like the egg he found would reveal something to him.

Honestly, Charlie was too old for a game of hide-and-seek with eggs, but everyone else was crashing through the trees. Shouts of delight and the roar of "no fair" that followed reminded Charlie of a happier time.

With a shrug, Charlie strode along the narrow animal trail, peeking under bushes and digging through grass. Eventually, a bright pink egg shimmered under the swaying leaf. Charlie picked it up, the small orb cool in his palm.

"Ah. You found one of the starter eggs." Sandra clapped her hands.

He rolled the egg in his fingers, feeling a tiny scratch on one side. When he turned the egg to examine the blemish, a tiny red dragon appeared, perched on a tree branch, a quizzical expression on her face. Charlie wasn't sure how he knew the illusion was female.

It all started with a dare.

He gasped. Her voice had been in his head.

"Did you hear it?" Sandra took the egg from him. "Ah, yes. I haven't heard this one. Interesting. I wonder what it means." Her intense gaze accompanied her curiosity.

Since Charlie had no way of knowing, he gave her a lopsided grin and turned his attention to the egg.

"Every egg will have an illusion? That's a lot of essence to waste on a story." People didn't even expend energy to perform menial spells anymore. This only emphasized how differently the villagers here viewed magic. No wonder the war mages wanted to take over this side of the boarder.

She frowned. "No one is using magic. Long ago, a witch spelled the eggs to tell our stories. He died, but the illusions remained. Each year, the elders select eggs and release a story. Sometimes it's an old one from before the war, and other times it's a recent one that we've never heard. Occasionally, there's a story with only dragons, but most are incredible dragon rider adventures."

He gently took the egg from her. "I'm sorry. I didn't mean ... Well." He was bumbling his apology, but she grinned, anyway.

"You'll see. Dragon stories are the best." She ran down the path between the trees.

They searched the forest, digging through stones in the streams, even climbing trees to check bird nests. After an hour, Sandra found an emerald egg at the edge of a stream. Charlie helped her retrieve it from the mud holding it in place.

"Now that we each have an egg, we need to assemble the clues." She held the egg tightly against her chest, her face scrunched in concentration.

"What did yours say?" A green dragon appeared every time she stroked the egg.

"'Change takes courage.'"

"Do you know what it means?"

"Nope. That's part of the challenge. You'll see."

They meandered through the forest, joined by others who'd found their eggs, until they wound up behind David's barn.

Heather grinned. "Good, you have the starter egg. You'll get to see the whole story."

She led them to a series of raised benches with thirty holes of various sizes. It didn't take long to figure out that each egg would only sit properly in a specific spot.

Charlie placed his egg in the first spot. The tiny red dragon appeared, spoke, and then tapped her talons once. Eric leaned forward and put his egg in the second spot. A blue dragon revealed the next line and then tapped his talons twice. Each correctly placed egg produced a dragon, and the story unfolded.

It all started with a dare.
Diane was a girl who chafed at unjust restrictions.
Laurel was a dragon who dreamed of a different life.
Both seeking change, without any power.
Laurel rescued the girl from certain death.
Their resentment of traditions bound them together.
Diane dared Laurel to break one rule.
To make a change that would help them all.
They trained in secret.
A girl destined for a life without dragons.
A dragon too young to choose a rider.
Both wanted the same thing.
To have a choice.
To ride together.
But they were caught.
Or possibly betrayed.
And they were punished.
But the world seeks change.
Traditions grow stagnant.
Questions are necessary for survival.
The dragon and the girl formed the rarest of bonds.
Of one mind, they rose to the challenge.
Breaking rules long past their usefulness.
They embraced new pathways.
They freed people and dragons from discontent.
Choice won.
Not because they broke traditions.
Because they asked the right questions.
Change takes courage.
Do you have the strength to do the same?

As soon as the story was complete, a full-sized dragon appeared on the barn roof. It swooped over Charlie. Wind blew his hair, and the power of the dragon's wing beat pushed him back a step. The other kids cheered and chased the golden illusion down the road.

The village had been transformed. Booths from the weekly markets lined the village square, but that was all he recognized. Illusions danced over the booths. Dragon-shaped cakes floated above Melanie's stall. Music filled the air with joy, and Sandra dragged him from one stand to another, each filled with delights he'd never seen. There were the wooden figurines of dragons in flight, and of dragons holding books in their talons. Pendants etched with dragons or inscribed with encouraging phrases twisted and sparkled in the setting sun.

A stage had been set up at the far end of the square. The long black curtains rippled, cycling the image of a moon as it shifted from full to crescent and back.

Jason would love this, but he wasn't there. Charlie watched a puppet show with his new friends and ate too many golden moon cakes, and the ache eased.

Everywhere there was joy, people celebrating the harvest and the coming season of dragon rider training. Villagers demonstrated their riding skills on ropes strung overhead, balancing on the ropes, leaping, and back-flipping, before sliding down the support poles. No one mentioned that they may never get to be dragon riders, or that riders were still trapped in their minds at the healing center.

Maybe they believed that dragons would survive this curse. Maybe their belief would make it happen.

Charlie hoped so. The villagers were connected to dragons in a way he could never have imagined.

He was careful to keep his shield up. With so many people around, he wanted to enjoy the festival, confident that all his emotions were his own.

Sandra stopped at an odd-looking booth. Books flapped like birds over a man smoking a pipe. "I think you'll like this one." She pointed to a narrow blue leather journal, which then landed in the merchant's waiting palm.

He winked. "Of course. This young man doesn't know our history."

Charlie found himself unable to escape the man's gaze as the world around him fell away.

Suddenly, Charlie stood on a hill, a tall brown dragon in front of him and a scared pregnant woman beside him. There was no village, no crops, and no roads, but he knew it was Silverstream. The first contact unfolded. Bravery filled his chest as he communicated his need to build a home for his family. The dragon's respect washed over him. And time sped up as buildings rose, streets appeared, and people filled the valley below the mountain keep.

The villagers and dragons lived in symbiosis. Each provided something the other needed. And in return, dragons found companionship with special people who became riders, able to fly across the world and bring news back and forth.

Dragons were important. Without them, the village was isolated, trade almost impossible, and the world inaccessible. The villagers protected the dragons until the world understood they were friends.

Time shifted. So many relationships and challenges. Storms and floods. Earthquakes. Forest fires. The villagers and dragons endured them all together. And then came the Great Wars. Magic that broke the land until villagers joined the fight to protect their home.

Charlie blinked, suddenly free of the illusion that had shown him hundreds of years. He'd grown up in a town where dragon sightings were rare. The first dragon he'd seen up close had been in

Bloodstar's tent. He hadn't understood their intelligence or their connection to their riders. But now he did.

Maybe Jason was right to warn them. Maybe he was destined to be the voice for dragons. Charlie didn't know for sure, but a pressure released in his chest.

Jason wasn't choosing the dragons over him. He was trying to save them.

When Jason returned ... *if* he returned, Charlie would help.

Dragons were worth saving. And once they'd done everything they could, he would convince Jason to settle in Silverstream.

Jason thought he needed to do everything alone.

He was wrong.

Everyone in this village loved dragons. Charlie would convince Jason to accept their help. Because there was no way that one sixteen-year-old boy could do it all alone.

Charlie followed Sandra from one booth to another, until the sun set and a hush settled over the festival. The illusions disappeared and darkness filled the square.

"It's time to light the way to a prosperous future." Heather opened her palm and produced a blue glow. Sandra giggled and lit a pink one.

Glows didn't take much energy, but it had been years since Charlie had cast the spell. It only took a single thought before a green orb hovered over his palm. He grinned, excitement fluttering in his stomach.

Some people expended the little bit of essence to join in, but many simply used candles. The villagers wove through the forest, chanting to the golden harvest moon and casting tiny spells across the fields for a fallow period of restoration so the spring planting would be fruitful. Some people added their desire for strawberries and others for carrots. Nightberries grew wild, but even those empty bushes received a blessing from many of the children.

Charlie made a fervent wish that Jason would return soon. He didn't want to imagine a future without his brother.

The evening ended with a spectacular show. The entire story of Diane and Laurel rolled across the sky as four illusionists combined their powers. Music and a vibrant voice transported Charlie into the vision. Sometimes he was the dragon, and other times the girl, experiencing their adventure as if it were his own.

By the end, he believed he could do anything.

He fell asleep with the song in his head: "There once was a lady so bold, who never did what she was told ..."

There were no rules to stop him. There was only belief.

QUESTS END
JASON

The weeks passed in a blur of flying, sleeping, and eating. Each evening Zanthor landed so Jason could sleep in his tent, sheltered from the increasingly colder nights. Jason would mount Zanthor as the dawn sun broke through the darkness and lit the clouds in vibrant shades of pink and orange, ready to fly over an ever changing landscape on the way to the next village or keep.

Jason mentally shouted his warning while Zanthor's coven dropped stones at least an hour's flight from the keep. Their safety was always at the front of Zanthor's mind. Jason never met the dragons that made up the coven, but he felt like he knew them. Ronin, Gregor, Fallyn, and Morgan.

After his message, a dragon would often grunt their acknowledgment in Jason's mind. Sometimes they tried to speak with Zanthor, but he blocked them, and Jason would repeat the warning. Occasionally, Jason had to endure the invasion of a dragon mind as they scanned his memories of the curse.

He was getting better at focusing on only the relevant details, and they didn't dig deeper. So far, only Zanthor knew of Jason's power and what he'd done to Karyn after she died.

As the days passed, Jason's magic shifted completely from heat to cold.

The flights were colder than winter in the balmy town of Cromwell, where Jason had grown up. Even his nightly campfire couldn't warm his magic. Now, he fought to control the ice in his veins.

Once they landed next to a lake, and Zanthor had to leave him alone for a few days. The isolation ate at Jason after spending so much time with Zanthor in his head. The futility of his quest and the uncertainty of his future overwhelmed him, and Jason froze the lake in an outburst of power.

He'd always known his magic was influenced by temperature, but he'd thought his emotions made him hot. That's what he'd learned with Heather. Turned out, his emotions acted as fuel, increasing his magic no matter what temperature it was.

Jason was exhausted, numb to his emotions, and yet the ice was constantly ready. His power was driven by more than the temperature of the air. At least he did thaw out a bit when he sat close to a fire.

Flying to the keeps wasn't the whole mission. Dragon riders lived in nearby villages, and they had to be told too. Those journeys were the hardest for Jason.

Even with Zanthor's senses they couldn't know how the villagers would react to seeing a dragon, so Jason had to be dropped off far enough away that Zanthor couldn't be detected. Hiking alone through overgrown forest or over unsettled hills took longer than Jason wanted, sometimes days. But it was a necessary precaution to keep them both safe.

Most of the villages were small and tight-knit. People didn't trust strangers, and Jason had to earn their acceptance, lengthening the time he spent there and delaying the quest. Once they believed him, their relief at learning their fallen riders with fever brain didn't have the plague caused the relationship to shift. Hope made them trust. Each village promised to avoid mind-speech and help the dragons that fought to survive. At least that meant fewer would be shot from the sky.

Whenever the coven had to retrieve more stones, Jason stayed in the village for a week. Dragons could only carry so many at a time. He cherished this time, finally able to warm himself and eat hot food. The villagers craved news about relatives in other villages and the state of the war. Jason spent his time wrapped in blankets, with a constant supply of hot soup, while he gathered notes and messages to pass on to the next village in his journey. This made visiting much more pleasurable than simply delivering a warning.

Jason loved talking about the flight. He'd been amazed at waterfalls that were wider than a building and cliffs that rose above forests, lakes that wound through mountains, and rivers that rushed over jagged rocks only to meander slowly through fields of wheat. Tiny houses, far from any village, hid on mountainsides. He'd flown over forests of Oldwood and Nightwood and over fields of blossoms that glowed in the moonlight. Often a herd of deer would race away from the dragon shadow as it whipped across the ground.

There were wonders he could only experience on the back of a dragon, like lightning as it jumped between clouds before shooting down to the forest, or traveling though rain clouds to bask in the sunlight above, and looking down at a cloudy world with no trees, roads, or villages.

But he'd seen devastation too. Burnt remains of villages. Churned fields of broken trees and corpses. Deep scars that ripped through meadows, trees, and houses, the after-effects of a war mage's spell. And then there were the plague tents. They were everywhere, not just at the two army camps. They were in the cities, in fallow fields surrounded by deserted farms, and in abandoned villages.

Twice Zanthor discovered a dead dragon far from a keep. They landed and Jason built a fire to burn the corpse. At those times, he wished he could call on his heat, but it was gone.

Tonight Zanthor flew along the Dragon Mountain Range. The moon was full, and the sky filled with clouds. Jason knew he should sleep while he could, since this flight would take most of the night, but his body hummed, as if the air had charged him with energy.

Klaw Keep was isolated, situated on an island off the eastern coast. There was no village nearby, so they wouldn't land, but it also meant that the coven may not accept Jason's warning. They were known to distrust humans. To reduce the risk to Zanthor and Ronin, they were flying over at midnight, hoping to flee before the dragons woke.

The sea was visible between the clouds, and Jason could hear the waves crash against the cliffs. He'd never been to the sea. Maybe that's what kept him awake. He leaned over, trying to see as much as he could, wishing they could fly over in daylight.

"It's safer this way. There's no place to drop the stones except at the keep." Worry filled Zanthor's mind.

Ronin flew slightly ahead, preparing to drop the stones and fly away before anyone could ask him what he was doing. The other dragons had been told to rest in a valley far from the island keep.

The stones tumbled to the ground, waking dragons with their thuds, and Ronin swerved out to the sea.

"Now." Zanthor's voice was barely a whisper in Jason's mind.

Jason sucked in a huge breath. He knew it didn't make any difference to how loudly he mind-spoke, but it felt more like shouting when he did it. Besides, the dragons were already alerted to their presence, and he had to ensure they didn't try to communicate with Zanthor or Ronin.

"Beware. Dragons have been infected by a magical curse that spreads through mind-speech. Isolation is the only way to slow the deadly disease. The coven at Dawn's Keep is dead, and other covens have been infected. Archive stones have been dropped to aid with

communication. When a cure is found, it will be shared at the keystone at Dragon Library."

Usually, this was when Jason would feel a presence in his mind. But this time there was nothing. No sense of dragons at all.

"Maybe they're asleep?"

Zanthor tilted his wings, and they flew over Klaw Keep for another pass.

"They're aware."

Jason repeated the warning, but still found it odd that he couldn't sense the dragons. His senses were enhanced whenever he was with Zanthor. Sometimes they returned to normal after a few days in a village, but sensing emotions had helped him connect with the villagers, so he'd learned to embrace this ability.

Zanthor continued flying away.

"Did they hear me?"

"I believe so. They must know to block mind-speech already." Jason would have to be satisfied with that answer. Zanthor closed himself off to any mind-speech to protect his coven. While they flew over a keep, he would speak only with Jason. He also wouldn't try to sense the residents of a keep, but usually Jason could.

They traveled swiftly back to the valley where the others slept.

Jason sighed. One last keep and village to visit and then Zanthor would take him back to Silverstream. His quest was almost done.

Tomorrow he would've warned all the dragons. There was nothing left to do.

WHITECLIFF KEEP

GREGOR

R onin was recounting his days as a youngling when a scent whispered through Gregor's nostrils. Light and citrus. He sniffed, unsure if it came from the orchard below him. His knowledge of human farming was limited to the vegetables the coven collected from the villagers after harvest. This was similar to the lemons and oranges that Seri had shown him at the library.

Zanthor had returned the night before with Jason, after they'd warned Klaw Keep. The boy still slept, so Gregor, Seri, and Ronin had flown to the lake to feast. Today, they would fly to Whitecliff Keep, the end of their journey, and probably the last time he'd see Seri.

The scent grew as he thought of the last coven to be warned. The one led by Sarcruze. The stories about the dragon had ranged from romantic to terrifying, a warning to younglings to learn from his mistakes. No one wanted to leave the coven, so it worked. But now that Gregor had experienced life away from his keep, he realized the stories had been incomplete.

Not everyone agreed with coven traditions. Zanthor had been trying to enlist aid for dragon riders, before the curse changed everything. Sometimes the way things were done didn't work anymore. Seri's coven was very different from Gregor's old coven. Less mired in the past, more focused on the future. Zanthor, though young in dragon years, had been able to voice his opinions. Every coven was different.

Now, Gregor was treated as an equal. He snickered, careful to keep his musing private. Younglings were never considered equal, but his opinion had weight. His power was respected by Zanthor, and therefore by the rest of their small coven.

The scent dissipated until Zanthor left with the boy and they followed. Now it was sharper.

"Gregor?" Seri was quick to notice. Probably because of her ability, but he wondered if it was more. Nevertheless, warmth filled his chest at her attention.

"I smell something citrusy. It's not like the other times. Reminds me of home." And it did, which was odd, since this wasn't a scent he would associate with Dawn's Keep.

"That's a good sign, since this will be my new home."

Other than a few mishaps, not including the time Gregor had fallen in the cave, Seri believed his emotional reaction to the scents were as important as his physical ones.

Over the past month, the others had come to depend on Gregor's power. If he detected mold, then Zanthor had them drop the stones far from the keep. If he didn't smell anything, then they were able to leave them closer but still out of range of mind-speech. Since the covens needed to quarantine themselves, it was best if dragons didn't have to fly far to retrieve the message stones.

Zanthor couldn't protect Seri and the others in her coven from mind-speech, so they flew half a day behind, often landing late in the night. But currently they were together, flying low over the farmlands and forests bordering Misthaven, the dragon rider village closest to Whitecliff Keep.

"Do you see it?" Gregor turned his head, testing the intensity of the scent.

"No. But I can sense the calmness in you. Or wait ... Was that dread?"

He shielded his thoughts and tilted his wings, turning into the wind current and then dipping back. She wasn't supposed to notice his uncertainty, not without the coven bond.

But of course, Zanthor had. *"You're troubled by our direction. Do you think they've been infected?"*

It wasn't that. There was no fear. No mustiness to hint at mold or decay. The citrus scent made Gregor feel safe, but when he shifted to follow it, anxiety tightened his chest, an overwhelming sense of change. *"No. It's not the curse. But something is different with this coven."*

Zanthor's sympathetic sigh filled his head. *"We are constantly in a state of change. Maybe your power is telling us that Sarcruze has found a cure."*

Gregor hoped so, but the scent lessened. So it wasn't a cure. Maybe he was worried about Seri. She would join the coven at Whitecliff Keep. Citrus tickled his snout. It was about Seri, but not completely. He didn't get any response to the normal range of questions. His power could be so frustrating.

"I don't know, but it has something to do with Seri." Gregor didn't bother hiding his concern for the turquoise dragon. Zanthor would understand.

"Sarcruze will protect her. We'll find a safe place in the mountains, to ride out this curse. We are a small coven, but you're everything to me." Zanthor's words held his heart, reinforcing Gregor's trust in their future. Zanthor would take care of him and the others. They would survive.

As they drew closer to Whitecliff Keep, the scent grew stronger.

Eventually, Seri could see the magic too. *"It's different. Colors winding together, all flowing toward the keep, forming a rope instead of individual threads."*

Zanthor dove, gliding through the wind currents, his speech thoughtful. *"I don't know what your powers are trying to tell us. But I'm confident there is no danger, since Gregor doesn't smell mold.*

Still, to be safe, I want all of you to stay away while I drop the archive stones and Jason warns Sarcruze. The boy is good at sensing dragon intent. We will know if something is wrong."

At his words, another scent wove through the overpowering citrus. Lilac and a human spice. Maybe cloves. Gregor wasn't as comfortable with those scents. But this was the first time he'd smelled so many at once.

He informed Zanthor, but since no one could figure out what it meant, Zanthor left them in a mountain meadow to fly into the morning sky.

Gregor didn't know what transpired on Zanthor's pass over Whitecliff Keep, but suddenly he was enveloped within Sarcruze's coven. Hundreds of voices filled his subconscious. Emotions swept through him, and he fell to the snow-covered ground. Memories rose and fell, a torrent of voices, images, and experiences.

Seri, Ronin, and Zanthor were there, holding him in their hearts and easing the pressure of exposure. Insulating the grief. Filling him with love. He breathed deeply and stood, the ache in his soul easing. He belonged.

Sarcruze was there, a steady presence. A leader with experience. Zanthor felt like a true friend, a mentor. But Sarcruze's authority strengthened Gregor. Steadied them all.

Gregor became aware that Garianna and the others from Seri's coven were inside the coven bond too. Seri was to be protected at all costs. The coven's awe for her was in conflict with his own feelings. He buried his thoughts deep in his subconscious. She was the Oracle and not simply another youngling.

A coven memory flickered. Of Sarcruze gathering dragons to form this new coven, away from the restrictions of Dawn's Keep. He had earned the respect of coven leaders. This was why Seri's leader trusted Sarcruze to keep the Oracle safe.

Tension eased from Gregor's shoulders. There were many dragons with abilities. Many dragons to fight the curse.

"Come home." There was so much behind the command. Sarcruze imparted his acceptance of this responsibility and the love that only a coven bond could provide.

Gregor shot to the sky, hope renewed, his grief absorbed, and the weight of the curse lifted. As a coven they would prevail. Dragons were stronger together. No human could harm them.

From now on, Gregor could be a youngling again. He could grow and learn to use his ability. There were others with powers like him. As the only younglings, Seri and he were adored. Covens protected their younglings, and there hadn't been one in Whitecliff Keep in a long time.

The love that had been missing since his coven had perished flowed over him now. Not that Zanthor hadn't loved him, but these were older dragons who treasured him for simply existing.

The bonds tightened, filling him with strength. All the dragons from Seri's old coven had powers too. He was one of them.

Sarcruze didn't care about their powers. He would protect all the younger dragons now in his care. His acceptance and power flowed through Gregor.

It had been too long since Gregor felt this safe.

He flew with his family to Whitecliff Keep, to his new coven, confident that dragons could survive any challenge together.

The citrus scent had dissipated along with his anxiety. Only a slight whiff of lilac lingered, but not enough to dampen Gregor's joy.

He was home.

MISTHAVEN

JASON

Five months later, Jason stretched and admired the view of Dawn's Keep. The dragon corpses were gone. It had taken many trips back and forth, even through the snow, to clear out the keep, but they'd done it. Just in time. The snow had started to melt, and spring was around the corner. Green tendrils were already poking through the ground around the archive stone.

The furious flight with Zanthor and the other dragons to warn all the covens seemed like a dream now. He'd hoped to get to know more about dragons, but Zanthor had been his only connection. None of the others had spoken with him, and usually they flew out of range of his human mind-speech. He'd always been aware of Gregor, though, as if his heart remembered the young dragon. But after Zanthor flew over Whitecliff Keep, that connection disappeared.

Probably for the best. After Jason spent a day and night with the villagers at Misthaven, Zanthor had returned him to Silverstream.

That was the last he'd heard from the dragons, his part in their quest done.

But Jason still didn't feel like the curse was done with him yet.

Heather had continued to work with Jason to control his magic. After a week on land, his heat had returned. Obviously, flying in the cold wind currents had been instrumental in snuffing it out. The heavy rains, followed by a mild winter season, had reduced the severity of his heat magic. But he'd had enough to enhance the fires and cremate the dragons in less time than normal.

The villagers believed that dragons burned faster than wood. Heather had cleverly enlisted a crafter to transform the sparkling ash into colorful pottery. Between the ash from the "lightning burst" and the quick burning corpses, Jason's magic remained a secret that only a few knew about.

At one point, a rumor of two dead dragons in the forest caused new fear. But Jason and Heather had hopped on Warhog and destroyed the corpses before anyone could find them.

One of the most interesting side effects of using his power had been that when he cremated certain dragons, a dragon rider would wake from their coma. Eleven had recovered, though one still lay in the Healing Center, trapped in fever brain visions.

Satisfaction rolled through Jason. He'd done everything he could to help the dragons and to reduce the risk to the villagers. His power was under control, and he no longer feared exposing his magic. Even Charlie had experimented with his magical ability with animals. But something prevented Jason from settling, from calling Silverstream home.

David trudged through the snow. "It's done. They're at peace. You did well."

Jason nodded, unable to speak. He felt Karyn's presence as if she were next to him. He'd fulfilled his promise to her and more.

These dragons were gone, but there were other keeps with corpses. More dragons to set free. He hoped the nearby villagers would honor their dragons by burning their bodies and thus release comatose dragon riders from fever brain.

But he needed to focus on the living.

"I feel like I need to do more for the dragons. For those fighting the curse." Jason didn't know how to explain better. He owed his life, and therefore his power, to dragons.

David turned back to their camp. "Some people are traveling south to check the other keeps. You could join them, or come north with me to Misthaven. My sister lives there, and I want to make sure she's all right."

A memory of flying over Whitecliff Keep, surrounded by mountains and trees on one side and the sea on the other, made him ache. Gregor was there. His heart thumped that erratic rhythm that he hadn't felt since he'd left the dragons. Before he'd lost his connection to the youngling, Jason had felt a sense of belonging, of family.

Despite their isolation, the villagers had been welcoming during his time with them. He didn't have anything left to do in Silverstream.

The yearning to know if the dragons had survived made his decision. Jason would go to Misthaven and find out what had happened to his dragon friends.

The group that headed to Misthaven was small. Heather, Jason, Charlie, David, and Melanie each rode a horse. Jason glanced at Charlie on Warhog and smiled. The horse had become part of their family. It wouldn't be right to leave him behind.

Traveling north during winter had its challenges, but the tension in Jason eased. He enjoyed being alone with these people. They'd gotten to know each other while burning dragon corpses, but now they could share stories of their lives and talk about the future. The gloom and sadness were gone.

By the time they reached Misthaven, Jason felt like they were his family.

The villagers were as welcoming as before. No dragon riders were sick. In fact, they traveled to Whitecliff Keep often to speak with the dragons there.

Jason joined them on their next trip up the mountain. He hadn't been able to reach Zanthor with mind-speech. If it wasn't for the riders' lack of concern, he would've been worried. They said that the coven leader, Sarcruze, had blocked mind-speech. Which made sense, given that's what Jason had warned every coven to do.

But for some reason, he'd thought he'd be exempt.

So now he hiked to Whitecliff Keep to speak directly with Zanthor.

They set up camp on the bare rock outside the keep entrance. Dragons flew in and out, weaving around each other in a chaotic pattern that was beautiful to watch. He couldn't see the whole keep from his vantage, but it was similar to Dawn's Keep. A rock slide had formed a bowl at the top of the mountain. Alcoves, natural and carved, dotted the sides, while the floor of the keep was packed from dragon weight.

Wind buffeted Jason, making his stance unsteady. One edge of the keep was open to the cliffs that towered over the crashing sea. No one entered the keep.

A female dragon, the largest he'd seen alive, came out to speak with them. Fiona. She broadcast to the entire group with mind-speech.

"We're leaving. Vaylor will keep in contact, since we expect more dragons will come seeking refuge. Whitecliff Keep will act as quarantine. In order to prevent infection, we require your help." She pointed to a pile of communication stones. *"These enable dragons to speak to each other, but mind-speech is still dangerous for all. Your verbal speech can be understood by dragons. It would help everyone if some of you could tell the incoming dragons about the danger, help them settle into the segregated areas, and inform Vaylor of their arrival."*

Immediately, some riders offered their help.

Jason was about to put up his hand when Zanthor slipped into his mind. *"No, little one. This task is not for you."*

Jason's heart leapt. *"How are you? And Gregor? Have you found a cure?"* He couldn't help the rush of questions, even though he knew they were leaving because of the curse.

Zanthor's chuckle did more to ease his worry than his words. *"We are well. The coven is moving to ensure we stay that way. I'm happy I can see you before I leave."*

Warmth eased into Jason, as heartfelt as a real embrace. He'd missed this level of connection. *"But you'll return, right?"*

"We will survive by hiding from other dragons and the world. We can't look for a cure." His sadness gripped Jason's heart. *"When this is over, you'll make a fine dragon rider."* The endorsement flowed through Jason, straightening his spine. *"I must go. Thank you for all you've done for us."* Then Zanthor was gone.

Though Jason peered at the dragons moving in the keep, he couldn't see one that could be Zanthor, or any that he knew. Over a hundred dragons filled the grounds, walking and resting, busy with whatever occupied dragon lives.

Even though he knew this would be the last time he would feel them, Jason wasn't ready to let them go. He let his awareness of them fill his soul. This was his last connection to Karyn and soon it would be gone. The finality in Zanthor's mind had been clear.

Jason may never see another dragon alive in his lifetime, not unless the curse was banished.

SEER'S WARNING
SARCRUZE

Sarcruze flew low, skimming the treetops. He loved flying at night while most of the coven slept. Their minds were always there, deep in his subconscious, easily accessible. But when they slept, he had a respite from the constant hum of emotions and thoughts.

He wasn't far enough to lose contact. That was one of the curses of being a leader. Though he'd never tested it, he was certain he would be connected no matter where he flew to in the whole of Drakkoia. But this moment, this nexus of night, gave him a break.

Sleep eluded him, anyway. Especially now. So many choices to make. So many lives to save.

He'd relocated his entire coven and those early survivors to a crater deep within the Dragon Mountain Range. The younger dragons had wanted to name it Jason's Keep to honor the boy's effort at warning all the keeps. He hadn't cared enough to protest. The keep, with its thermal hot springs, was simply a place to hide, until it was safe to return to their homes.

Only Vaylor had stayed behind at Whitecliff Keep to oversee the quarantine process. But it had been tough. The dragon riders at Misthaven had helped with communication. The stones worked, though they were rudimentary. But keeping dragons apart for two weeks was key to ensure no one was infected.

Sarcruze had collected small groups of survivors over the past few months. Never more than five. But a new wave had arrived.

He couldn't show weakness at the keep, but here among the stars and trees, he could give in to the weight of his decisions. His muscles loosened as he stretched his wings, turning his glide into a slow spiral over the lake. He'd taken twice as long to fly to the meeting point to ease the tightness in his body. There was plenty of time to prepare.

The most recent additions to the coven had included a rare Seer, Tayla. Despite her blindness, her reputation for accuracy superseded any Seer before her. He'd been shocked to see her condition when she arrived. The eighty-five-year-old dragon was gaunt, and her exhaustion made his own bones ache.

Only two others from her coven had survived. A thirty-year-old powered dragon, Drekan, and Renalia. At first Sarcruze had worried that Renalia would demand to lead the coven. She had the right of age, being a decade older than his one hundred and nine years. But she'd bowed and accepted his leadership, pushing Tayla to speak.

The Seer's words were branded into his memory. He'd kept the exchange hidden from the coven, but now her premonition could replay at will.

"You can save no more. A dragon flies over the land, cursing all in her path. She must be stopped. If she reaches Whitecliff, all is lost. For dragons and humans, alike."

Tayla had collapsed afterward and had slept since. Renalia spoke little of their flight, only saying they'd encountered much fear and distrust from humans, and the journey had taken far longer than expected. From their state, he surmised they hadn't eaten in weeks. His mate, Fiona, had made it her quest to nurse them back to full health.

Sarcruze grinned. Any thoughts of Fiona always filled him with pride and strength. She was a constant light in all this darkness. With her by his side, he could survive anything.

Tilting his wing, he brushed the tops of the trees, enjoying the sensation. He was once again grounded and connected to the world.

He landed next to the river winding through the lush valley and walked to the narrow archive stone he'd placed next to the Nightwood tree grove. Seemed like it was ages ago, but it had only been three months.

Vaylor bowed over the archive stone, barely restrained desperation transmitting clearly.

Sarcruze shielded his mind and touched the stone with his talons. Fine lines etched into the stone glowed and seeped into his consciousness. The stone held memories and reports, but one of the younger powered dragons had transformed it to allow conversation.

Sarcruze tapped into the glowing rune that imitated mind-speech. *"What is it?"*

One of the reasons Sarcruze had entrusted Vaylor with the task of ensuring the refugee dragons followed proper protocol was his unflappable disposition.

"They think we're withholding a cure. Two more showed up yesterday, showing the first signs of fever brain. The humans guided them to the quarantine cave, but I'm not so sure the blockade will hold them. I don't think we can help any more." Vaylor's fear consumed him, images of dragons attacking each other transmitting from the archive stone.

And that was the real fear. At first the curse had made dragons too sick to move. They'd died quickly. But now that the curse had slowed, infected dragons were more dangerous than before, unable to discern reality from the fever brain visions. But underlying Vaylor's terror was something more disturbing. He worried that he would be forced to reveal the location of Jason's Keep.

If that happened, the coven would be lost. Sarcruze grunted, suddenly saddened beyond belief, aware the decision he'd made would destroy many dragons. But they'd finally hit the tipping point between saving dragons and surviving the curse.

"Tell me what they say. How many are clear of the curse?" Sarcruze asked.

They discovered early on that an infected dragon etched inconsistencies into the communications stones, their logic affected before they showed symptoms. Brave riders had led those dragons to the caves, trapping the dragon until the curse killed them. But Vaylor was fine, his communication clear and sharp.

"They believe the Oracle will save them. Somehow, they've decided that Jason is a powerful human mage who can reverse the spell. You have them both, and will only save those you deem worthy." Vaylor's shoulders drooped, his wings quivering. *"There have been fights. Unnecessary injuries. Some will die because of stupidity. I don't have the powers of leadership or of a coven bond to control them. And more are arriving every day. We now have over twenty dragons."*

Jason's Keep could hold them. There were only one hundred and twenty-seven dragons there now. But it was too early to break their quarantine. Too soon to tell if they were free of the curse.

There was no cure.

Only isolation.

With the plague taking longer to spread than those first frantic days, Sarcruze hoped the curse had weakened. That it would die a natural death, or dwindle into something like the human cold, an annoyance but not deadly.

The Seer's words made more sense now. The next infected dragon could evade the riders and infect those in quarantine. Vaylor couldn't hold out against twenty dragons. His fear was valid.

"Your mission is over. It's time. We can't save any more."

Shock ran through Vaylor's body, followed by an intense wave of relief.

Sarcruze couldn't allow him to return to Whitecliff Keep. He couldn't save the ones in quarantine, even though they deserved a chance. The risk was too great.

His heart hurt. Options tumbled over each other, resisting this decision. So many dragons had already died. They'd tried so hard to fight this horrible human curse. But now there was nothing he or anyone could do. It pained him to assign as many dragons as he saved to a certain death. But if he didn't take this step, then he feared no dragon would survive.

Sarcruze dropped his shields and opened his mind to Vaylor. The dragon's relief flooded through him. Vaylor had been strong because he had to, but the responsibility had worn him out.

Together, they buried the archive stone. No one would know of its existence or find any secrets. The location of Jason's Keep hadn't been etched into the stone, but it did contain reports between himself and Vaylor, as well as all the names of the dragons he had taken in. He didn't want anyone to find it. To think they'd been unworthy.

All dragons were worthy of living, but they were on their own.

Sarcruze hoped with all his heart that Drakkoia would find a way to restore balance to magic and the world.

It was a hope he clung to as he sent Vaylor north to Jason's Keep. Because that's all he had left to give.

Sarcruze flew south, to a forest lake near Misthaven. He had one more task before he shut his coven away from the world.

This one ate at his soul. But the Seer's warning had been clear. The dragon flying to Whitecliff was a danger to everything he'd accomplished. Even sacrificing the dragons at Whitecliff Keep might not be enough to stop it. He just hoped the boy was strong enough to do what had to be done.

DRAGON'S REQUEST
JASON

After the dragons left, there was only Vaylor at Whitecliff Keep and his answers to Jason's questions were abrupt. *"The coven is safe. No cure yet."*

The sense of duty in the dragon's thoughts had rolled through Jason. This dragon would die to protect his coven. But there were no more answers.

Jason stayed at Misthaven. Life went on. He learned how to prepare logs and build a home. Charlie, naturally drawn to the animals he could hear, tended the barn animals. This village was completely self-sufficient, since trader caravans rarely traveled their way.

Occasionally, a dragon flew overhead but none of the dragon riders caught fever brain. It seemed even the plague didn't travel this far north.

Heather had become more to Jason than a mentor. He couldn't help grinning every time he thought of her. She accepted and admired him. She was strong and opinionated. He was pretty sure he was falling in love with her, but the only one he could ask for advice was David and he'd been away.

Jason jogged past the barn and waved at Charlie feeding the pigs. Heather would be taking down the laundry from the line now. It was his favorite time to meet her. No one bothered them while they were working, and it was quiet behind the wash house.

Her deep red hair was tied up, the back of her neck exposed as she reached to squeeze the clothespin to release the dry garment. The setting sun cast rays through the trees that highlighted her, like a painting of a fairy-tale woman in a field.

As usual she sensed him before he could surprise her.

"You left it late. I only have two more to take down." She turned and frowned at him, the teasing tilt of her lips belying her tone.

He reached over her head to pull down the offending clothing and leaned in for a light kiss. They'd spent hours kissing and hugging. If someone had told him how much fun it was, he would've tried it a lot sooner. Or maybe not. He suspected that Heather was the reason his heart raced, while his mind quieted in a way he'd never thought possible. She was peace.

Heather rewarded him by pulling his head closer, and for a moment, he deepened the kiss. They hadn't gone much further yet, but he hoped they would soon. Every encounter left him aching and wanting more.

His mother had taught him to honor a woman, and let her set the pace of a relationship and simply enjoy the journey. But there were times when his body screamed at him to speed up.

Their tongues tangled in an intoxicating dance, and he tightened his grip, suddenly hot and breathless.

Jason's power rushed to his lips, and he abruptly ended their kiss.

Heather giggled. He tried not to be offended, but this was getting ridiculous.

"I think your magic is jealous." She danced away, grabbing the basket and the clothes he'd dropped on the grass.

Maybe it was, or maybe she just made him too hot.

Jason sighed and rubbed the back of his neck. "I'll figure it out." It was a promise. His magic had to stop getting in the way of his need to be with Heather.

"Jason." The presence of an ancient dragon pressed into Jason's mind. Sarcruze. The way dragon names popped into his subconscious still surprised him. But this dragon was older than any he'd heard before.

Heather tugged his hand. "Jason, are you all right?"

He smiled down at her wide, brown eyes. "A dragon has contacted me. I'll see you later at dinner." He didn't know if it would take that long, but the power of Sarcruze's presence in Jason's mind told him this was important.

"What do you need? Are Gregor and Zanthor all right?" Jason couldn't help asking. He missed those two dragons most of all.

"They are well. Do not concern yourself with them." And Jason felt the dragon's promise to always keep them safe. *"I need you to do something."*

The pause was long enough for Jason's power to roll through his body at the premonition of danger. He waited, though. This was not a dragon to push or interrupt.

Sarcruze's sigh filled Jason's entire body with a fatalistic determination.

"I've seen your magic." Zanthor had explained how being a leader allowed him to access the coven memories. Jason's heart raced more. Obviously, Sarcruze knew about him cremating dragons with his power.

"I'm not one to depend on human magic, but you have a strange connection to dragons. I can sense you through Gregor. Zanthor thinks it might have to do with the sorcerer's spell. Nevertheless, I feel your desire to help. Your guilt at surviving. And this power you have. It's like a constant presence in your body now."

Jason walked through the field and into the forest, as if drawn by a force.

"I want to help." Jason infused his thoughts with his admiration for dragons and his remorse at their plight.

"Your power is more dangerous than you know. If it were another time, we would destroy you."

Shock at the threat stopped Jason's momentum. Dragons would kill him over something that he had never chosen? Something that was a part of him?

Sarcruze continued, ignoring Jason's reaction. *"But I have need of your power, so I must adapt."*

There was more behind the statement. Something about upholding traditions, which meant nothing to Jason since he didn't know dragon culture at all. He only knew how things had been since the curse.

"Traditions define a dragon, guide our lives, and sustain our dominance over humans."

"I didn't mean to offend." Jason found himself apologizing without knowing why. This was not a dragon to upset. Drawing on his power, Jason built a wall of flame around his mind, to keep his thoughts hidden.

Sarcruze's chuckle echoed in Jason's skull. *"Good. You have learned control."*

Not that it would stand up to a mind as strong as Sarcruze's, but there was no sarcasm in the old dragon's tone. A hint of relief, maybe. He was difficult to read.

Suddenly, Jason's memories of using his power flashed through his mind, backward. He'd been right. His shield was useless. His lack of control when he'd first seen the dragon corpses at Dawn's Keep replayed twice.

"This was not in the coven memories. Your power is unlike any I've seen a human wield."

Before Jason could respond, Sarcruze pushed images into his mind. A long flight to a crater deep in the Dragon Mountain Range. Dragons flying from Whitecliff Keep to Jason's Keep.

He couldn't help the pride at having a keep named after him.

Maybe Sarcruze thought Jason could use his power to stop the curse. Though he couldn't figure out how.

"No. I need you to ... In our history, some dragons have had to be destroyed for the safety of the many. Long before humans used magic, when dragons ruled all the land, traditions were built to guide leaders. In my lifetime, only one dragon was killed to protect a coven. Their mind could not be saved." The weight that followed pressed down on Jason, and he realized he was far from the village, on the path to the lake.

"Traditions are necessary."

Jason wasn't sure he was supposed to hear that, but Sarcruze was struggling to ask him to do something.

"What do you need?" If it was important enough for Sarcruze to share dragon culture, then it must be something dire, but Jason would do anything to help dragons.

"Your power is not good or bad. We have power in our size, our strength, and even in our ability to outlive humans. But logic and foresight rule how we use our power. Dragons could've destroyed humans. We could've ruled over them. But the world needs balance. I want you to remember that when you embrace your power. Find your balance."

Jason shook his head but kept walking. This wasn't making much sense. Of course he wanted balance.

"I see loyalty in you. Empathy. But what I'm about to ask you may not seem that way. It is a kindness. It is a balance of sorts."

The lake was surrounded by trees, the setting sun blocked by the mountain. Sarcruze moved, separating from the shadows, and Jason gasped. The mahogany dragon was larger than a hill.

"I need you to kill a dragon with your power. Traditionally, I would take on this burden. But the curse has infected this dragon's mind. I can't get close enough, and I will not risk the coven."

It was as if Sarcruze knew Jason's biggest fear. That he could hurt someone with his power. That he could become a monster.

But to ask him to do this?

Cremating corpses and burning down trees didn't hurt anyone. Didn't destroy a soul.

Absolutely not. Jason could never use his power to kill.

But Sarcruze let Jason feel his agony behind the request, at the necessity of destroying a dragon when all he wanted to do was save as many as possible. It must've taken Sarcruze a lot of soul-searching to make this decision.

Jason shook his head. It didn't matter. He couldn't do it. He'd worked too hard to control his power. This could destroy him.

"I will not beg a human. If there were another way, I would do it. I will protect my coven in every way possible. The dragon is on her way to Whitecliff. Our Seer has foretold that if she lands, we will not survive."

But Sarcruze and the other dragons were in Jason's Keep. They were safe.

"The dragon will find us. It has been seen. She must not reach Whitecliff Keep."

So Jason was supposed to kill a dragon based on a Seer's vision? There had to be another way.

"Feel your connection to Gregor. He's been transmitting his certainty of death all day."

It was an odd request. Gregor was too far away, but when he thought of the youngling, Jason's heart beat faster, harder. His power swirled, building. He might not be able to read Gregor's thoughts, but their connection still induced fear in Jason.

"I can't. Using my power to kill ... I won't. But I will stop this dragon from reaching Whitecliff Keep." He would enlist the help of the dragon riders. They would know how to capture a dragon.

"She will escape." Sarcruze's certainty eroded Jason's determination. *"Your fire is mercy. The curse has ensured the dragon will suffer and die, anyway. And fever brain makes her dangerous to humans."*

Sarcruze was sure of it, but Jason wasn't. He would try every option first.

"That is your choice. I will leave this burden with you. Thank you, Jason." He felt the bow implied in Sarcruze's words.

The large dragon leapt effortlessly into the sky and flew into the clouds, his presence gone from Jason's mind.

Jason wasn't as convinced that one infected dragon could be powerful enough to put the coven at risk, but the future was always changing.

Seers weren't always clear in their forecasts. The dragon might not be infected. She might not even come. There'd been no dragons for weeks.

But if a dragon did appear, Jason would stop them from reaching Whitecliff Keep, from finding Jason's Keep and killing his friends.

There had to be a way that didn't involve him using his power to kill.

DRAGON ATTACK

JASON

David and the dragon riders returned to Misthaven in the morning. After Jason outlined the problem, they devised a plan to trap the dragon.

The riders tied the riding straps together to form a huge net while the villagers dug a large pit in a clearing near the road. But Jason would be the one who had to convince the dragon to land.

Once the tasks were done, David gripped Jason's shoulder and stared into his eyes. "If she is one of the older dragons, she'll be too big for the pit and our nets won't hold her. We'll have no choice."

Jason nodded. There were ten villagers ready to shoot the dragon if that was the case, but that was the same as killing her.

"Are you ready?"

Ready to harm a dragon? To trick her into either a quick or slow death? He'd never be ready. "Yes."

Charlie stood by the pit, giving Jason an encouraging grin. They'd covered it with loose branches. Once the dragon fell through, the others would throw the net over and secure it to the ground with the metal cleats lining the pit.

So many things could go wrong. The pit might be too small. The nets might not hold. And the dragon could ignore Jason's call. The dragon riders were taking a huge risk exposing themselves to mind-speech, but they all agreed that Sarcruze wouldn't have made his request if it wasn't crucial.

Waiting for something to happen was the hardest. The day passed with no sighting. Villagers exchanged places, taking the opportunity to eat before resuming their vigil.

As the sun set over the trees, a series of whistles signaled that it was time. Someone had spotted the dragon.

Jason licked suddenly parched lips. This had to work. He refused to think of the alternative.

He caught a whiff of rot but couldn't identify the source.

For a brief moment, he felt Sarcruze in his mind. Resolve steadied his hands.

Jason scanned the sky, tension growing with each moment that passed. Finally, a dragon flew below the pink and orange clouds, tiny but identifiable from the wingspan.

This was it.

"Help. One of our villagers is trapped." After much discussion, the dragon riders had assured him that dragons were empathetic creatures and would try to help when asked.

Jason expanded his mind and tried to sense the coral dragon. He repeated his request, still unsure if the dragon could hear his feeble mind-speech.

And then he was inside her mind, desperate to find other dragons. Ones that lived. Jason straightened, suddenly sure that connecting with another dragon was the only way to survive.

He mustn't be alone.

Jason struggled to keep his mind separate. This desire wasn't his. It was Wynter's.

Her memories twisted into disconnected shapes and colors, the past mixed with the present. It reminded him of his own fever brain during the plague, of rocks with mouths that spewed chaos. But this was a dragon mind, filled with scents, and sounds that collided with emotions. So much more than a human mind could handle.

Wynter was indeed infected with the curse, but her resolve to connect was stronger. As if this one thought kept her from giving in to the fever brain.

Shock shot through Jason, his power flooding his body.

She was young, no more than ten years old. Too young to be alone. This dragon, no bigger than a foal, was only looking for a family. To belong. Her loneliness made his chest ache.

Suddenly, Jason was inside Charlie's mind, inside Heather's, and with the next breath he knew everyone in the village.

He slammed up his mental shields, his power forming a barrier of fire, shutting out their thoughts and keeping him safe.

Charlie groaned and fell to the ground, swiftly followed by everyone else.

Jason's mind was on fire, his power protecting him from whatever was happening to the others. They writhed on the ground, unable to capture the dragon, unable to do anything.

Wynter had mental powers. She was inside all of their minds. Even now he felt her trying to get past his shield. Her desire for connection was so strong that he wanted to help her. He wanted to let her in, but he couldn't.

Every person in the village was trapped in her fever brain-induced hallucinations.

He had to do something.

Sarcruze had been right.

This youngling would infect every surviving dragon. With this much power, this much connection, they would all experience the visions. They would all be infected.

Maybe Wynter's power was broadcasting mind-speech or forging a mental bond. Either way, she would ensnare everyone in her path with her chaotic fever brain. She may have already turned entire villages comatose on her journey.

Wynter landed beside Jason, her head wobbling on her small frame. She leaned into him, her body fragile, her translucent wings tucked tightly against her body, as if holding in her pain.

"Why will they not speak to me?" Loneliness and anguish poured from her. She'd lost her coven and couldn't survive without a new one. She'd even take a human family. Anyone to love. To take care of her.

Jason felt himself waver. His own magic fought hard to protect his mind, but her power was stronger. He didn't have much time.

"They can't. You're sick, and now they are too." Jason hoped she still had enough grasp of reality to understand what he was saying. *"You must release them."*

Puzzlement berated Jason, her emotions amplified by her magic. *"But I'm not holding them. Why will no one speak to me?"*

The force of the dragon's pain rocked Jason backward. He thrust out a hand for balance and touched her soft head.

Wynter gazed up with swirling eyes. *"You feel me. You will talk to me."* The strength of her command broke through Jason's shield.

Chaos flooded through him. Heat and ice. Vortices and rainbows. Every scent he'd ever smelled, and many he hadn't, attacked his nose. His tongue bled, his ears rang, and his body was not his own.

He was a youngling. So very alone.

Anguish swept through Jason, and he lunged for his magic.

He must burn his way to his soul. To himself, buried in the chaos.

The heat grew, a beacon of magic, of his essence. That would ground him against this plague. He'd been here before. He'd survived.

Because of Charlie.

Jason found Charlie's soul glowing in the maelstrom of wind and twisted colors. And there, he found Heather and David. They writhed in the shadows of the colorful display.

Jason's heat burned a path to them.

He must save Charlie. He must protect his family.

As his power cleared his mind, the world rushed into focus.

Jason hadn't moved. He stood touching the small, frightened dragon, while Charlie and the others lay unmoving on the ground. He didn't know if they lived or not.

There was only him and Wynter.

A sob caught in his throat. Sarcruze was right. He had no choice, even though he'd thought he would. Even though he'd created a plan to avoid it.

With a cry of agony, Jason released his magic, burning away Wynter's flesh, the curse, and finally her desperate soul, longing for connection.

He wanted to say something. To send the youngling to her death with final words. But there were no words that would make this right.

Jason collapsed in the tiny pile of coral ash.

He'd used his power to kill. Maybe that made him a monster, but in the end he had no choice.

SACRIFICE

SARCRUZE

Sarcruze felt the death of the dragon even though he was sequestered at Jason's Keep. The youngling wasn't one of his own, and it would've been too dangerous to open his mind to her, but he'd maintained his connection to Jason.

The boy didn't know. Sarcruze set the link deep within his subconscious. Humans weren't even aware of how much of their minds was accessible. They focused on the obvious and missed the invisible connections and activities within their brains.

He'd felt the boy's hope for a peaceful solution and mourned for his loss of innocence. Jason was merely a youngling. Dragons protected their young from as much pain as they could.

At the first burst of fear, Sarcruze had taken to the sky, shutting out the coven so he could focus on Jason. He'd spun over the ice-covered mountains, flying high above the clouds.

The pain of that death, the intense heat, had been brief, the boy's desire to harm as little as possible evident in his control of the fire. But Sarcruze had felt it all.

Wynter had been barely ten years old, far too young to die. Jason's fire had consumed her, and for a moment, Sarcruze had felt as if he burned.

But then it was over. The boy's grief washing away the heat.

Sarcruze mourned for Wynter, for the choices he'd made, and for Jason. That one act had broken the boy, shattered something essential to his soul.

Jason would eventually find peace. One thing about being pushed to the breaking point was learning exactly how far you would go to save those you love.

And then something would happen to move that line.

Protecting the coven had required too many hard choices. But Sarcruze had persevered, no matter how battered his soul became. Leaving the last survivors at Whitecliff had almost broken him. But experiencing Jason's magic, and allowing him to reduce a dragon to ash, had pushed him beyond his limit.

He'd destroyed a dragon soul.

Certainly, Jason had done the act, but he'd convinced the boy and killed a youngling.

Sarcruze was responsible.

He flew until his wings ached, rising higher into the sky. Soon, each breath burned in his chest. He must not give in to the doubt that tried to find another way, to undo the damage, to lessen the ache in his soul.

The curse was to blame. After all he'd done and would do, his coven had to survive.

Tucking his wings tightly against his torso, he dove for the ground. As the wind rushed over him and the sky lightened, a peace settled. At the last second he opened his wings and shot over the trees. Flying always brought perspective.

He'd done what was necessary. He would continue to use what he could to beat this curse, even if it meant using magic. But when they were safe, when this curse was banished, he would ensure that magic never became the ruling force in his life ever again.

JASON'S QUEST

JASON

Jason spent the whole night thinking about himself, his power, and what he'd do if his brother didn't wake up. He moved those he cared about into the meeting hall, but dragging unconscious people across grass and gravel roads was a lot harder than he'd expected.

At least Charlie and Heather were comfortable, with pillows tucked under them on the wooden floor. For hours Jason sat between them, holding their hands.

No one moaned or cried out. No one had a fever. They simply appeared to be in a deep sleep. It was enough to give him hope that his monstrous act had saved them, and they would recover. That whatever spell had trapped them in Wynter's mind had dissipated.

She was gone. According to the magic rules he'd grown up with, the villagers should've been released with her death. Even the dragon riders trapped in fever brain had woken when he'd cremated their dragons. But this was dragon magic.

It didn't follow the rules.

As the first rays of dawn lightened the sky outside the hall window, Jason stared down at his brother. If Charlie didn't wake, he'd find a mage to cure him. Even if it meant revealing his power.

Charlie had saved his life, and he'd spent it trying to save dragons.

Jason brushed Charlie's overgrown hair off his forehead. His brother had changed so much in the past year. He didn't need Jason to do everything for him anymore. But that didn't mean that Jason should've left him to fend for himself. He'd been selfish. Focusing on what he wanted and accepting Charlie's help as if it was due to him.

But Charlie deserved better. They were family. His brother understood that. He'd been there when Jason struggled with his power. He'd followed Jason from Silverstream to Misthaven. He'd supported every decision that Jason made.

A deep sigh filled Jason's soul, because he'd made another decision during the long night, one that would involve another quest. If Charlie survived this, then it wasn't right to drag him along. Melanie had taken care of Charlie when he'd left for his great dragon quest. Maybe his brother was better off without him and his problems.

Charlie shifted, his breathing lighter. Between one breath and the next, he opened his eyes. Sounds of motion and people waking up surrounded Jason, but he kept his gaze on his brother.

"Hey. Why are you watching me sleep?" Though his voice was croaky, Charlie's eyes were clear as he sat up.

Jason laughed and hugged him. Everything would be all right now.

Heather murmured and turned over, her usual resistance to waking from a normal sleep. They would all be fine.

Jason stood. He'd fill them in later, but for now he needed to check on the villagers outside. They would be disoriented and uncomfortable.

"See you at breakfast. You might be hungrier than usual."

Joy lifted his steps as he strode from the hall. He didn't need to enlist the mages or hunt for a cure. Charlie had survived.

Jason stretched, working the kinks out of his neck and shoulders, and gazed at the mountains, to the dragon keep.

"Vaylor?" He wasn't surprised when there was no answer.

He'd made a critical decision during his vigil through the night. His power was dangerous, but he was in full control of it. He hadn't burned the trees or the grass when he'd destroyed Wynter, despite his fear. All the houses and buildings were untouched.

Yes. His magic could destroy. But turning dragon corpses into colorful ash somehow honored them. Rotting corpses would only fuel the fear that dragons were responsible for the plague. If there weren't any, then dragons would be remembered as the saviors they'd been.

Moans and complaints filled the air. Jason rushed from one villager to the next, handing them water, and helping them get up. Charlie and Heather joined him, and soon everyone had recovered. Most of the villagers didn't seem to be suffering any after-effects of Wynter's hallucinations. They didn't remember anything, thinking they'd simply fallen asleep.

But the dragon riders rubbed their heads, and their eyes held a haunted expression. Jason hoped it wouldn't last.

"You did it." The sadness in David's voice as he held Wynter's ashes soothed Jason's soul. This man understood how difficult the decision had been.

"I had no choice."

David winced. "Guess not. My head hurts and I can still see rainbows over everything, but I'm sure I'll be fine. We'll all be fine."

This time. There were still more infected dragons out there. Dragons with powers that could hurt people. Jason couldn't destroy another living dragon, but he had the power to hurt them. He could use that to force a dragon away or to contain it. He was in control of his magic.

Once everyone was back to normal he would speak with Charlie. He'd vowed to treat his brother as an equal, so together they would decide what to do. If Charlie wanted to join him on his quest to cleanse the keeps and honor any fallen dragons along the way, then Jason wouldn't stifle him. His brother was strong enough to make his own choices.

It would be a long journey, taking a year at least. Maybe more.

Jason didn't want to do it alone.

But if Charlie wanted to stay behind and live a normal life, Jason would accept that and be happy for him. David and Heather would probably help, and maybe some other riders. He didn't need his brother to be there. Charlie deserved the chance to be who he wanted to be.

Maybe the dragons would find a cure and return. Maybe they'd hide for years and wait for the sorcerer who cast the curse to die. After all, a spell shouldn't continue without the caster.

Of course those rules might not apply anymore, at least not with dragons, or with curses.

Charlie ran up behind him. "Whatever you're planning, I'm in."

Jason grinned. His brother knew him so well. But this time, he'd give Charlie a choice. No more dragging him along and ignoring what he needed. Charlie had a mind of his own. Jason wouldn't tell him what to do or try to influence his decision. This was about being together.

"I've thought of a quest, but I need your input. And if you want to do something else, say so."

Jason wouldn't kill again. Not for anything. So, he couldn't put his brother in danger ever again. Sarcruze had said something about power not defining him. He wasn't a monster if he didn't use his power to do horrible things. So Jason would focus on the good things he could do with his power.

Too much of his life had been about death and magic. The two had melded together in his mind. But it didn't have to be that way.

Magic wasn't pain and death.

It was simply a part of him. He was the one who chose how to use his ability. And he chose happiness and life.

ORACLE
SERI

Their trips to the other keeps had stopped a long time ago, but Seri knew they were running out of time. One of the scouts had returned with news that the Nightwood Keep had been infected. They were almost as isolated as Whitecliff Keep.

Everything they'd tried had barely slowed the plague. Sarcruze's coven might survive the longest, hidden from the world at Jason's Keep, but the curse would find them.

The inevitability of this weighed on Seri. Garianna and the others expected her to know the answers. The mantle of Oracle had never been so useless.

Seeing magic didn't grant solutions.

The only thing Seri knew for sure was that unless they countered the curse with magic, all dragons would die. It might take another year or more if they were lucky. This plague wasn't like the human one. This one was driven by magic. It would never end.

She strode up to Sarcruze, Garianna close behind her, as usual. Seri held her head high and kept her tail straight. This was not the time to show her doubts.

Sarcruze finished speaking and turned to Seri. His mood was somber, but his eyes still whirled with pleasure.

For some reason, he treated Seri with respect, while pretty much ignoring Gregor. She didn't know if it was the prophecy or because she reminded him of someone. Once in a while, she'd get a flash of a turquoise dragon a little older than herself. But Sarcruze was adept at hiding his emotions and thoughts, so she had to wonder if he was letting her see those memories.

She shook her head, casting aside her musings. That wasn't why she was there. *"The only way we will survive this curse is to find the source of magic."*

He would see the logic in her thoughts. She concentrated on her research, on how human magic was countered by more magic, and on how this meant that all their attempts to outlast the plague would fail. Her conclusions were solid. Seri had tested every one. They needed magic and a lot of it.

"You believe you've found this source?" He didn't ask her to justify her premise.

Respect and acceptance lay in his demeanor, helping her to continue.

"No. But I know where to start. In the northern part of the Dragon Mountain Range. I can see threads of magic originating from that direction. I'm certain that if I can follow them, I can find the source. The human legends say it's an unfreezing lake. I believe that means the lake is heated by a volcano."

It was the only thing that made sense. Ice and snow encased the northern part of the continent so all the lakes would be frozen. But when Gregor was trapped in that volcanic shaft months ago, she'd seen magic act differently. His power had sent him into the gap between the pillars. She didn't know if the source of magic was a volcano or a lake, but it might save them.

"I can't risk sending you. The prophecy may be happening now, and we need you here."

Zanthor approached and laid a talon on Seri's shoulder. *"Then we should all go. If this is Seri's destiny, then we need to trust in it. Sometimes we have to leap into the abyss to find our way."*

There was so much underlying Zanthor's words that Seri could feel the shift in the air. Magic swirled between the two dragons with everything they didn't say.

"It's too big of a risk." Sarcruze wilted, his shoulders sagging and weariness clouding his eyes. *"After everything, to lose to a human curse…"*

Zanthor's belief in Seri's quest radiated through him. *"Then let me do it. I'll lead the coven on this journey. I'll take the burden this time. You've done so much, carried more than any leader should. Let me help you with this."*

Sarcruze's nod was slight, but Seri felt the subtle shift in magic before Zanthor became their leader. Shock held her still. She'd never heard of a leader transferring power without a fight or a death. But obviously that's what just happened.

She focused on the magic as bright threads from every dragon in the keep wound around Zanthor. They were still attached to Sarcruze, but they wove between both dragons, as if sharing the coven bond. Suddenly, the threads around Sarcruze faded, still there but muted. Seri blinked, restoring her vision to normal. Something unusual had happened with their bond. Zanthor was their leader, but the coven was still connected to Sarcruze.

Zanthor turned, seeming to grow in stature. *"We have a new quest in our battle against the curse. Prepare yourselves. Tomorrow, we will travel deep into the icy north. We will find the source of magic. And we will survive."* Power and conviction rang through his words.

No one questioned the shift or the quest. With nods and murmurs of assent, the dragons prepared for the long journey ahead.

Seri believed in her quest, but she'd never thought this would be what it took to make it happen.

As she walked to Gregor to see if his power could help, dragons bowed.

"The Oracle has found the path. We're saved."

Pressure built between her shoulders at their whispered reverence. They trusted the Oracle.

It didn't matter that she was only a youngling, or that she didn't know if any amount of magic could reverse the curse.

Seri only knew that they had no options left.

Stay and die, or find the source of magic and hope that it could protect them.

SOURCE OF MAGIC
GREGOR

Gregor followed the scent of lilac that had pulled him northward when he'd fled Dawn's Keep almost a year ago. If he'd known then what would happen, he would've flown deeper into the snow-covered mountains.

He could've avoided so much pain.

But then he wouldn't have found his friends, or become a part of this amazing coven. He would never have met Seri.

Gregor flew beside Zanthor as they led the dragons to their last chance at survival.

Even Seri, with all her research into the source of magic, didn't know what to expect at the end of their journey. No one had ever explored beyond the ice spires of the ancient Dragon Mountains. Even though they carried supplies, they didn't know how far they would need to travel or if they could find game to sustain them once they ran out.

Everything depended on Gregor's ability to know the right path. Gregor closed his eyes. What if he was wrong? He still didn't really understand his power. Some scents called him while others pushed him away. Sometimes, an emotion would accompany the smell, to guide him.

He'd asked many questions, but the scent held steady.

There was no other path. No cure.

He could be leading them to their doom instead of to their salvation. The scent didn't change when he asked if they would survive or perish. His power wasn't forthcoming on specifics. Something dragons needed lay to the north.

Zanthor flew slightly ahead of Gregor, confidence in every stroke of his longer, light-blue wings. He was almost invisible against the cloud-free sky, his skin changing slightly as day turned to evening.

"Either way, we will die. Better to try something than to quiver in Jason's Keep, waiting for the plague to take us all." Zanthor's mental tone soothed Gregor's churning mind.

A hint of a newly opened rosebud reinforced the feeling that they were going the right way. A sense of hope.

The plague would kill them if they did nothing. It was only a matter of time.

With a stroke of his wings, Grego flew toward the scent of lilac, following the pull deeper into the mountain range, far beyond any source of food or shelter.

Gregor flew over endless ice fields, surrounded by ice-crystal forests. His breath froze in his nostrils, which didn't affect his power, since it was all in his head. Even with his arms clasped tightly across his chest, the cold seeped into his body, freezing his bones. His feet and wingtips tingled, a warning it was too cold, even for dragons.

Suddenly, the scent grew, so potent his eyes watered. He sneezed violently and gasped out, *"Here. It has to be here."*

Below them, a steaming lake wound through the valley between two frozen mountain ranges which stretched to the horizon.

Zanthor sent a sigh of relief to Gregor. They could not have flown much farther. Zanthor tucked his wings against his body and dove to the lake edge. Without hesitation, the others followed, perching on icy outcrops and deep snow banks along the lake.

Gregor circled once, hoping he hadn't led them to their deaths. There was nothing alive. Even the trees were buried under snow.

As soon as he landed, Seri clapped her talons with delight, as if her exhaustion had disappeared. *"You found it, the source of magic. I can see the magic swirling through the air currents. The entire lake is breathing."*

Gregor coughed as he attempted to stop his relieved laughter at her enthusiasm. She'd picked up a few bad habits from the humans she studied with at the university. He must act serious in front of the others. The older dragons already thought him immature. But a spark of excitement sizzled from his head to his tail as she confirmed that he'd been right to follow his power. And there was something special here. His fatigue from the long flight was gone, even his hunger had diminished.

"What now, Seri?" Gregor had gotten them there, but he had no idea what they had to do.

Seri hummed as she stepped into the lake. The air shimmered around her, and the water rippled, racing across the surface to the far end and back.

For a brief moment, Gregor could almost see the colors of magic before he remembered to withdraw his mental connection from Seri.

"We go into the Source. Magic will protect us." Her tone held only wonder, not a hint of doubt.

With an encouraging grin, Seri walked deeper into the lake, tucking her wings against her back, until the water covered her head.

"The Oracle is right. No turning back. No room for doubt." Zanthor's voice, filled with his own power of conviction, rumbled deep within Gregor's skull and melted away his fear. *"To survive we must immerse ourselves.. The Source will make us stronger. We may sleep for an hour, a week, or longer. We may sleep until the world is free of the plague. But magic is our only chance of defeating the curse and returning to Jason's Keep. Be brave. Dragons will endure."*

One by one, the dragons slipped into the water. The scales of the mature dragons, those over the age of thirty, shimmered as they swam to the bottom, filling the lake with moving strips of color.

Just before Zanthor stepped into the lake, he clasped Gregor's talons.

"You may be the first to wake, as you're the youngest and can't breathe underwater as long. You must ensure it is safe before you wake us. Use your power. I can trust you to know this for us." He laid his forehead against Gregor's in a deep sign of respect.

Gregor gulped. It was a huge responsibility. His entire coven depended on his ability and the inconsistent *knowing* that came with it. What if he was wrong?

Zanthor slipped beneath the surface, his hide transforming into a swirling rainbow.

Steam rose over the lake, marking the center of each ripple as a dragon dove deeper into its depths. Gregor walked through the shallows, enjoying the warmth that eliminated the coldness that had been in his body for too long. He hoped Seri was right and that all this magic would protect them from the curse. Many in the coven expected a cure, but they weren't infected. Magic couldn't reverse something they didn't have. So he had to believe in Seri's theory.

He swam to the deepest part of the lake and dove to the bottom. Even though dragons could breathe underwater, he'd been too afraid to spend more than an hour practicing after nearly drowning at the basalt cliffs. Worry filled his chest. He reached for his coven, but they were already asleep. Even Seri.

He needed a scent. To know this was the right choice.

Would he survive?

His power didn't answer.

STORM'S KEEP

JASON

Two years later, Jason's quest was done. He'd traveled to every dragon keep and cremated their remains. Charlie and Heather had been with him every step of the way, from east to west and then all the way to the southern tip of Drakkoia.

They'd scaled mountains, sailed to the island with Klaw Keep, visited Dragon Library, and gathered friends along the way.

Melanie and David had helped, enlisting dragon riders and people with useful magical abilities. Their caravan exchanged colorful pottery and trinkets for trader coin, enabling the group to purchase food and supplies for the long journey. Lonely villages had welcomed the news they shared of the world.

Jason sighed wearily. His heart still ached at the number of dragon riders who'd been trapped in fever brain from the curse. Many woke when his magic destroyed the right dragon corpse, but he couldn't free them all.

The last cremation at Storm's Keep had been the hardest. Until they got there, he'd held out hope that some dragons had survived the curse. But the entire coven was dead, recently perished, their bodies still whole.

Memories of Karyn's death and his futile journey to Dawn's Keep had slammed into him. All his efforts to save the dragons hadn't stopped this devastation. Power had rushed to his fingertips, but it was no longer a wild thing to control.

It was comfort.

A part of him that no one could take.

The quest had been harder than he could've imagined, starting with the dragons left behind at Whitestone Keep. They'd died quickly after being infected by Wynter's mental blast. Killing her had done nothing to stop the curse.

The villagers had set up pyres, insisting that Jason needed to conserve his magic to honor all the dragons decaying in more isolated keeps. He's set off on his journey with hope and determination.

It was easy cremating dragon corpses in the mountain keeps. A quick flash burn, contained by the rock walls, was all that was needed. Unlike the forest keeps. Controlling the fires that had burned the Nightwood trees had proved impossible. Entire groves had been lost. Two keeps, built on mountains weakened by wartime spells, had collapsed into rubble from his power. One day grass and trees would grow over them, leaving no sign they had ever existed, just a hill. Water would naturally fill the depression, hiding the sleeping alcoves.

This was the last keep, the last chance to find survivors. Jason wiped the sweat from his forehead and stretched. Now what?

"You've done enough." Heather rubbed his back and kissed his cheek. "Let's go home."

Jason gathered her into his arms. His strength. His rock. She'd been there through it all with him. They were young to marry, but he knew he could love no other as much as her. They were stronger together.

"Yes. I'm ready." He kissed her deeply. "Thank you."

She blushed. He loved that she still reacted after almost two years together.

Heather pulled free and walked across the empty keep to gathered their supplies. He followed her to the patiently waiting Warhog.

Charlie grinned as he loaded the last sack of ash into the back of the wagon. His brother was ready for the great quest to be over. They'd fought over silly things, each day a different challenge. But after time alone with his animals, Charlie always came back, settled. No one else knew Jason as deeply as Charlie or could push him to rage with a well-timed smirk. But there'd been more laughter and joy than arguments, as his brother grew from a lanky boy into a muscled sixteen-year-old young man.

They would camp at the base of the mountain and transform the fifty bags of sparkling dragon ash into bowls, urns, and cups before starting the two-month journey back to Misthaven. David and Melanie had decided to return to Silverstream on the way.

Maybe they should travel up the coast instead of through the winding roads. They hadn't had time to explore the villages far from the keeps, and Charlie might enjoy some companionship his own age. Jason had resented his own sudden responsibility at sixteen. His brother deserved a chance to enjoy life and explore who he wanted to become. He'd supported Jason long enough.

Besides, they might entice skilled tradespeople to join them in Misthaven. There were many who desired the quiet isolation away from the rulings of the new government.

Jason sighed as they left the keep. He'd done everything he could to keep the memory of dragons pure. People wouldn't find rotting corpses to fuel the rumor that dragons caused the plague. Instead they would find empty keeps. Maybe that would help them long for the return of dragons. Maybe not. But he'd done all he could to honor dragons, to honor Karyn, and her heart in his chest.

It was up to Sarcruze now. Jason knew deep in his soul that he may never know what happened to the coven at Jason's Keep, but he hoped they had found a way to defeat the curse. The world needed dragons.

A peace settled in Jason's heart, lifting a weight off his shoulders. He clasped Heather's hand as they traveled down the mountain trail in the wagon.

It was time to go home.

EPILOGUE - VALLEY KEEP

JASON

The past seven years had been both difficult and amazing. Jason was married to Heather now, and they had two girls and one healthy baby boy. Life had settled into a comfortable rhythm of family, working their small farm, and helping Misthaven grow as a community.

The dragons never returned to Whitecliff Keep and none had been seen since the days of Jason's quest. Once a year, he hiked up the mountain hoping for some evidence that the coven had survived. But the etchings in the archive stone never changed, and soon grass and trees took root in the ground.

Some of the dragon riders wanted to bury the archive stone, so no one could vandalize it. Jason wasn't ready to admit that dragons wouldn't return.

He'd visited David in Silverstream a few times, but travel was becoming dangerous.

Over the years, magic had dwindled. At first the war mages were blamed, the devastation from their spells a recent memory. But eventually the blame shifted to the Dragon Plague. Despite his best efforts, Jason hadn't been able to find the dragons who fled their keeps. People didn't know about the curse. They only knew that dragons fell from the sky to rot. It was enough to fuel the rumor that entire villages became infected from their corpses.

The plague finally stopped when dragons no longer flew the skies, and their keeps were empty. People needed hope for a future without war, disease, or fear.

Eventually, dragons were to blame for the loss of magic too.

Only witches with strong abilities could wield magic, causing a rift between those who could and those who couldn't. They were in high demand, performing spells for cities and villages, but even they couldn't harness enough power to satisfy everyone. A new industry of machines evolved to replace magic.

Healers became the profession of choice, able to supplement their magic with herbs, salves, and common sense. Something shifted. Healers were no longer remembered as magic users. They were saviors. They stopped the Dragon Plague.

Jason didn't know when or how, but hatred of magic had grown. Now, mobs hunted down witches and mages with a frantic passion, burning them in their homes or drowning them at sea. Spell books and anything containing references to magic or dragons were burned, buildings where magic had been taught were torn down. All evidence of magic was being wiped from history.

Misthaven had been safe, far from the anger and fear.

Until now.

Smoke warned him long before the mob arrived. Jason had always been sensitive to fire.

"Get up, Heather. Gather our things. It's time."

She rolled out of bed, determination in her eyes. They'd prepared, knowing it was only a matter of time before the zealots came to Misthaven.

They had a plan. David had visited six weeks ago, begging them to join him on his journey north through the Dragon Mountain Range. A new community was being built, Valley Keep, where they could live off the land, isolated from the rest of the world. Many magic users had already fled there, leaving secret notes behind for those who sought refuge.

Heather carried the baby, while Jason gathered their backpacks. He'd miss this home, the memories, and the love in the walls.

Charlie was outside, tacking up Warhog and his wild mare, Wonder. He'd grown into a tall, strong man far too early. Sandra was at his side, handing him the saddlebags.

"It's time." His eyes were filled with excitement. Charlie had wanted to leave two weeks ago when a trader caravan passed through warning them of the witch hunters.

But Jason hadn't wanted to move Heather and the baby so soon. They'd lost two already, after their girls, and this two-month old boy was fragile. Heather was worn out, but they had no choice.

The smoke was closer. He could see it now. The fools must've started a forest fire. He didn't understand it. Burning the forests wouldn't help anyone.

But logic didn't drive these people. Magic had resulted in thirty-four years of war. Magic had defined society, making many who didn't have abilities of lower class. Hatred and fear drove an entire generation of plague survivors who would do anything, kill anyone, to destroy this perceived evil.

With one last look at the home he'd built for his family, Jason helped Heather and the baby into the back of the wagon next two his two brave daughters. As long as they were together, they would survive.

Jason, Charlie, and the last of the Misthaven residents rode hard and fast for the Dragon Tail Trail north of the village. An explosion rocked the ground. The horses reared, but Charlie quickly quieted them and pushed them down the trail. There was a chance their group of twenty would be followed, but if they could make it through the narrow pass, they could release the rocks that David had told them to use. Anyone following would have to find another trail.

Jason bit his lip, hoping that the rock slide hadn't been triggered already. David had warned them that it was too dangerous to keep the pass open for long.

Jason looked back. Flames shot over the trees. The village was on fire. But fire was his power.

With a whisper and a thought, Jason swirled the distant flames into a tornado and sent it in three directions. One blocking the trail he was on, one forcing the mob back down the road toward the forest fire they'd created, and one blocking the road to the next village along the coast. He could give those villagers time to escape.

The power wouldn't last long, and the flames would die faster than if he'd left them be, but no one would be able to follow them for half a day. That should give them enough time to escape, even if the pass was blocked.

He turned forward and caught Charlie's smirk. Jason's power hadn't fluctuated like others. Instead, it had held steady. He'd learned to harness it. To embrace it. And to channel it from a distance.

Jason wished he'd known this long ago when he'd first joined the army with his brother. He wished he'd known it when infected dragons had been a threat. He could've forced Wynter away. He could've shielded the dragons at Whitecliff Keep. He wouldn't have spent so much time being afraid of his power, of hurting Charlie, or of becoming a monster.

They rounded the bend and slowed. The passage was clear. A sharp whistle sounded from above the tree line. A person waved from a treetop.

Jason made the symbol with his hands and was waved through. The road would remain open for as long as possible to offer refuge to the dragon riders and the magic users being forced from their homes.

Heather leaned her head on his shoulder. "Are you ready to start over again?"

Jason rubbed her head and grinned at Charlie. "As long as we're together, we can do anything."

He was ready to face the future.

Valley Keep would be their home, and Jason would teach his children to love dragons. Because deep in his dragon heart, he knew they would return.

Thank you for reading Curse of a Dragon Heart.

If you enjoyed this book please leave a review wherever you purchased the book or on Goodreads to help others discover this series.

To hear about the writing process, get sneak peeks into upcoming books, and read excerpts, sign up for my newsletter at **https://www.bonniejacoby.com/subscribe/**.

For more information about other books in the series visit my website at **https://www.bonniejacoby.com/**.

ACKNOWLEDGEMENTS

This book was originally a short story that was supposed to become a novella. It grew because so many characters wanted a chance to tell their side of the story. Yes, I listen to the voices in my head.

So I thank those voices. I know. Weird.

I'm grateful for Leslie Wibberley, my cheerleader, friend, and critique partner who reads everything I send her. Her enthusiasm keeps me from questioning my process. Thank you to Eileen Cook and Jenn Sommersby Young for loving what I write and getting what I mean. Lastly, I couldn't have done this without the support of my family, my writer family on The Creative Academy for Writers, and my readers.